Proof of Our Resolve

Chris Hernandez

TACTICAL

Proof of Our Resolve
Copyright © 2012 Chris Hernandez

First Edition

Because of the dynamic nature of the internet, any web address or links contained in this book may have changed since publication and may no longer be valid.

Proof of Our Resolve is a work of fiction. Names, characters, places, and incidents are the products of the author's imagination, experiences, or are fictitious. Any resemblance to actual events, locales, or persons, living or dead, is entirely coincidental.

The views expressed in this work are solely those of the author and do not necessarily reflect the views of the publisher, and the publisher hereby disclaims any responsibility for them.

Published by Tactical 16, LLC
Colorado Springs, CO

eISBN: 978-0-9855582-3-9
ISBN: 978-0-9898175-0-9 (hc)
ISBN: 978-0-9855582-9-1 (sc)

Printed in the United States of America

For my family.

CHAPTER 1

The Tagab valley was not the most dangerous valley in Afghanistan, and Kapisa province was not the most dangerous province. But to the small convoy of American soldiers traveling between the two main firebases in the province, all the statistics showing how much worse other areas were didn't make much difference. All the soldiers cared about were the five Improvised Explosive Device attacks that had taken place in the last four months on that stretch of road, plus the dozen or so direct fire ambushes. They remembered the Afghan army truck that was blasted to pieces and the two Afghan soldiers whose bodies were indistinguishable from the charred wreckage, they had seen pictures of the French armored vehicle that was hit dead center by an IED and blown off the side of the road.

Twenty-four American soldiers convoyed south in two poorly armored humvees and four gigantic armored trucks called MRAPs, Mine Resistant Ambush Protected personnel carriers. They kept their eyes open, heads moving and weapons ready. All hoped they wouldn't get hit by an IED and some hoped they would get into a good firefight. They knew that the opposite was more likely though, that they would meet an IED and miss an ambush. Not because the statistics said that was more likely, but because that would just be their luck.

For this mission, Sergeant First Class Jerry Nunez's infantry platoon was escorting a small detachment of Civil Affairs soldiers heading to a meeting with village elders at Firebase Walden. Nunez, pronounced "noon-yez", was thirty-six, small and thin, beginning to develop grey hair and a tiny spare tire. He was nothing special, just a Texas National Guard infantry platoon sergeant whose soldiers had been assigned to work alongside the French army at Firebase Pierce, the northern of Kapisa province's two firebases. Nunez's four MRAPs had the simple mission of escorting the two Civil Affairs humvees to the firebase, and then heading back north. All told, the mission should last no more than three hours. If nothing went wrong.

The first half hour on the route had been IED-free, but they were getting close to the ambush hot spots around Landakhel village. Nunez checked his map, gauging the distance to the northern edge of the village, and keyed the radio to speak to the Civil Affairs soldiers in the humvee in front of his MRAP.

"Slasher 4 this is Colt 4."

The Civil Affairs Lieutenant answered, "This is Slasher 4."

"About a kilometer and a half from here we hit Landakhel village." Nunez said. "The compounds are going to be in real close, plus rock walls where there have been a lot of IED attacks. Keep your gunners down from there until we get to Walden."

"Colt 4 Slasher 4, copy."

The lead vehicle's commander called to Nunez on the radio. "Colt 4 this is Colt 3, my gunner is looking ahead through his scope, normal activity in Landakhel."

Normal activity was a good thing. The people almost always knew the locations of emplaced IEDs, and they stayed away from them. Unlike in Iraq, the insurgents in Afghanistan didn't want to kill their own civilians. The Taliban even warned civilians to leave areas where they were going to conduct attacks.

"Colt 3 this is Colt 4, tell me when you're two hundred meters from the village."

"Roger."

Inside Nunez's vehicle his driver, Vlacek, blurted out, "My dick hurts." Prior to this announcement the conversation had been about the advantages and disadvantages of running missions in an MRAP instead of a humvee, so this was an odd turn.

Nunez turned his head toward Vlacek and asked seriously, "Severe masturbation injury? Friction burn?"

Wilson offered his assessment from where he stood in the gunner's position, his head exposed above the "teacup" of armor mounted on the roof of the MRAP. "Naw sarge, he's been hanging out with the Afghan army a lot lately. He's made progress, he's pitching now instead of catching."

"Well good for you, Vlacek," Nunez said. "I hope you found one that looks nice and feminine. Maybe the colonel's chai boy, I hear he's pretty much a girl."

Vlacek was a twenty year old hick, a good ol' boy from Flatonia, Texas, and the rampant homosexuality in the Afghan National Army disgusted him to no end. Like the rest of the US troops on the base, Vlacek had seen that every senior ANA officer had a dedicated servant, called a *chai* boy for their alleged primary duty of serving tea to their boss. Their actual job, however, was to provide sexual favors whenever their boss demanded it. Nunez respected the Afghans as fighters and sometimes was amazed at their bravery, but he did not think he had ever seen a gayer group of men anywhere in the world. He just accepted it as the way the Afghans were and didn't let it bother him. Vlacek, on the other hand, came unglued whenever someone jokingly accused him of being gay, which was at least several times a day.

"Fuck that shit, man!" Vlacek protested. "My dick hurts because I ain't been drinkin' enough water lately. I ain't doin' no faggit shit. If it keeps burnin' when I pee I think I need to get doc to gimme an IV."

Wilson answered, "Sure thing. Fag."

"Fuck you, Wilson."

"Don't take it out on me, you're the poojabber," Wilson said. "Try having sex with a woman someday, it's not as scary as you think."

"Man, I been with twice as many women as you have," Vlacek said. "You talk all funny and shit, the girls where I'm from would say you sound like a queer."

"Sounds like them's some quality women down there, Czech. Hook me up with your sister when we get back, I'll try her out and see if she thinks I'm a fag while I've got her bent over the hood of my truck."

Vlacek turned in the seat and swung at Wilson, hit him on the left thigh and drew a sharp "Ow!"

"Fuck you man, my fuckin' sister's twelve years old!"

"No problem, I'll wait a year. Thirteen's legal in hick country, right?"

From the back of the MRAP, Corporal Rodger Quincy surprised them by saying, "You two guys are idiots." Quincy was the quietest man in the platoon, a twenty-three year old black soldier built of muscle carved from solid rock. He was always reading, working out, running with a full pack or emailing his parents in East Texas. He could do anything, never had to be watched while he did it, and never, ever complained. Nunez had complete trust in him, especially in his skill with his M249 Squad Automatic Weapon.

"Y'all hear that?" Nunez asked. "Quincy called y'all idiots. He never says shit, and when he does, it's true."

"Yeah, Vlacek, you hear that?" Wilson said. "Quincy called you a retard."

"Fuck you, Wilson. He said it to you too."

"Liar."

"Pause the idiocy a second," Nunez said as he keyed his radio. "Colt 3 this is Colt 4, how we looking?"

"Colt 4 this is Colt 3, everything still looks normal, nothing weird so far."

"Roger. Gunners, get down." He let go of the mike switch. "Alex, that means you too."

Wilson always wanted to keep his head up, just like he always had in Iraq. He replied, "Yeah, yeah, whatever," and dropped his head until his eyes were even with the edge of the gun shield.

"Maybe I should ask the guys on the other trucks if their dicks hurt too," Vlacek said.

"Yeah, that's a great idea, Vlacek," Wilson said. "You should probably ask everyone to take pictures of their dicks and email them to you too. Then you can give them all a taste test. God damn, Czech, you're a hick motherfucker."

Vlacek pulled his knife off his body armor and announced "Wilson, stand still. I'm fixin' to stab you."

In a microsecond the humvee forty meters in front of Nunez's MRAP disappeared in a black cloud of dirt, smoke and flames. The explosion was so sudden that Nunez didn't realize what it was until the solid concussion wall hit them, knocked Wilson off his feet and stopped their huge vehicle in its tracks. The first sound was like glass and steel being shattered, covered an instant later by the solid *WHUMP* of the concussion. Something large and square flew sideways out of the cloud and a tire flipped straight up through the smoke.

Someone on the radio yelled "IED! IED!" at the same time Nunez registered Wilson scream into the intercom, "My ear! Fuck, my ear! I think I blew my eardrum out!"

"Motherfucker!" Nunez screamed. "Vlacek, pull up closer! Pull up closer!"

Vlacek hit the accelerator. The MRAP lurched forward and knocked Wilson off his feet again just as he regained his balance. Nunez steadied himself and reached to key his radio.

A sideways, finger-wide scrape magically appeared on the windshield in front of him as an insurgent ricocheted a round off the thick bulletproof glass. Nunez jerked his head left to look out of Vlacek's window. Vlacek leaned as far back in his seat as he could, staying away from the large circular spider web impact mark another round had made as it struck the outside of the window, inches from his head.

Nunez keyed his mike and yelled "Small arms fire, nine o'clock! Small arms fire, nine o'clock!" In his peripheral vision he saw Wilson stand and swivel the turret left.

Vlacek jammed on the brakes. "Fuck, I cain't see, Sarge! There's too much smoke! I don't wanna hit nobody, or drive into a crater!"

A voice yelled over the radio to Nunez, "Four, dis' Two! Can you see the humvee in front you? Can it roll, or does we hook it up?"

The standard procedure for an IED strike was for the vehicle in front of the disabled vehicle to back up to it, hook up tow cables and pull it out of the kill zone, or for the vehicle behind it to push it to safety. Right then, seconds after the detonation, nobody could see through the smoke and dust enough to tell if there was anything left to tow or push.

Nunez keyed his mike and yelled, "Slasher 4, this is Colt 4!"

No response.

"Two this is Four, we can't--"

Wilson opened up with the big .50 caliber machine gun mounted on their vehicle. Nunez let go of the radio mike and yelled to Wilson, "What the fuck are you shooting at?"

With his microphone keyed so everyone in the convoy could hear him, Wilson yelled, "Muzzle flash, inside a compound window, 150 meters, 9:30 o'clock! There's two compounds, it's the one on the left, the one on the left! Watch my fucking tracers!"

"This is 3, contact left, contact left!" In the background Nunez heard Corporal Eli Gore on 3's M240 machine gun let off a long burst from their position at the front of the convoy.

"Fo' dis' Two, can you see the humvee? We need to get it outta there!"

Without identifying himself on the radio, someone yelled out, "Gunners scan five and twenty-five, look for fucking secondaries!"

"--er the left, cover the left!" someone else screamed on the radio.

Nunez felt himself going into overload. Too much shit was happening at once. *Think, man, think*, he said to himself. *Don't let this get out of your control.*

He keyed his radio again. "This is 4, everybody stop fucking screaming! Everybody stop screaming. Colt 3, continue to suppress. Colt 2, get to the CA humvee and find out if the guys who got hit are okay."

Nunez thought a second. If he didn't go after the Taliban within the next minute or so, they would get away clean. On the other hand, if he did go after them, he and his soldiers might find themselves in the middle of an ambush that none of them would walk away from.

Over the intercom he asked, "Wilson, how many targets do you have?"

Still firing, Wilson yelled, "Just the muzzle flashes from the one room in one compound, Sarge!"

Nunez keyed his radio. "Three this is Four, how many targets do you have?"

The lead MRAP's commander answered, "Four this is Three, rounds came from one compound, the same one that your gunner was talking about. I think it's just one guy."

"Roger," Nunez said, trying to figure out how many soldiers he could spare to search for the Taliban. He had to leave the drivers and gunners with their vehicles, and the medic plus one of the truck commanders would have to stay with the downed humvee. Nunez wouldn't have many soldiers to work with.

He said, "I need all the truck commanders and dismounts except 2's to meet me on the passenger side of my MRAP now. Gunners continue to suppress, 2 keep working on that humvee. Maintain fucking security, and let's go!" Nunez saw Vlacek looking at him with wide eyes, and said to him, "Keep an eye on us and don't go anywhere." From the turret, Wilson said between bursts, "Be fucking careful, Jerry."

Nunez tore off his headset, popped his door and climbed onto the step below the doorway. The dust cloud in front of his vehicle had dissipated enough to reveal the back end of the Civil Affairs humvee, sticking up at the wrong elevation and angle for it to be in one piece. Nunez couldn't see what was in front of it because of the smoke and dust, but several small fires burned around it. He hoped he wasn't about to find the total loss of the vehicle and its crew.

Nunez shoved the heavy door closed, stood on the step and leaned to his right so he could see the compound that Wilson was shooting at. An RPK machine gun, basically a long-barreled AK rifle with a bipod, made its familiar hollow bamboo noise as a lone Taliban gunner fired bursts out of the compound's window. The rounds weren't coming near Nunez. He couldn't see the muzzle flashes, but tracers from Wilson's, Sergeant Jeff Albright's and Gore's machine guns peppered the window and area around it.

To Nunez the two small compounds looked closer than 150 meters away. Both were in the open, separated from each other by about fifteen meters. The compound on the left had a single window, just an open square hole in the wall, to the left of the front door. Some compounds in Afghanistan are almost the size of city blocks, monstrous multi-story castles interconnected with other gigantic compounds, an absolute nightmare that an entire infantry battalion would have a hell of a hard time clearing. Others were like these two, a fifty meter square single story cluster of rooms inside a walled courtyard. All of them had mud-brick walls that anything up to and including .50 caliber rounds couldn't penetrate. Whatever the size, every compound was a fortress.

The ground in front of the compounds had a few small depressions that might be usable for cover, but other than those few spots the area was wide open. Behind the two compounds several others were scattered among dense vegetation. Nunez jumped to the ground with gunfire ringing out from above him as Wilson continued to fire into the window.

Quincy jogged toward him from the back of their MRAP, then 1's dismount Private First Class Manuel Trevino and Truck Commander Sergeant James Powell sprinted over from their truck at the rear. Trevino was young, dark, chubby and harmless-looking. He looked nothing like Powell, thin-faced and lean, always mad, always ready for a fistfight. Powell usually manned the gun on the MRAP commanded by their platoon leader Lieutenant Klein, and was only in command of the truck because Klein was in Bagram for a meeting. A few seconds later 3's commander Staff Sergeant Eric Lattimore ran in a crouch toward them, skirting the burning humvee while he searched furiously for secondary IEDs. With his square glasses Lattimore looked like a young college professor, and was as smart as one.

"Lattimore, where's your dismount?"

"I had already sent Lyons out to help out with the CA humvee when you called. It's completely wasted, Sarge. Lyons is looking for the crew now, Doc is with him. The CA guys from the other humvee are fucking hysterical, they won't be helping us any."

God damn it, Nunez thought. *You'd think that with six vehicles and twenty-four soldiers in this convoy I could get more than five fucking guys together to take this compound.*

"Fuck. Okay, it's just us five. We're going to sprint across the field to that compound while the gunners cover us, then we get in there and clear it. We don't go anywhere else, just clear that one compound and get back here. Keep your eyes open for other bad guys in other places besides that compound. Any questions?"

"You sure you wanna do this, Sarge?" Powell asked. "If we get pinned down in the open, or if there's a bunch of Taliban in that compound, we're all fucked."

"Yeah Powell, I know. I know. Let's get ready. Trevino, get to the corner of the MRAP and start putting 203 rounds into that compound, then join us when we move."

"Roger Sarsh," Trevino answered in his thick south Texas Mexican accent. He hustled over to the front of the MRAP, dug into the pouch full of 40mm grenades mounted on his left thigh and loaded one into the grenade launcher tube mounted under the barrel of his M4 carbine. Nunez got on the radio and said to the soldiers staying on the road, "We're about to move to the compound. Gunners suppress until we're twenty meters from the compound, then cease fire and maintain 360."

Then he remembered that he hadn't even notified the Firebase about the ambush. He continued, "Two, call for QRF and get a medevac going." The Quick Reaction Force would be composed of a platoon of French Mountain Troops, and Nunez hoped they would get there soon. But soon usually meant half an hour or so.

Trevino steadied himself along the edge of the MRAP's bumper, aimed as well as he could and fired. He had no grenade launcher sight on his weapon, and his shots were little more than guesses. The grenade impacted short of the compound.

Powell yelled, "Adjust, you're short!" Trevino loaded and fired again, and missed just to the left.

"Fuck the 203. Let's go." Nunez looked back, saw his soldiers tensed up and ready behind him, and sprinted around the corner of the MRAP. His four soldiers followed him. Trevino, already the heaviest and slowest, lagged behind and distracted himself by trying to load his 203 on the move. Nunez led them in an arc to the left, and yelled "Get on line! Get on line!" as they moved. They spread out into a skirmish line, evenly spaced with all their weapons ready to engage the enemy.

The weight of the gear bouncing on his chest and shoulders, combined with the summer morning heat, had Nunez gasping for breath within the first fifty meters. The rocks and folds in the ground caught at their boots and made them stumble. Nunez kept an eye open for depressions deep enough to dive into if rounds came toward them. Tracers whizzed toward the compound to their right, making them hunch lower as they ran. To Nunez's left, Trevino thunked a 40mm grenade toward the compound and managed to hit the wall to the right of the door. Lots of smoke and noise, no effect. Dust and mud chips flew from the compound wall as rounds from three machine guns hit it. The big .50 caliber rounds made fist-sized flashes as they slammed into the wall around the window. The Taliban fighter inside the compound fired a burst at them with his RPK, and the advancing soldiers heard the distinctive *sk! sk! sk!* noise as the rounds went low over their heads.

They ducked and shifted a step or two left. On the second burst Nunez saw two rounds hit the rocks a few feet to his right. A shallow depression was in front of Nunez, and he tried to increase his speed and dive for it. Instead he just bounced one foot off a rock and fell on his face onto a jumble of stones. He heard the unmistakable sound of an M249 machine gun being fired close by, and rolled to his left to get up. From the ground, he saw a sight he knew he would never forget.

Quincy was crouched, bent at the waist with his machine gun pointed at the compound, no longer running. He walked at a slow pace, firing long bursts toward the invisible Taliban in the window. His face was all lines and creases, muscles rippling through his sleeves and pant legs. He ignored the third burst as it raised clouds of dust and scattered shards of rock around him. To his right, tracers whizzed by from Wilson's .50. Nunez wished he had time to take a picture. Quincy looked plain heroic, the model of the American combat soldier. No hesitation, no fear, all power and danger and determination.

Nunez scrambled back onto his feet and ran to catch up to the other three soldiers. He flicked off the safety on his M4 carbine and fired one round toward the window as they ran, then realized there was no point, he was just wasting ammunition. The left corner of the compound got closer, the cover fire from the guns on the MRAPs stopped and suddenly they were there, hugging the corner of the compound for cover.

Quincy took a position closest to the window. Nunez hit the wall close behind him and grabbed the back of Quincy's body armor as a signal for him to stay put. Nunez took several deep breaths, trying to heave some energy back into his body, and turned around to give another quick brief to his other three soldiers. They were stacked up along the wall to the left of the window but several feet away from it.

"Fo' dis is Two, y'all good?" Staff Sergeant Harris asked from his vehicle, back on the road.

"We're good, Harris", Nunez heaved. "Any more movement in the compound?"

"Nothin' else," Harris responded. "We didn't see him when he shot at y'all, we just seen da' impacts. The Quick Reaction Force is on da' way."

"Roger, we're about to enter. Keep y'all's eyes open."

"Roger."

Nunez turned to his soldiers as he pulled out a grenade from a pouch. "Okay, I'm going to frag the window, then we move past it to the door. Powell, you stay at the back and make sure nobody pops out of the window after we pass it. We'll enter in the order we're in now, except that I'll be in the middle. Everyone good?"

They all nodded except Quincy, who gave a sharp "Got it." Nunez pulled the strip of green duct tape he had wrapped around the grenade's lever, thumbed the safety clip from the fragmentation grenade and squeezed the pin ends straight to prep it for use. He put his hand on Quincy's back and whispered, "Okay, move up." They crept toward the window, which was quiet and had been since they reached the compound. Both of them lowered themselves as they moved closer to the square, empty opening. Quincy stopped two feet away and knelt down. Nunez stood up, leaned as far forward as possible, yanked the pin from the grenade and sidearmed it into the window.

He and Quincy stutter-stepped backwards as they heard the grenade bounce off the back wall. Four seconds later the *WHAM!* burst out of the window, blew dirt in a fan away from the front of the compound and intensified the hay and manure stink that had been present since they reached the wall. Nunez slapped Quincy on the back and he jumped forward, straining to keep his large frame under the window. Nunez followed him in a duck walk, kept his carbine pointed toward the window with his right hand and motioned for his other three soldiers to move up with his left. As the five of them passed under the window Powell lifted his carbine over his head and fired two three-round bursts into the room.

Six feet past the window Quincy reached the door. This one was wooden instead of metal, a double door with a medieval looking lock in the center where the two doors met. The door wasn't particularly sturdy looking, but since none of them had a shotgun to breach it with, it could still bring their clearing operation to a quick halt if it had a decent lock.

When they all stacked up on the left side of the door, Nunez grabbed Lattimore, who had moved into the spot behind him, and moved him into the spot behind Quincy. He had to keep himself in the center of the stack, to maintain better control. Keeping one hand on Lattimore, he keyed his radio.

"Two this is Four, have you guys seen anything else?"

"Negative," Harris answered. "Aftah' he fired a few bursts at y'all he stopped shootin', as far as we could tell. We never had eyes on 'im, we just seen smoke from his weapon."

"Roger," Nunez said. "Keep an eye on the back corners of the compound, and make sure you get positive ID before you shoot at anything. We might come running out if things go to shit inside."

"Roger. We got yo' backs."

Nunez let go of the mike and said to Quincy, "Quincy, can you breach the door?"

Over his shoulder Quincy said "I'm going to kick it, and if that doesn't work, I'm going to shoot it and then kick it again."

"Okay, good plan." Nunez turned toward the wall, so that he could address the soldiers on either side of him. "You guys all know what to do. If the guy in front of you goes left, you go right. We clear every room, we don't leave anything undone. Try not to frag anything unless you have a good reason. Hooah?"

To his left and right, his soldiers nodded. Trevino, second from last in the stack, still breathed heavily, and Nunez knew it wasn't from the exertion anymore. Nunez took a couple of deep breaths, trying to bring his own heart rate down. He knew that he could call this off now, forget about entering the compound, and nobody would criticize him for it. He could make up whatever reason he wanted in order to justify that decision; he only had five guys, he thought there were too many Taliban inside the compound, he had too many casualties from the IED already...whatever excuse he felt like using, it would work.

Nunez saw and understood Trevino's fear, sensed the thought behind Powell's eyes, *This is a bad fucking idea and when we all die it'll be your fault.* Nunez took one last, long breath, then tapped the bolt forward assist on his carbine like he always did in high stress situations, making sure his weapon would fire when he needed it to. He put his hand on Lattimore's shoulder. Every man in the stack behind Quincy put one hand on the shoulder of the man in front of him, a means of physical communication.

"Quincy, whenever you're ready, we're behind you."

Quincy's shoulders raised as he breathed in, then he took two steps forward and kicked the lock from an angle. The doors bent at the center, the lock bowed but didn't break. Nunez expected Quincy to shoot the door, but instead he took a step backward and kicked the lock again. The doors popped open and Nunez readied himself for the rush inside. Over Lattimore's shoulder he saw Quincy recover his footing and start his charge through the doorway. Nunez and Lattimore moved together behind him.

A machine gun exploded inside the compound. Quincy screamed "Fuck!" and threw his left hand out to steady himself against the doorway. He fell, and Nunez felt something like panic flood his brain as he lost sight of him. A second burst of gunfire ripped the space in the doorway. The rounds made *thunk!* sounds as they punched holes through the right side door.

Lattimore threw himself backwards hard, hit Nunez square in the chest and knocked him off balance. As Nunez struggled to keep his footing his mind registered one odd-sounding impact among all the others. In his peripheral vision he saw a helmet pop into the air above the place he last saw Quincy, spin end over end and fall out of sight again. The helmet was only in view for a fraction of a second, but like everything else that was happening, it seemed to Nunez to fly in crystal clear slow motion.

Nunez sprang to the right to get around Lattimore and bounded the few feet to Quincy. His heart sank as he saw Quincy lying in an unnatural, contorted position, just like most dead people he had seen at work as a cop. Quincy was on his left side, his left leg and arm crunched under his upper body and his right arm behind his back. A small bloodstain was visible under him, and above his right temple a large, bloody welt marred his scalp. Nunez grabbed the handle on the back of Quincy's body armor and yanked so hard he nearly wrenched his shoulder.

In a flash Lattimore and Trevino were there, reaching past Nunez to grab whatever handhold they could find. The three of them pulled Quincy clear of the doorway as rounds screamed through it. After Quincy was behind cover Nunez looked up and saw the machine gun lying in the open in the doorway, at the end of a streak of blood. From nowhere, a sudden realization hit Nunez.

Quincy stopped running so he could stay close and protect me, Nunez thought. *That's why he was walking when I looked up and saw him. He slowed down in the open, under fire, so he could protect me. And I just got him killed.*

Behind him, Trevino blurted out, "Fuck man, hees dead! Sheet!"

"Shut the fuck up, Trevino!" Nunez snapped. "He's not fucking dead until the fucking medic says he's dead!"

Nunez took another look at Quincy and thought, *Fuck, he really is dead. God damn, I fucked this up.*

"Powell!" Nunez yelled. "Stay here and treat Quincy! Lattimore and Trevino, stack on me!"

"Are you fucking serious?" Powell screamed back. "What the fuck are you trying to do? Fuck this compound, we need to get Quincy back to the vehicles!"

"Powell, I got this! Stay here with Quincy, we'll get him back to the road as soon as we clear this place! Lattimore, Trevino, let's fucking go!"

Trevino popped up and stepped behind Nunez as Nunez moved toward the door. Lattimore gave Powell a serious look, then ran forward and forced his way between Nunez and Trevino. Nunez understood what Lattimore was doing; Nunez had ordered Quincy to be first through the door, and Quincy had been killed. If Nunez was going to continue this mission, his mission, he had to be first through the door himself, to take the risk he was ordering his people to take. And Lattimore was willing to take that same risk, before he let a lower-ranked soldier do it.

At the head of the stack, Nunez tried to steady himself, thinking of what he would do as he made entry. He pictured the impacts of the rounds that had come through the doorway, and had the impression that they had come from the far side of the compound, not from the side or from a very steep angle. When he hit the doorway, the threat would probably be right in front of him. He coiled his muscles in preparation for his movement, then took another look at the machine gun lying in the doorway.

He said "Wait!" over his shoulder and let his weapon hang on its sling so both his hands would be free. He crouched and lunged forward, grabbed the gun and jerked it back to him. Nobody fired at him in the split second he was exposed in the doorway. Nunez fumbled to his feet with the SAW in his hands, then stuck it around the corner and pulled the trigger, dumping a long burst into the open courtyard.

When the bolt slammed home on an empty chamber, Nunez dropped the smoking machine gun, reached back with his left hand and slapped Lattimore. Then he grabbed his carbine, ducked his head and pulled his elbows in close, and hooked to the left through the doorway. He barely noticed the sound of the woman and children screaming from across the courtyard as he charged through the door. Just inside the door to the left was the entrance to the room whose window the Taliban fighter had been firing from. It was empty except for brass shells littering the floor.

Lattimore came through the door behind Nunez. Trevino stumbled through the doorway and fell on his face before bouncing back onto his feet three feet inside the threshold. Other than the room next to the main door, nothing was on that wall or the side walls; all the rooms were across the courtyard, spread out all along that side of the compound. A small, mud-brick storage shed stood to the right side.

"The room they were shooting from is clear!" Nunez yelled. Then he realized that the three of them were standing in the open like flaming fucking morons. Nunez sprinted toward the far left corner of the courtyard, yelling out, "Get the fuck out of the open! Stack on me!"

Lattimore and Trevino bounded to Nunez. They bunched up on the wall next to the door to the far left room, all three of them breathing so heavily they could barely talk. Nunez made out a woman's voice shrieking from one of the rooms, along with a mix of children's screams, and he wondered if he had just shot them with Quincy's machine gun.

"Okay...we do this...real quick", Nunez huffed between gasps. "Don't be afraid...afraid to shoot...but watch out for fucking civilians."

"Roger."

"Okay, Sarsh."

Nunez threw the first door open and charged inside. The room was a kitchen of sorts, with a cast-iron stove and piles of wood along with bags of rice laid neatly along the walls. It was a small room, and it took just seconds to determine nobody was inside. Nunez led his two soldiers back into the courtyard, heading the stack again as they prepared to clear the next room. Nunez was unnerved a little by the fact that the woman and children were still screaming.

The next room was someone's bedroom, also empty of people. The doors to the next three rooms were unlocked, and each was mostly bare and unoccupied. Past the fifth room around a corner Nunez discovered a short alley leading to another wooden door. That door was standing open, and shells were scattered around the doorway. The door led to a walkway, with thick vegetation on one side and the wall of another compound on the other side. The walkway curved to the left and disappeared from view.

Nunez peered around the corner into the small alley and thought, *Mother-fucker. He got away. He shot at us from the livestock room, then moved to here and shot Quincy from this doorway, then hauled ass.* Considering the screaming from one of the next rooms, Nunez added, *Well...maybe.* Then he sprinted past the alley, leading Lattimore and Trevino to the second to last door. The screaming came from this room.

As he stood outside the door, the thought crossed Nunez's mind to toss a grenade into the room before they entered. He forced the thought away, knowing he wouldn't do that without some indication that enemy was inside. There was no question civilians were in there. A Taliban fighter might also be inside with them, pointing his machine gun at the door and maybe even using the woman and children for cover. But he wasn't certain there were any Taliban inside, so he wouldn't prep the room with a grenade. If there had been spent shells lying near the door, or if he heard the sound of a weapon being charged inside the room, if he had any evidence at all that a bad guy was inside he would have steeled his heart, accepted the guilt and thrown as many grenades as it took to make sure the room was safe before his soldiers took one step through the door.

He reached for the steel handle and pushed without success; this was the only locked room in the compound so far. He stepped around and kicked the door as hard as he could. The door flexed but held, and the screaming inside increased in pitch and volume. Nunez kicked again at what looked like the weakest spot. The second kick seemed to do nothing at all, other than hurt Nunez's foot and leg like hell. Furious, Nunez kicked the door several more times until he was in so much pain he had to stop. The door held.

Trevino ran up and respectfully bumped him aside, saying "Lemme try, Sarsh." Trevino was only five foot six inches tall and way overweight at 210 pounds, most of which was fat instead of muscle, and was burdened with almost sixty pounds of gear. Trevino took several steps back from the door and then charged it with all the speed he could muster. He hit the door sideways with his left shoulder, and the force of the impact knocked the center wood panel from the door but left the frame around it in place. The bottom of the frame caught Trevino's ankle and he fell hard onto his left side inside the room.

Nunez tried to charge into the room but Lattimore was there first, jumping over Trevino as he scrambled to his feet and moved from the exposed spot on the floor. The shrieking was loud enough to hurt now. Nunez charged into the room. A woman in a sky blue *burqa* cowered in a corner behind a large table and shielded two small boys behind her. This room was the largest in the compound, with several pieces of simple wooden furniture inside. A quick glance through the room was enough to show that the woman and children were the only occupants.

"Shut the fuck up, bitch!" Lattimore yelled. The woman slapped her hands on her head and shrieked even louder.

"What the fuck is she wearing a burqa inside here for? Don't they uncover themselves inside their houses?" Nunez asked. "Do we even know this is an actual woman?"

Over the screams, Lattimore said, "Sounds like a fucking woman. You want me to check her?"

Nunez thought it over. Throughout their training, for both Iraq and Afghanistan, he had been told over and over, do not ever touch a woman. They had been taught to order women to stand with their arms outstretched and pull their clothing tight in order to see if anything was hidden underneath. During the training, it just seemed to be assumed that an interpreter would always be available. Nobody had ever told them what to do when they were confronted with a hysterical woman, or at least what looked like a hysterical woman, in a compound they had just been shot at from, with one of their soldiers lying dead outside, and the possibility that Taliban were in the next room.

"Yeah, check her," Nunez said.

Lattimore walked toward the woman, who kicked herself further into the corner while she wailed. Even with her eyes nearly covered, Nunez could still read the terror in them.

Lattimore repeated "Shut the fuck up!", reached down to grab the thin *burqa* material in a fist just under her neck and yanked her to her feet. Nunez almost told him to take it easy but changed his mind, directing Trevino to stop watching Lattimore and cover the door instead. Lattimore grabbed the bottom edge of the *burqa* and yanked it up hard, revealing a dark green, satiny Afghan dress underneath. The woman tried to slap Lattimore's hands away as he pulled the material farther up, finally revealing her face. Lattimore dropped the *burqa* and turned to Nunez to say "It's a woman, and she's fucking ugly. No weapons." Behind him, the woman wailed in protest and pulled her *burqa* down while the two boys, not more than a few years old, screamed in terror.

"Okay, let's get the fuck out of here." Nunez stepped to the door, stuck his eyes and weapon out of the doorway, then jogged outside. He scanned the court-yard again before setting up on the last door. Trevino and Lattimore came out right after him, and without a word they entered and cleared the last room, which turned out to be a storage room filled with bags of rice, beans and dried cow shit the Afghans use to heat their homes during the winter. They cleared what they thought was the storage shed but which turned out to be the compound's outhouse, nothing more than a bare four walls with a shit-splattered hole in the center of the floor. Nunez just had to stick his head into the outhouse to clear it and then said "We're done, let's go."

Lattimore exhaled, relieved. He took a step toward Nunez and slapped him on the shoulder, giving a look that Nunez really couldn't read. Then he turned and headed toward the main doorway, yelling "Lattimore coming out, Lattimore coming out!" Trevino trotted after him, and Nunez walked out backward, watching the other door to the courtyard.

When he turned around to walk out of the doorway he saw for the first time at all that was left of the Civil Affairs humvee. The back end pointed at the sky from what had to be a crater. The roof and turret were missing. Nunez couldn't see any indication of a front half.

He turned to his right and was shocked to see one of the Civil Affairs sol-diers kneeling down working on Quincy, who was laid out straight with a black nylon tourniquet on his upper left thigh and a bloody Israeli bandage underneath it. A second bandage was wrapped around his head, and a black stretcher was unfolded next to him. Staff Sergeant Powell stood behind the CA soldier, pull-ing security. Nunez couldn't believe what he had to be seeing, and asked Powell what was going on.

"Quincy's leg is pretty fucked up, but we got the bleeding stopped. It looks like one round hit his helmet and knocked it into the side of his head. He's still out cold, but he's a lucky motherfucker."

Nunez took a moment to absorb the relief he felt washing over him; he had been certain Quincy was dead. The fact that he was still unconscious was a bad sign, but he was alive. Nunez knelt down and put his hand on Quincy's left shoulder, felt him breathe and thought to himself, *Thank god, Quincy. Thank god.* Then he sobered up and asked Powell, "What about the CA guys, any of them make it?"

"They're fucked, all dead except for the gunner. He went with the roof when it blew, and he's seriously fucked up. He's pinned under the roof, but he's still alive. Doc's monitoring him and the guys are trying to lift the roof off of him."

"Did you see the gunner?" Nunez asked. "How the fuck did he survive that hit?"

"I haven't left this spot," Powell said. "This CA guy told me what was going on, and Harris has been talking about it on the radio. If you had been listening you might have heard all that."

Nunez gave Powell a hard look. "Yeah, whatever. I was a little busy. Next time I'll let you run everything."

"Maybe you should. I would have kept everyone at the vehicles instead of doing this John Wayne bullshit."

"Good fucking thing you're not in charge then, isn't it?" Nunez shot back. "Enough of your shit, Powell. It was my call to go after the guy. If you have a fucking problem with that, go whine to First Sergeant or Klein."

"I'm not whining," Powell said. "I just think it was stupid to try to clear a compound with five guys. And you guys didn't find shit, did you?"

"We cleared the compound," Nunez said. "The guy got away. It is what it is. We'll talk about it later."

The CA soldier spoke up. "Hey, if you guys are ready we need to move him back to the MRAPs. Help me get him onto the litter."

The five soldiers grabbed pant legs and body armor and half lifted, half dragged Quincy onto the stretcher. Trevino covered their backs while the rest of them hefted the stretcher and struggled to keep Quincy from falling off. Lattimore carried Quincy's machine gun in his right hand and one handle of the litter in his left. Quincy's damaged helmet, which the CA soldier had placed on

Quincy's chest, fell off and Trevino picked it up. As they stumbled to the road, Nunez heard first and then saw the comforting sight of two OH-58 Kiowas, observation helicopters, providing cover from above.

As they moved, Nunez wheezed to the CA soldier, "Are you a medic?"

"No, I just switched to a reserve CA position for this deployment. I used to be a forward observer. Back home in California I'm a paramedic."

"Fuck, I'm glad you're here."

"Thanks."

The group reached the MRAPs, where Harris, Colt 2's commander, waited to help stage the litter on the safe side of the MRAP. Harris was calm, like he almost always was. He was twenty-six, black with the light skin of his mother, who was still back in his hometown of New Orleans. As they placed the litter on the side of the road Nunez looked again at the CA humvee, not surrounded by smoke and dust anymore, although small fires still burned near it.

"Hey Sarge', I'm still waiting on a' arrival time fo' the medevac bird," Harris said to Nunez. "But don' worry, it on the way. The French are almost here also."

"Okay. Walk with me, I need to get a handle on where we're at now," Nunez told Harris. "Lattimore, stay here and make sure Quincy's ready for the bird."

"Roger, Sarge."

"What the fuck?" Powell protested. "I'm right here, I can make sure he's ready. I've been with him the whole time."

"Yeah, I know. Lattimore, you got it. I'll be back in a few." Harris and Nunez walked toward the destroyed humvee. The back third, all that was still intact, was ass-up in a crater that was at least six feet wide and spanned almost the entire road. Nunez walked around to look at the front of what was left of the humvee and Nunez was shocked again, for the third or fourth time that morning.

The Civil Affairs lieutenant was still strapped into one of the back seats. His corpse hung forward against the seat belt straps, helmet gone and head black, sleeves and pant legs torn open, both feet blown off of lower legs that were all shredded flesh and exposed bone. Everything forward of the back seats was just gone; the rest of the humvee was barely recognizable, a scattered mass of burned and shattered engine parts, splintered fiberglass shell, broken radios and seats.

"What the fuck?" Nunez asked, astounded. "Why is he still in there?"

"Shit Jerry, he dead," Harris said. "Every motherfuckah who could help was workin' on keepin' tha' gunner alive, then after they got him sorta stable the CA paramedic dude took off to help you guys out. And we still had to find the TC and driver. Doc took five seconds to confirm the LT was dead, then we had other shit to do."

"God damn," Nunez said. "Where are the TC and driver?"

"They in pieces, all over the fuckin' place. We found they body armor with they chests still inside, and we found most of one of 'em, but we're still missing a head and an arm and legs, I think. Lyons been gatherin' 'em up."

"Did you tell the French to bring body bags?"

"I told 'em we had confirmed KIAs," Harris said. "They shoulda figured it out from there."

"Okay. Fuck, this sucks." Nunez looked at a small group of soldiers gathered about twenty five meters west of the road. He pointed at them and asked, "How's the gunner?"

"He pinned by the roof, but he breathing and he have a decent pulse. Doc say his legs are fucked, tha' edge of tha' roof broke both his femurs and he'll probly' lose both legs above the knee. But last I heard, his vital signs were good. I don' know how tha' fuck he survived that blast, Jerry. Look how far from the road it blew him."

"Fuck man, I don't know either," Nunez said. "He must be one seriously strong fucker. Listen, I need to get back on the radio and get an update. You monitor what's going on with that gunner. Cool?"

"I got it man, you go ahead," Harris said.

"Thanks man."

Nunez turned to walk back to his MRAP so he could get on the vehicle radio. When he turned he saw the CA lieutenant again, and thought he and Harris should get him out of his seat. Then he changed his mind and walked past the humvee to his vehicle. Someone else could get him, after QRF showed up.

Before Nunez could get his headset on he heard heavy small arms fire to their south, at least a kilometer away. The MRAP gunners edged their weapons south while the dismounted soldiers hunched down a little, looked over their shoulders and then went back to what they were doing. Nunez pulled his headset on and listened for radio traffic.

The French were being ambushed as they rolled north from. The shooting was over in less than a minute. As Nunez looked south he was relieved to see the French vehicles come around a curve through Landakhel.

The eight French armored vehicles, called VABs, stopped when their first vehicle was parallel with the rear of Nunez's convoy. One of the VABs lumbered over a small rock wall bordering the road and moved out toward the pinned-down humvee gunner. The back doors of the other vehicles opened and French soldiers climbed out, pulling on backpacks as they set a loose perimeter a few meters east of the road. Nunez saw a few of the gunners throw handfuls of spent shells from the roofs of the VABs, clearing the refuse left by their short engagement.

The soldiers wore uniforms with a camouflage pattern that looked like the old US military green Battle Dress Uniform, with new and modern body armor covered with magazine pouches, global positioning systems and rifle grenades. They carried FAMAS carbines that looked futuristic but had been in service since the 1970's.

Some of the French Mountain troops had told Nunez that their regiment was the third best in the French Army, after the paratroopers and the Marine regiment. But the mountain troops, every one of them, were in amazing physical condition, disciplined, aggressive as hell, proud and eager for combat. Nunez had been surprised at how much he liked and respected them all, since like most other Americans he had heard nothing but negatives about the French army. And the French seemed proud to serve alongside Americans, another thing that surprised Nunez. Some of them even wore US military combat patches on their right sleeves. They were especially fond of 101st or 82nd Airborne patches, the patches of the units they knew had helped liberate their homeland more than sixty years earlier. Nunez was not ashamed at the relief he felt when he saw them.

He got out of his MRAP to give the French platoon leader a quick rundown on what had happened. The platoon leader spoke good English, like most French officers and a good number of the enlisted men. Nunez told the lieutenant about the compound they had cleared, and the lieutenant decided to have his men clear it again, and the compound next to it.

The lieutenant spoke into his radio, and one of the French squads that had and gone prone on the side of the road rose up as one and jogged toward the compound that Nunez had cleared. There was no firing from either side this time, and when the squad filed through the doorway the woman inside started shrieking again. The squad cleared the compound in less than three minutes, then filed back out and stacked on the next compound. This one took longer, and a radio call from inside the compound grabbed the lieutenant's attention.

"My soldiers have found a car battery and wire inside the compound," the lieutenant said. "They are going to secure it and remain inside."

"There are no people inside, lieutenant?" Nunez asked.

"No, there are no people."

From that point on, Nunez didn't have much to do. The French directed the recovery of the humvee and the pieces of its occupants, freed the gunner by hooking a chain from a VAB to the edge of the roof to lift it off his legs. They directed the medevac birds to a landing zone, sent Quincy and the wounded gunner to safety while most of Nunez's platoon watched in silence. Lattimore and Powell insisted on helping carry Quincy, who was now conscious and in agony, to the bird.

The French had one of their interpreters speak to a very infuriated-looking village elder who had been called by the brother of the woman inside the compound. The three of them were irate over the fact that an Afghan woman had been touched by an American. When Nunez went through the frustrating, nonsensical, must-be-followed-in-order-to-show-proper-respect-for-all-Afghans-involved ritual of asking the interpreter to ask the elder to ask the brother to ask the woman why the Taliban had been shooting at his convoy from her compound, the reply that came back down the chain was exactly what he expected: "It was not my compound. You have made a mistake." And he couldn't explode at them about the insurgent who was shooting at them from the window, about Quincy getting shot in the leg and almost taking a round through the head, about the spent shells inside the compound and at the back gate. He just had to hold it in.

From the time the IED exploded until the time they remounted their vehicles, turned around and headed north almost thirteen hours had passed. After the initial chaos that seemed to fly by, everything else took forever. The recovery of the bodies, the Explosive Ordnance Disposal team's assessment, the recovery of the car battery and the wire that had been buried so that nothing was visible unless someone walked over it almost sixty meters from the road, the arduous task of putting every little piece of humvee they could find into the back of a truck, a crane operator's careful lifting of the engine and large pieces of vehicle frame, all the things that soldiers rarely think about but that have to happen after a catastrophic IED strike.

Just after dusk Nunez shook hands with the French platoon leader and ordered his soldiers to mount up and head out. The remaining Civil Affairs humvee headed south with the French. The bodies went with the French also, stuffed in body bags and draped over the jumble of vehicle parts in the back of a truck.

The short trip back was made mostly in silence. The little bit of radio chatter was all business, and at least in Nunez's MRAP there was almost no talk at all. Wilson made one feeble attempt at a joke just as they reached the gate to Firebase Pierce.

"Hey Vlacek."

"Yeah."

"New rule. No more talking about your dick while we're on missions."

"Funny. Yeah, sure."

When they arrived at Pierce, they weaved through the serpentine path made by the huge concrete barriers at the firebase gate, passed under the powerful halogen lamps and the machine guns mounted in guard towers manned by bored French soldiers. The gunners cleared their weapons and Nunez got on the radio to tell them to forget about refueling, he just wanted them to get some food and go to sleep. They pulled into their parking spots in the small open area near their tent, and drivers got out to help gunners dismount crew-served weapons while truck commanders stripped off their gear.

Nunez stayed in the vehicle to record information he would need for his After Action Report: approximate times, grid locations, approximate number of rounds they had fired, pictures of the RPK bullet impacts on the armor and windows of Nunez's vehicle, the names of the three Civil Affairs soldiers who had been killed and the one who was wounded, details about Quincy's wounds. It was going to be a long report, with a lot of attention paid to it at battalion headquarters.

"Hey, Sarge."

Nunez turned in his seat to see Lattimore and Harris standing at the open back door, looking past Wilson's legs toward the TC's seat.

"Yeah, what's up?"

"We're going in, you need us to do anything?"

"Nah, not tonight," Nunez answered. "I'll need statements later, but tonight get some food and kick back. Just make sure I get the statements by noon or so tomorrow. I'll need them before I put you guys in for awards."

Lattimore and Harris gave him blank stares. Soldiers never really knew how to respond when they were told that their bravery deserved to be publicly recognized.

Nunez continued, "I'm putting Quincy in for a Bronze Star with a V for valor. Lattimore, I'm putting you in for an Army Commendation medal with a V. Harris, you and Lyons and Doc were running around under fire trying to help out the CA guys, you deserve Army Commendation Medals with V's too. So does Trevino. And Powell. I think we should put the CA guy in for something also, he did a good job out there."

Behind Lattimore and Harris, Powell walked past the back of the MRAP with a pissed off expression on his face, eyes fixed on a spot in front of him, not looking toward the three other senior NCOs in the platoon. Lattimore watched him walk away, frowned and turned back to Nunez.

"You want a statement from him too?"

"No. But I guess we'll have to have one. I'm sure it'll say I fucked everything up in every possible way. It'll probably say I'm the one that planted the IED."

Smiling, Harris said, "I can jus' copy his 'den, that's what mine was goin' to say too."

Nunez needed the comic relief. Laughing, he responded, "Prick."

"Don't worry about Powell, Sarge," Lattimore said. "He'll pout for a few days and then be back to normal. I think tomorrow morning the four of us should get together and go over the details for the statements, so nobody bitches about something not matching up. We can talk things out with Powell then, if we need to."

"Yeah, that's a good idea," Nunez agreed. "We'll do it right after maintenance."

"Awright, I guess if you don' need nuthin', we'll head in," Harris said.

"Hang on a second...I know I just told you I'm putting you in for medals, but I still need to say it to you," Nunez said. "Y'all did a badass job out there. I'm sorry it turned out the way it did, but that wasn't because of anything you two did. Tell all the guys they did good too, especially Trevino."

"We'll tell them," Lattimore replied. "And Sarge, tomorrow sometime we'll get Quincy's stuff ready to send back home."

Fuck, I hadn't even thought about that, Nunez realized. *I guess nobody expects him to come back.*

"Yeah, okay. We'll get it tomorrow."

"No, we'll get it tomorrow," Lattimore said, pointing to himself and Harris. "You have other shit to do, don't worry about it."

Nodding, Nunez said, "Okay." The word was almost a whisper.

"Later boss."

"Later."

Harris and Lattimore walked away into the dark. Above Nunez, Wilson finished locking the turret hatch and leaned down over Nunez's shoulder. He was on his second deployment as Nunez's gunner. They had first been teamed up during the big Texas National Guard call up early in the Iraq war. At that time Wilson had been a twenty year old part time college student who spent half his week in school, half his week moving boxes of junk food from warehouse shelves to delivery trucks, and one weekend a month loading 120mm rounds into the main gun of an M1A1 Abrams tank in a Guard unit near his hometown of Victoria, Texas. When he was called to active duty he became a victim of the Guard's practice of pulling soldiers from their home units, sticking them with strangers plucked from other units, and sending them off to war.

Nunez was at that time a thirty-two year old displaced infantryman, and he and Wilson had been teamed up on a vehicle with a lonely cavalry scout in a so-called artillery battalion half full of soldiers who had never seen an arty tube in their lives and would never see one in Iraq. Together they had all spent a year running around the highways of Iraq in poorly armored humvees, escorting supply trucks to bases around the country. Wilson changed his specialty to infantry after that deployment and volunteered for Afghanistan when he found out Nunez was going. They had served together longer than anyone else in the platoon, were friends outside the military, and almost never spoke to each other as supervisor and subordinate.

"Hey Jerry, we're done, you coming to the house?" Wilson asked, talking about the big, open tent that Nunez's platoon occupied.

"Not yet, man. I got a ton of shit I need to write down for the AAR, then I have to call battalion headquarters and make sure they have all the details right. You know there's a bunch of staff officers back there spazzing out over this whole thing. Hopefully they have an update on Quincy too."

"You need to chill out a little Jerry, just do all that shit tomorrow," Wilson said. "Maybe you have to make the phone call, but the AAR can wait. Nobody expects it tonight."

"Nah, I'm awake, might as well get it done now. I doubt I'll be able to sleep anyway."

"Jerry...that's bullshit. You're making an excuse to not come inside."

Nunez looked at Wilson for a few seconds. "Yeah, maybe I am. I guess I need a minute or two alone to sort this through in my head. I keep thinking about what I did wrong. What I should have done."

"There's nothing to sort out," Wilson said. "The CA guys got hit by an IED. That's not your fault. You went after the Taliban when they fired at us, and Quincy got hit. That's not your fault either. It's a war, Jerry, shit happens. We both know that."

"Maybe it was my fault and maybe it wasn't, Alex. I shouldn't have gone into that compound with three guys, or with five guys. If there had been three or four Taliban in there who really wanted to fight, we would've all been fucked. All that shit that happened today was done by two guys, just one guy with an IED and one guy with an RPK. That's all there were, and they fucked us up that bad. If there had been more..." he said, his voice trailing off.

"There weren't more," Wilson interrupted. "And you know that five guys is enough to clear a small compound. I think you're looking for a reason to beat yourself up."

"There are a lot of reasons I should beat myself up, Alex. Do you know how many times we left our backs uncovered when we cleared that compound? How many times we got tunnel vision so bad that we forgot to look around? Fuck, Alex, I didn't even hear the radio, not once the entire time we were in there. Jesus man, what if you guys had seen more Taliban coming and tried to warn me? I wouldn't have heard it. I wouldn't have heard shit."

"But that didn't happen, Jerry," Wilson said in obvious frustration. "We can what if this shit to death. This isn't anything complicated, stop blowing it up into something worse than it is. We got hit, and we lost guys. That's going to happen in a war, and it's not your fault. Ease up on yourself, man. You did good."

Nunez's eyes snapped upward. "I did *good*? How the fuck do you figure I did *good*?"

Wilson squatted down so that his eyes were almost even with Nunez's. "Jerry, what do we always say, every god damn mission, that we should do if we take fire? We always say that if you run when you get hit it just encourages the enemy to shoot at us more. We said the same thing in Iraq. We always talk shit about the transportation companies and VIP convoys protecting idiot colonels and generals who just unload rounds and run away whenever someone shoots at them. Spray, Pray and Run Away, right? The Taliban aren't afraid to ambush us, Jerry. Fuck, I wouldn't be afraid to ambush a regular American convoy. But in this platoon we say we should go after them, that we need to kill them, or at least scare them so bad that they think about it next time they feel like fucking with us. And that's what you did today, Jerry. You haven't just been talking shit, you did exactly what you said you were going to do. And even though that Taliban gunner hit Quincy, I bet he shit his pants when he saw you guys coming after him. I was proud to see you guys charge across that field to that compound. I was even prouder to see that after Quincy got hit, you guys stacked on the door and went in anyway."

"Well...yeah, we've always said we should go after the enemy. And yeah, we said it in Iraq. But Alex," Nunez said, "we never had to actually do it in Iraq. We never did it here either, not until today. And I don't feel like it turned out so good. Quincy probably doesn't think much of my decisions today."

"Jerry, we're an infantry platoon," Wilson said. "It's our job. If Quincy had been on the gun and I had been the dismount, I would have been first in the door. And if I had gotten killed, I wouldn't come back and blame you at all."

"That doesn't make any fucking sense, but thanks," Nunez said. "Look, I'll be in in a few, I just need to sit out here and get myself ready for all the second guessing and shit talking I'm going to hear in the next couple of days. Powell's probably sending official complaints about me to his congressman already."

"Powell just runs his mouth, but he's one of us. He'll bitch and make smart-ass comments and then do whatever you tell him to do," Wilson said.

"Yeah, maybe. We'll see. Go ahead and go on in man, I'll be there in a few minutes," Nunez said. "Promise."

"Alright, but don't convince yourself to commit suicide by jumping from the top of the truck or anything like that."

Nunez gave Wilson a deadpan look. "Fuck off, Alex. Trust me, if I decide to off myself I'll tell you first so you get first shot at all my stuff."

"I'll be waiting...seriously bro, don't stay out here alone too long. It's bad for you."

"Gotcha."

Wilson climbed over the gear strewn around the back of the MRAP and went out the back door, locking it behind him. Nunez laid his head back against his seat and closed his eyes. He rubbed his eyes and ran his hands down his face. *Sometimes being a leader sucks*, he thought. *Having to make these choices sucks. Losing your guys sucks. Losing your guys sucks worse when it's your fault. Deal with it, dipshit. Deal with it.*

He reached over and popped the door, managing to get one foot out before hesitation took over again. *We've only been here three months*, he thought. *Six or seven more to go.*

He kicked the door open again and half-crawled onto the step, then pulled his body armor off and threw it onto his seat. From the step he cleared his M4 carbine and M9 pistol. Looking into the darkened firebase, he thought of graffiti he had seen in a bathroom stall in Kyrgyzstan, at the airbase where they stopped before entering Afghanistan.

I wish I was
Where I was
When I wished
I was here

Nunez yawned and ran his hand over his face again, finally feeling the fatigue from the day's events, and looked at the moonlit mountains off in the distance. The air was warm and thin, the night crystal clear and beautiful. The faint glow of a cigarette intensified and ebbed as a French soldier took a drag in a guard tower, reviving the pangs of Nunez's old nicotine addiction, something he had beaten years before.

He jumped from the step, closed the MRAP door and locked it with its padlock. A dirty medium sized black and white mutt, an unofficial firebase pet that had survived the French camp commander's halfhearted orders to his soldiers to kill every dog on the base for disease prevention reasons, sat a few feet from Nunez's door. The dog tilted its head and looked at Nunez with a puzzled expression. Nunez slapped his thigh and whistled, and the dog trotted to him to press its nose against his leg. He took a few seconds to pet it, savoring the tiny bit of affection they shared. Then, wishing for all the world that he was somewhere else, he walked into the darkness toward the platoon office to start his report.

CHAPTER 2

Klein, Nunez, Powell, Harris and Lattimore crowded into the small conex box that served as the intelligence team's office, looking at the maps and pictures of bikinied women on the walls but still listening intently to the intel sergeant's briefing. The intel sergeant was regular army but was under a "relaxed grooming standards" memo, the idea behind it being that an American with a beard and civilian clothes would be better able to connect with the Afghan population. He was in a pair of jeans and an AC/DC T-shirt, and had a full beard, moustache and long hair. Even though his appearance was allowed by the military, whenever colonels and sergeants major came to the firebase he hid so that they wouldn't see him and demand an explanation for it.

"This is what we've found out so far," Sergeant First Class Durrand said to the group. "The IED cell that took out the CA humvee isn't the same one that's been hitting vehicles on that route over the last four months. These guys just moved to this area because they got pushed out of the Uzbin valley down south. A Special Forces team took out two of their commanders but missed the actual bomb makers, and the Taliban area commander shifted them here until the heat's off. This team has six guys left, we think. We talked to the intel team in Uzbin and got some background on this cell, and apparently these guys know what they're doing. The cell that's been hitting us here for months has had some pretty spectacular successes, but they miss more than they hit. And they don't usually use as much explosive as this new cell always does. Basically, the existing cell was good, but this new one is better."

Nunez remembered what was left of the Civil Affairs soldiers after the IED strike. He shot a sideways glance at Lieutenant Klein and whispered, "Well, isn't that fucking great news." Klein, at twenty-seven, looked and acted less like a confused new lieutenant than like the regular army infantry sergeant he had been three years earlier in Iraq. His full name was Henry David Klein, Henry D. Klein, and as soon as he was assigned to their platoon Nunez had christened him Lieutenant Homie D. Klown. Even the soldiers in the platoon who were too

31

young to have watched *In Living Color* in the early 90's thought it was a cool nickname. Klein was smart enough to know that if he bitched and whined and ordered them not to call him that it would only entrench it as his nickname forever, so he kept his mouth shut about it.

Klein frowned and spoke up, "Hey Durrand, is there any chance these guys will get pissed at each other and start fighting among themselves? I mean, is maybe one cell Taliban and one cell someone else?"

"Man, I wish," Durrand sighed. "No, these teams are both Taliban. No other insurgent networks have broken into the IED business in Kapisa yet. We haven't been told this specifically, but I'm sure the two teams are under orders to work together or else. I mean, you're right, there probably is some conflict between them, since the leader of the old cell is now under the leader of the new cell. The old guy will be pissed about it. Every Taliban is stepping on every other Taliban and trying to claw his way to the top, they all want to be in command of everyone else. They're worse than our officers."

Everyone in the office smiled at that. Even Klein, who said, "Yeah, blow me, douchebag."

"Oh sorry sir," Durrand said, smiling back. "Didn't see you there. Anyway, we can't expect these guys to fight each other, even if they don't like each other much. And this sucks, but what'll probably happen is that since the old cell has the local knowledge and the new cell has better capabilities, they'll probably merge into a cell that's better than either one of them could be individually. But I guess I don't have to tell you guys that. You've already seen it."

"That's no shit," Powell said.

"What about the actual fighters, not the guys who build and detonate the IEDs, but the fucks who are just there to shoot?" Nunez asked. "Like that cocksucker who shot Quincy? How many of those are there?"

Durrand raised his eyebrows. "That's a good question, and the answer is 'I don't have a fucking clue.' We don't know if there are dedicated fighters in either of these cells, or if the guys take turns being fighters or being bombers. Maybe the cell only handles IEDs and uses local Taliban fighters for support. My gut feeling is that we'll never know, and it won't make any difference anyway. For you line guys, all you really need to know is that the tactics have changed. With the old cell, they just blew their IED, hauled ass and hoped for the best. These new guys, when they were operating down south they always followed an IED with an ambush. So from now on, if you take an IED hit, you should expect small arms fire along with it." He paused a second, then asked, "Speaking of Quincy, how's he doing?"

"He's good," Klein said. "He's in Germany now, getting ready to go back to the U.S. As far as we know he's going to be fine. How close are we to pinning down a good location for this cell and taking it out?"

"We're not close," Durrand said. "We're nowhere near close. We know they move around a lot, and we think they individually change locations every night. The only real pattern we know of is that they mostly stay in the Alasai valley, but that's a big area. And you guys know how bad Alasai is. If we have to go in there to get them, it's going to be a motherfucker."

They nodded. None of them had been in the Alasai, but every soldier in Kapisa had heard all about that valley. It was Taliban territory, a haven where insurgents could always find shelter, food, medical attention, ammunition and freedom to operate. Soldiers from the 82nd Airborne had held outposts in the valley two years before but the unit that replaced them had decided not to man those outposts, under the mistaken assumption that the valley had been pacified.

The valley was quiet while the 82nd was there. Two years later it was pure Indian country, a place where coalition soldiers were ambushed every time they dared enter. French and Afghan army forces had pushed into the valley on patrols twice during the previous month, and both times the ANA had lost several killed before pulling out. In those two engagements the French had suffered a few wounded but no one killed, and had pulled out with the ANA after expending tens of thousands of rounds of ammunition, firing dozens of tank main gun rounds and anti-tank missiles, and calling in repeated air and mortar strikes.

Durrand continued, "The cell's orders are to not all meet up except when they're going to conduct an attack. So unless we get a heads up that they're going to be together someplace to make a hit, we'll be trying to track a bunch of individuals, and that shit's not gonna work. Even if we get enough intel to take out one or two we can't really expect to defeat the cell, at best they'll probably just move to another area like they did this time. Hopefully we'll catch them all together for an attack, but I wouldn't count on that. These guys are smart."

"If they're so fuckin' smart, how'd two of them get caught in Uzbin?" Powell retorted.

"One of them pissed off a family member, and the family member went to the team in Uzbin to get even," Durrand answered. "That was pure luck, it had nothing to do with anything the team had done. And it just so happened that when SF hit the guy's compound, his co-team leader was there too."

"Probly' bangin' each other," Harris observed.

"Yup. The SF guys killed one and badly wounded the other. It would be nice if something like that would happen now, but we can't count on it, and I bet the cell learned a lot from that experience," Durrand said. "Oh, and the family member who ratted them out was found decapitated and hanging from a tree two days after the raid. So no chance he'll help out again."

"What about French intel?" Lattimore asked. "What are they getting?"

"Pretty much the same thing. They've actually gotten less information than we have about the new guys, and they're pretty pissed because they were getting close to pinning down the old cell's operating patterns."

"So what's your suggestion for us? What do we need to do differently now that these guys are in the province?" Klein asked.

"I wouldn't say you need to do anything different, you just need to be more aware of what's around you. I mean, the basics are the same. They want to blow us up and shoot us like usual, they're just a little better at it now. When we're outside the wire, we still need to look for changes in normal patterns of civilian behavior, fresh dirt, crap on the side of the road that looks out of place, all the normal shit. And I hate to tell you guys this, but chances are you won't spot anything before the IED blows. Like I said, these guys are good. I know nobody saw shit before the detonation three days ago, even though two of your trucks and one CA truck rolled right over it before it blew. And that was over a hundred pounds of buried HME."

The men in the room looked at each other. Lattimore and Harris had driven over the IED, a hundred plus pounds of Home Made Explosive, a mixture of fertilizer and fuel oil. That IED had shredded a humvee, and it probably would have killed at least one or two guys if it had detonated under an MRAP. Nunez would never say it, to himself or anyone else, but he was relieved the triggerman had the discipline to aim for a humvee instead of one of their MRAPs.

"Alright. Anything else we need to know?" Klein asked.

"Not right now, that pretty much covers it. I'll let you know if we get anything new. Right now just keep your eyes open, and if you take a hit do what you did last time. I wasn't there so I can't say for sure, but it sounds like you guys almost took one of those cocksuckers out when you charged that compound. They don't expect us to do shit like that, so keep it up."

"What's the name of the guy who's in charge of the new IED cell?" Nunez asked.

"His name, we think, is Maulawi Rahman. We don't know his first name. Maulawi is a religious title, something like 'Deacon'. His radio call sign is 'Shafaq'. He's probably in his early thirties, based on all the experience he's supposed to have. We've heard different things about him, but all the reports more or less agree on some things. We're pretty sure he got his IED training in Pakistan, and that he fought in Ghazni province before he came back to Uzbin. We don't know if he's from Uzbin or what, but that seems to be his home base.

"We know he's got some foreign fighters working for him. A lot of the reports say his foreign fighters are Chechens, but you have to take that with a grain of salt. The Talibs think we're terrified of Chechens, so they claim that every foreign fighter is from Chechnya. The ANA captured four supposed Chechens in Konar province a few months back, and when they were interrogated it turned out they were from Uzbekistan. But Rahman's probably got some Pakis, and maybe a Saudi or two. We don't know."

"Roger that. Thanks bro."

Klein and the others stood up and each shook Durrand's hand, then walked out of the intel team's office toward the French chow hall. They didn't talk much, mostly they just took in what Durrand had told them. None of the information was good news.

The French chow hall was almost all the way across the firebase from the intel office. The soldiers walked through the open area in the center of the base, past the helicopter landing zone and the huts of the soldiers whose only job was to refuel and rearm the helicopters, past the rows of French armored personnel carriers, scout cars and wheeled light tanks. After they passed the motor pool they shook hands with several French soldiers lounging around their tents, giving friendly jabs to those who were wearing the French-issue running shorts that looked like white silk Daisy Dukes.

The men walked through the line at the chow hall, getting what looked like French food but was according to the French not even close. They sat at one of the long tables inside the tent and ate in silence for the first few minutes, until Klein spoke up.

"From now on all gunners have to actually wear those stupid harnesses so they don't get blown out of the hatch if we get hit. And everyone inside the vehicle wears seat belts. No more ignoring that order. Got it?"

They nodded. "LT, what do you say we start pushing for battalion to let us step up our patrols around Landakhel?" Lattimore asked. "It would be nice to run across these guys and kill some of them in a firefight, instead of waiting for them to hit us."

"I already asked for that. The company commander thinks it's a good idea, but battalion is worried about us losing more guys. The French are pushing their leadership to let them patrol more and to push further from the road during the patrols. We're also looking into starting some joint patrolling at night."

"And we'll actually start doing this stuff when? In six months, after battalion presents a hundred power point presentations and has forty staff meetings to discuss it?" Nunez asked.

"Hopefully within a month. Quit bitching. You're right, but quit bitching."

"How about the Afghan army?" Lattimore asked. "Can't we get them--"

WHUMP! The sound of a distant explosion carried through the air into the tent. Conversation stopped at every table, and everyone's eyes rose in alarm.

"That outgoin' mortar fire?" Harris asked.

"I don't think so, it sounds too far away," Powell said.

Small arms fire rang out, in the distance somewhere to the south of the firebase. At first there were a few shorts bursts, then several seconds of sustained firing from at least ten machine guns. At another table a French officer heard a call on his handheld radio, exclaimed "*Merde!*" and ran out of the tent. Everyone else dropped their food and followed him, toward the southern wall of the perimeter.

The firing sounded louder outside, but Nunez could tell it was well out-side the base. As they sprinted toward the perimeter most of the French soldiers peeled away from the Americans, either headed toward the French armored ve-hicles or toward the Tactical Operations Center, the nerve center of the firebase. Nunez saw that French soldiers assigned to the quick reaction force were already at their vehicles, pulling on their gear and prepping their weapons. The Ameri-cans continued past them, puffing heavily and unslinging their weapons as they skirted the helicopter landing zone and support soldiers looking to the south.

The machine guns in the southern guard towers weren't firing. The gunfire outside the firebase hadn't let up, but the gunners in the towers either didn't have a target or were out of range. The perimeter was made of rows of Hesco barriers, big metal and fabric squares filled with dirt and laid out in a long row. The Hescos were maybe five feet tall and were stacked two high, and at hundred meter intervals platforms were built behind the Hesco wall for soldiers to occupy during attacks on the perimeter. At Firebase Pierce those platforms had only been used to take pictures of the breathtaking vista outside the base, since the Taliban had never been stupid enough to risk a ground assault. Now, for the first time since their arrival at Pierce, Nunez saw men run up the steps to the firing platforms and aim outward, preparing to defend the base.

Nunez knew before they made it up the steps that they wouldn't have a target; if the .50 caliber machine guns in the towers couldn't engage, then a bunch of guys with carbines wouldn't either. Out of breath, Nunez and the others cleared the steps and spread out along the railing, looking southward through their weapon sights into the Tagab valley below.

Roughly a kilometer away a French supply convoy was stopped and spray-ing fire into the compounds east of the road. At the rear of the convoy a VAB was laying on its side in a settling cloud of dust and smoke, next to a six foot crater. Another VAB had pulled up next to the crater, on the contact side to protect the damaged vehicle from enemy fire. Nunez could see a cluster of French soldiers on the "safe" side of the VAB, hunched around a few soldiers who were laid out on the ground and who had to be dead or wounded. Even with the low magnifi-cation on his scope, Nunez could see puffs of dirt from Taliban gunfire kick up around the wounded VAB and the one protecting it. He watched a French soldier stumble backward from the rear of the downed vehicle, dragging another limp soldier. The rescuer fell onto his back and two other soldiers grabbed them both and pulled them to safety.

Nunez grumbled "Motherfucker," to nobody, watching tracer rounds screaming east from the stopped convoy. All the tracer fire was outgoing; in Kapisa province the Taliban never gave away their position by using tracer rounds. He scanned the compounds where the tracers were impacting, not seeing any targets at all. The Taliban were masters of cover and concealment, and were probably firing from inside compound windows or heavy vegetation. French soldiers popped up from behind cover to fire volleys of rifle grenades toward the enemy, and as the quick reaction force vehicles cleared the gate the enemy fire stopped.

By the time the QRF arrived the Taliban were long gone, like they always were when coalition troops finally got their shit together and reacted to the enemy's actions. As the American and French soldiers watched the French secure the area and recover their wounded men and their damaged vehicle they spoke in hushed tones among themselves. Nunez, Klein and their soldiers repeated one collective thought: their desire to find the Taliban IED cell and slaughter every man in it.

CHAPTER 3

Klein walked into the platoon's tent, threw his carbine onto his cot and announced, "It's on, motherfuckers!"

Soldiers dropped their magazines and video game controllers and crowded around him. Nunez put his book on the floor, looked at the ceiling and thought, *Well, here we fucking go.* Then he stood up, walked to Klein and asked, "What's on and when's it happening, lieutenant?"

"We're going into the Alasai valley with the ANA and the French, and we're going in heavy. They're talking about a battalion task force, several hundred guys plus air cover and indirect fire support. The ANA and French are bringing their tanks, too. It's a big fucking operation."

A brief hush fell over the soldiers. It wasn't exactly an ominous silence, and as Nunez looked round the tent he recognized what it was. The silence was the sound of a group of men making the sober realization that they're about to do something very likely to get some of them killed.

"And what about us?" Powell asked. "Don't tell me, we're gonna stay here at the firebase and guard the gates while everyone else is gone."

"Nope." Klein said. "Not sure exactly what we're doing, but we're somewhere in the middle of it. The French are going to establish observation posts in the mountains, so they don't need us for that. And they did mention that they wanted our MRAPs out there, so we've got to be in the main body of the assault someplace. Or we're the Quick Reaction Force. We'll find out soon enough."

Nunez pulled out a notepad and flipped it open. There were lots of details to clear up, a lot of preparing to do. "What's the time frame for the op? Do we know if we're going as a full platoon, do we need any special gear or weapons? Do we know anything yet?"

"Don't know any of that," Klein said. "The French wouldn't say what the date is because they don't want the Afghan army to leak it, so we won't know that for a while. The way they were talking, it sounds like it's going to happen within weeks. And they said 'Your platoon will be involved', not that part of the platoon would be involved. I don't know anything more than that, and the French probably don't either. We'll find out when they find out. The overall mission commander is the Marine colonel in charge of the Embedded Training Teams, he'll be making the plan and then telling the French what's up. We'll find out pretty soon, we have another planning meeting scheduled in three days."

"Nothing more for now?" Nunez asked.

"Nothing more for now," Klein answered.

"Okay. Vehicle commanders and gunners, meet me outside in five minutes," Nunez announced.

They were seated at the wooden picnic bench outside the tent less than three minutes later. Nunez and his gunner Wilson, Powell by himself, Harris and Jeff Albright, Lattimore and Gore. They had notepads and pens ready when they sat down, bottles of Gatorade or cans of Coke in front of them. Powell and Albright were already smoking. Nunez had written a checklist and looked it over as they sat around him.

"Okay guys, sounds like this operation, if it happens, is going to be a big, big deal. We also know it's going to be confused and fucked up, since we'll have people from three different armies speaking three different languages working together, but I don't want any of the fuckups or confusion to be our fault. So here's the deal. I want every crew to do a full maintenance check on every vehicle, today. Don't skip anything. We need to know if there are any issues at all with any of the trucks, the last thing we need is a breakdown while we're rolling into the Alasai. Tomorrow we aren't scheduled for any patrols, so hit the radios and weapons. And Powell," Nunez said, looking at him, "don't bitch about us having to do this now even though we know the op isn't going to happen for a while. We need to know about any problems now, so we have time to get them fixed beforehand."

"Roger that, Sergeant," Powell said. "I wasn't gonna complain about anything."

"Yeah you were, just not to me. Everybody, go ahead and let your guys go to lunch, then we get on the vehicles. We should have plenty of time to get them checked out." Nunez looked down the checklist. "Also, I want a complete count on all ammo for each vehicle. I mean everything, not just the basic loads we all know we have. We need to know about all the extra ammo that we've stolen from other units and all the crap that's been in the trucks since before we got here, and whatever other ammo is hidden away and not on the books. If we need to steal more from someplace or cross-level between trucks, we need to know that now. The other firefights we've been in have been quick ones, this one might last for days and we can't risk anyone running out of ammo. I'll get us more grenades, I want everyone to have at least one. The ammo count can get done the day after tomorrow, if we don't have any patrols that day."

The soldiers wrote in their notepads, and Nunez thought about the last thing he was going to say and how his soldiers would react to it. Something else popped into his mind. He was grateful for the temporary distraction.

"Another thing. We need every one of our vehicles to have tow cables attached, front and back. I know we've talked about that since we got here and we've all figured we could get by with just one set per vehicle, but not now. Every truck has to be prepped to be towed or to tow another truck. I'll do whatever I have to to get more tow cables. This is just a gut feeling, but I can almost guarantee you that some of the vehicles rolling into the Alasai are going to get blown the fuck up during the advance. Hopefully none will be ours, but if we take a hit, we have to be ready to get our guys out of the kill zone."

The men wrote notes in their notebooks while Nunez gauged their reactions. None of them looked nervous, they were all business.

"And along that same line of thought," Nunez went on, "we need Doc to check every last aid bag and litter we have. If any bag needs anything, get it from the infirmary and if you can't, let me know. Every truck commander needs to check every individual first aid kit too. Got that?"

They nodded and jotted down Nunez's words. As they wrote, Nunez pondered whether or not he should give the last order. It was something they should have been doing since the beginning, but nobody ever wanted to think about it. *Well, might as well talk about the part nobody wants to talk about.*

"Lattimore, one special thing for you. I need you to go to the French logistics company and ask if you can get some body bags. Ask for four, we'll put one in each truck."

Lattimore looked back at him in surprise. The other soldiers stopped writing and lifted their eyes from their notepads. Nunez had just done something akin to violating an unwritten rule. The men in the platoon were combat arms soldiers. All had firsthand experience of seeing men in their units wounded, either in Afghanistan or Iraq. Most of them had been on missions where soldiers from other units were killed. None of them other than Klein had experienced it, but they knew on an intellectual level that men in their own platoon might die someday. Klein and Nunez were fanatics about medical training and the need to have gear ready in case one of their men was badly wounded, and the rest of the men accepted that as necessary. But none of them had ever trained, planned or equipped themselves for the death of one of their own. Nunez knew that to all the men sitting at the table, that seemed to be an invitation to bad karma that nobody should extend. Maybe other units thought it was normal to carry body bags in their trucks, but in this platoon they never had.

"You sure you want us to do that, Sarge?" Lattimore asked. "I don't think it's necessary. If we need to evacuate a KIA we can use the litters we already have. I'm not arguing or anything, but I think it would be a bad idea to freak out the Joes by bringing something like that with us."

"I hear you, Eric," Nunez answered. But what if it's a loss from an IED hit and we have someone in pieces, like the CA guys were? We can't put the pieces on a litter and tie it on top of an MRAP, and think how bad the guys would lose it if we had to put a dismembered soldier inside the truck with the dismounts."

Nunez looked around at everyone for a second. "Listen, I know how bad this sucks, that we don't want to think about it at all. But if we take a hit on this mission, even if we lose an entire crew, that doesn't mean the mission's over. It might mean we recover the bodies and sensitive items, and Charlie Mike on down the road with everyone else."

Some of the men nodded. "Charlie Mike" was the military's phonetic alphabet for the letters C and M, and meant "continue mission" to this generation of soldiers.

"You know I won't buck you on an order Jerry, but I still think it's a bad idea," Lattimore said. "I'll go to the French and get some bags, but hopefully you'll change your mind before we actually roll. Carrying a body bag on a mission gives me the willies."

"Hey Sarge," Harris said, "how 'bout we say that part of our job on the mission is to recover any KIAs the Afghan National Army has? Then we can tell ourselves the bags ain't fo' us."

Nunez smiled and rolled his eyes a little. "Hey man, whatever works. We can say the bags are for the ANA if it makes it easier."

"It does," Harris said.

Powell snorted in disgust and mumbled, "Faggot."

"Alright, that's that then. Anyone have any questions?" Nunez asked.

Nobody said anything. Nunez dismissed them to go back to their soldiers, which they did, except for Corporal Elijah Gore. Gore stood up, stretched, waited for everyone else to walk away. Then he walked to Nunez and asked, "So boss, you think this mission's gonna be that bad, huh? Or are you just trying to get me all terrified so that I'll want to climb into bed with you for protection tonight? I'm on to you, I know you're always trying to figure out a way to take advantage of me."

Nunez smiled and took a second to finish off his Gatorade before he answered. He was going to be honest with Gore, there was no reason not to be. Gore was the second oldest soldier in the platoon, one year younger than Nunez, and unlike most of the rest of the platoon they were both family men. Gore had been a generator mechanic in the regular army during his late teens and early 20's, and had then gone on to marriage and a decent job in Austin. Years passed, a child was born, his marriage failed, the World Trade Center was attacked, he remarried a divorcee who had two children of her own before she gave birth to his twins, and now he had five children to support. He told everyone he only joined the Guard for the extra money and the life insurance, but Nunez thought he was full of shit. If those had been the only reasons, Gore wouldn't have joined an infantry unit, not when he could have had a much easier life as a mechanic somewhere.

Gore was probably the most average soldier in the platoon, but he could do whatever he needed to. He was a little heavy, but not too heavy to pass the physical fitness test or walk for hours through rough terrain in full gear. He said he wasn't the smartest guy in the world, but orders never had to be repeated to him. And above all he was witty, a fun guy to talk to.

"Dude," Nunez said, "if I was going to hook up with one of you hot handsome men in this platoon I'd choose someone else," Nunez said. "You have too many kids, I wouldn't want to get stuck supporting them. But yeah, I think this is going to be a bad mission, Eli. We all know what happens when the ANA get info on upcoming operations, as soon as they know details the Taliban know too. The Talibs will know when we're coming, and that fuckhead Maulawi Rahman and his cell will have some big IEDs on that road into the valley. There's only one road, it's not like they won't know which way we're coming. I think we're going to take some catastrophic hits on the way in. I hate to say this, because I feel like shit for even thinking it, but the best we can hope for is that they'll hit the ANA pickups instead of us."

Gore nodded. The ANA rode out on missions packed in Ford Ranger pickup trucks, with two or three soldiers in the cab and as many as eight soldiers in the bed. A good hit on one of their trucks could kill eleven Afghan soldiers and cause the rest of them to refuse to move another step forward.

"So, uh," Gore said, with a nervous little grin, "you think I should maybe leave a little note for my wife and kids, you know, like just in case?"

"Eli, I think you should shut the fuck up and not say anything like that," Nunez said. "I know I just talked to you guys about preparing for losses, but that doesn't mean you have to roll into this thing prepared to die. I'm not going to say a fucking word to my wife about this mission, and I'm not leaving any goodbye letters to anyone. If I get killed over here my wife will be so pissed at me I'll never get laid again, so I won't let that shit happen. I'll be okay, and so will you." Nunez thought a second and then added, "But maybe we should both make sure someone knows to clear the porn off our computers if something happens. You know, just in case we get bitten by rabid camels after the battle or something."

Gore laughed, then spoke mock-seriously, "That's a good plan, Sergeant First Class Nunez. I mean, I don't have any porn so I'm not worried, but I'd hate for your wife to find all the gay German videos you watch in your cot every night."

Nunez smiled and said, "I only watch them because you're in them all, you homo."

CHAPTER 4

4:17 a.m., game day. Nunez and Lieutenant Klein stood outside Nunez's MRAP in the darkness, anxious but eager to get started. Spread out ahead and behind them, all along the eastern wall of Firebase Walden and in the open motor pool in its center, over a hundred Afghan, French and American vehicles idled in the darkness. Soldiers periodically jumped out of the vehicles to piss or smoke a cigarette, or to just move around and burn off adrenaline.

"All this fucking power, Jerry," Klein said. "All these troops and armored vehicles, just to take out a hundred or so guys in man-dresses with AKs and RPGs. If this was a straight up, face to face fight, we'd slaughter those fucks in ten minutes."

"Yeah," Nunez responded. "Too bad they know that, so it won't ever be a face to face fight. This will be the same shit like always, they'll use civilians as shields so we can't hit them with all our supporting arms. That, and those IEDs will take out someone and fuck the whole plan up. The Taliban aren't stupid, they'll make this a fair fight."

"Don't remind me about the IEDs, Jerry. I don't need to think about it anymore." Klein looked toward the front of the line of vehicles, sighed and said, "Man, I don't envy the guys in the lead sticks. Being in the first vehicles is going to suck. Those guys are probably taking bets on who's still going to be alive thirty minutes after they leave the gate."

Nunez thought back to his time escorting convoys in Iraq. At the start of every mission convoys would be lined up in the truck yard, their soldiers hoping someone else would be first to leave the base and face the IEDs waiting for them on the highways. Usually Nunez's team was lucky enough to be the third or fourth convoy, sometimes they were first.

Nunez knew what the Afghans and Marines in the lead vehicles were feeling. The sick, helpless knowledge that some enemy fighter was out there, holding a wire to a battery and watching a spot in the road, just waiting for their vehicle to drive over it. The soldiers and Marines wouldn't hear anything, wouldn't see anything, wouldn't know anything. One instant they would be charged on adrenaline, scanning all around for enemy, the next they'd be burned and shredded lumps of tissue.

In the last two months since Klein had first briefed them about this operation, Maulawi Rahman had shifted his focus from attacking American and French vehicles to hitting softer Afghan targets. Nunez went over the numbers in his head. The ANA had lost eight killed and seventeen wounded in six IED attacks. Afghan civilian construction crews had also suffered, losing four killed and seven wounded. The road construction had come to an abrupt halt, ruining the coalition's pipe dream of bringing prosperity and stability to the Afghan people by making it easier for them to move goods to the markets.

The Americans and French hadn't been completely ignored, though. The French had been hit two more times and taken five wounded after the ambush that Nunez had watched from Firebase Pierce's perimeter, but just like on that day they hadn't suffered any more deaths. Only one American military police patrol had taken an IED strike, but the IED cell had been way off their timing that day and had only blown a wheel off an MRAP and broken the driver's leg. Nunez's platoon hadn't been hit again, and had only been in two short firefights in the Tagab valley. Life for Nunez's men had been relatively safe, but that safety would end today. Today, Americans, French and Afghans were going to invade the Alasai valley, take the Taliban's safe refuge from them and kill every one that tried to resist.

"You know, the Taliban might not hit the first vehicles," Nunez said. "They might wait and take out a vehicle in the center of the column, so they can block the road and split the entire force."

"Shut the fuck up, Jerry. I can't do anything about that, so I'm choosing to ignore that possibility."

"Let me know how that works for you."

"It's not going to."

"You know what Durrand told me last night?" Nunez asked. "He said that not only do the Taliban know we're coming, they know about how many of us there are and what our objectives are. They even know the name of the operation."

"What a shock," Klein answered in a flat, sarcastic tone. "Does he have any idea where they got the information? I mean, I know it was someone in the ANA, but does he have any idea which one it was?"

"Nope, doesn't have a clue. All he knows is that the ANA got briefed on the operation, and within a few days the Taliban were talking about it."

"Well, that's just fucking great. I wouldn't want it any other way."

"Yeah. I guess it doesn't matter too much though. When the helicopters dropped the French teams onto the mountains around the valley this morning, I'm pretty sure any Taliban who didn't already know about the operation figured it out."

The radio on Nunez's chest crackled as the Marine colonel in command of the operation said, "Overlord 6 to all my units. We're late. Kick your ANA in their asses and get them into their fucking trucks. We need to move."

The assault force was supposed to have begun rolling at 3:30, but of course the Afghans had still been a confused mob at that time, so the start time had been pushed back an hour until they got their shit together. It had taken a superhuman effort from the Marines to do it, but Nunez thought the ANA looked more or less ready now.

"Well," Klein said, looking down the line of vehicles, "I guess it's time to mount up."

He put his hand out to Nunez. "Be careful, Jerry. Let's get all our guys back home after this, alright?"

"We will, Homie. And listen," Nunez said, knowing what he was about to say would sound corny, even though it was true. "You should know that there is no other place in the world I would rather be than right here, right now, with this platoon. No matter what happens, I have no regrets."

Klein nodded somberly. He gave Nunez's hand another squeeze and said, "No regrets, Jerry. Let's do this shit."

"Let's do this shit," Nunez echoed.

The two men stood in the darkness in silence for a second, until Klein let go, nodded and turned to walk through the exhaust fumes toward his MRAP. Nunez watched him go, wondering why he wasn't staggering under the weight of responsibility for the lives of all the men in the platoon. Klein disappeared behind a vehicle, and Nunez climbed inside his MRAP. As he put on his helmet and headset he rehearsed the plan again, making sure he had no last minute questions.

The vehicles in the assault force were organized into "sticks" of eight to twenty, the size depending on what the stick's purpose was. The French infantry sticks were composed of ten personnel carriers and light tanks. The Americans and Afghans had humvees, Afghan army pickups and maybe one old ANA T-55 tank or M113 armored personnel carrier. The Afghan engineer stick ahead of Nunez was the largest since it had the bulldozers, excavators, and cargo trucks full of building materials and all the troops they would need for security.

Afghan infantry sticks would be in the lead. French teams were already in the mountains, providing overwatch. The plan was for the vehicles to push one kilometer into the valley, then stop and dismount their Afghan infantry and US Marine mentors, who would walk alongside and in front of the vehicles the rest of the way to the objective. French vehicles and dismounted troops would be at their backs, intent on arriving at the objective with them. That objective was the government district center in the village of Alasai, five kilometers away at the far eastern end of the valley.

To prevent a pileup of a hundred vehicles on the narrow valley road, the sticks would leave the firebase at ten minute intervals. Nunez's stick included a platoon of Afghans and a few loose Marines who needed a ride into the valley. They would be fourth out the gate, after the engineer stick.

When they were halfway to Alasai village some of the Afghans and Marines would peel off and take the school in She Kut village, three kilometers into the valley. That school would become a combat outpost. The force would then take the district center 300 meters south of Alasai village and turn it into another, larger outpost. All the engineer assets were dedicated to building up Hesco walls around the district center and fortifying the building. Once the coalition's hold on the valley was secure, another small outpost would be built another kilometer east of the district center, right where the Alasai valley split into the Shpee and Shkin valleys.

Nunez looked out toward the ridgelines. The sky was still fully dark, but wouldn't be for long.

"This is Peleliu 1, stick one is rolling, stick one is rolling," a voice said on the radio.

At the front of the column a dust cloud kicked up as the first stick headed out the gate. The vehicles in front of Nunez's MRAP crept forward, choking up to the gate after the first stick was clear.

Vlacek cleared his throat and drummed his fingers on the steering wheel, complaining, "Shit, we still got thirty fuckin' minutes to go before we roll. Come on, let's get this shit done." In the back of the MRAP Wilson was laid out on the floor under the turret and their borrowed dismount, a Marine named Gammage, leaned back in his seat with his boonie hat pulled over his eyes, both of them trying to get a last few minutes of sleep.

Nunez yawned, quiet and still but nervous as hell. He checked his watch every few minutes, eager to move. He knew from experience that he would be anxious and edgy until the movement began. He would calm a little once he was concentrating on keeping the platoon together and moving. Then after the first shot was fired he'd be so busy trying to figure out what to do that he wouldn't have time to be scared.

The Marines in the lead ANA trucks gave updates on the radio. They had dismounted with their ANA and were walking so far unopposed to the east. But they were only seeing a few civilians outside their compounds, and all of those were well away from the road. Minutes passed. No contact with the enemy.

Nunez's stomach twisted as his imagination sprinted from one possible disaster to the next. He tried to stop it, but there were so many bad things that could happen, were no doubt about to happen. He went over plans again, reciting in his head what steps to take if one of his vehicles was hit by an IED, if a gunner was hit by small arms fire, if a vehicle was disabled by an RPG but the crew was uninjured, if a vehicle was hit and burning and soldiers were trapped inside.

"This is Overlord 6, stick two is rolling, stick two is rolling." Another dust cloud up ahead as the first French troops moved out, and the vehicles behind them inched closer to the gate. Still nothing on the radio but location updates, no contact. The sky was lighter now, enough so the soldiers could make out the mountain ridges in the distance.

"Damn, Czech, I would have sworn that an IED would have taken out at least one vehicle by now," Nunez said. "Maybe the Taliban are off today."

"Dang I hope so, Sarge. I hope they ain't waitin' for us or nuthin' like that."

More minutes ticked by. The French had their own radios and wouldn't be on the American net, but Overlord 6 gave updates. Several minutes after they left the gate, the French were within sight of the lead stick, preparing to dismount their men.

"This is Peleliu 3, stick three is rolling. Semper Fi."

Another dust cloud, and the engineer stick moved out. Two flatbed trucks loaded with bulldozers in the middle of the stick had a hard time making the sharp turn onto the Tagab valley road. The Marines had to stop the drivers of the ANA pickups behind the flatbed trucks from getting impatient and racing around them.

Nunez's stick pushed up to the gate. Two ANA trucks were in the lead, then the four Texan MRAPs, followed by another two ANA trucks. The ANA soldiers in the beds of the trucks smoked, checked their gear and weapons. Nunez watched two soldiers with RPGs put pink flowers onto each other's body armor.

Nunez closed his eyes and made a wish. *Man, I'm such a dick for thinking this, but...if someone has to get blown up, please let it be someone else. My guys are good guys, let them make it home.*

He yelled into the back of the truck, "Wilson, Gammage, wake up! We're rolling in less than ten minutes."

Wilson sat up, stretched and climbed onto the platform under the turret. As soon as he had his helmet and headset on he muttered into the intercom, "Damn, quit yelling at me Sarge, you're lowering my self esteem." In the back of the MRAP Gammage popped one of the air cover hatches, readying himself to stick his head out of the hatch during the ride in.

Minutes dragged by. Marines in the valley called out a group of military age Afghan males clustered around one compound north of the road, but the males went back inside and nothing else happened. The Marines, ANA and French who had linked up with them kept going. Not a shot was fired, no contact with the enemy.

"This is Peleliu 3, stick three has visual contact with the lead elements."

Nunez looked at his watch. Two minutes left to their start time. He pulled his two grenades out to make sure they were dummy taped correctly and set in the pouches the way he wanted them, made sure his magazines were rounds down in their pouches, confirmed his GPS was where he always kept it. He had already checked his gear many times. He was doing what soldiers had done for thousands of years, repeating small tasks before battle to keep their minds occupied, to prevent them from dwelling on the danger they were about to face.

One minute left. The sun hadn't cleared the horizon, but the sky was lit. The lead sticks had been able to use the darkness to cover some of their advance, but Nunez's stick would move in almost full daylight.

A Marine called on the radio, "This is Peleliu 1, we just heard shots fired way to the south, I think the Taliban are signaling to each other. No incoming rounds."

Their start time was seconds away. On the platoon's radio frequency Klein gave the order, "Drivers, lock and load." In each of the four vehicles, the drivers slapped their carbine magazines, pulled back on the charging handles and let them fly, tapped the forward assists and checked the safeties, then stowed their carbines out of the way. Then they pulled their M9 pistols from their thigh or chest holsters, racked the slides to chamber a round, flipped the pistols off safe and holstered them.

"Colt 4 this is Colt 1, start your move. Colt 4 Colt 1, start your move."

Time to roll, Nunez said to himself. He knew Gore, on the gun in Lattimore's truck, would be going through his usual start-of-mission ritual. As soon as the platoon received the order to head out the gate, Gore would reach down and lay his hand on each soldier's head, asking God in a whisper to protect them. For all of Gore's jokes, about anything and everything, when it came to the lives of his fellow soldiers he was all faith and devotion.

Nunez reached over and squeezed Vlacek's arm. Then, in the closest he ever came to prayer, he thought, *I hope to see all of you back at Pierce when this is over. Best of luck to you, my brothers.*

"Alex, tell the ANA to move out," Nunez ordered.

Wilson stood up and yelled to the ANA soldiers, "Hey, move out, gangsters! Move out!" The ANA didn't understand anything he said, but they got the gestures. Afghan gunners standing behind the 12.7mm "Dushka" machine guns mounted in the beds of the trucks pounded on the roofs, the brake lights briefly flicked on, and the trucks drove forward. As each MRAP reached the gate, every soldier and Marine except the drivers loaded their carbines and pistols. The gunners raised the feed tray covers on their M2 or M240 machine guns, laid the end of a belt of ammunition onto the feed trays, slammed the covers shut and yanked back on the charging handles. After the machine guns were loaded they readied their carbines and stuck them in the racks built into the insides of the turret armor. Wilson swung his .50 to the left as they cleared the gate, and each gunner behind him alternated his weapon's orientation from the truck in front of it.

"Overlord 6 this is Colt 1, clearing the gate, time 0503."

"Roger that, Colt. Come on, Texas, get out there and kick those motherfuckers' asses."

"Hooah Overlord, Texas is on it."

They made the turn onto the Tagab valley road, headed a short distance south through a deserted bazaar, and made the left turn eastward into the mouth of the Alasai valley. The landscape around them was stunning, one of the most beautiful places Nunez had ever seen. The trees and flowers were in full bloom, the streams full of clear, rushing water from the mountains. The compounds themselves were dull brown, but most of them had flags or banners with bright, satin colors flying from the roofs or hanging from windows. What the valley lacked, though, was the presence of normal human life. The only people visible anywhere were coalition soldiers.

"Hey Sergeant...First Class, I think I hear shots," Gammage said. There was no sergeant first class rank in the Marines, so Marines always had a hard time calling someone sergeant first class instead of Gunny, which was their equivalent rank. "A long ways off, to the southeast."

"Roger that Sarge," Wilson confirmed. "I heard them too. Maybe a kilometer away. They've stopped now."

Before Nunez could get on the radio to report it, Marines from the lead sticks were calling the shots in. But still no contact, and the lead troops were nearly two kilometers into the valley. They were moving slow, giving the follow-on sticks time to catch up and letting the dismounts check every possible place an IED could be hidden. Nunez's stick cleared a slight curve in the road and he saw the trail vehicle from the engineer stick a few hundred meters ahead of them. Marines and ANA soldiers had dismounted from the trucks and walked alongside the vehicles, searching for anything the lead sticks had missed.

"Colt 1 this is Colt 4, we've made visual contact with the engineer stick."

"Roger that," Klein answered. "We're almost two kilometers in, so far so good."

Nunez radioed Overlord that they were caught up to the engineers, and had nothing else to report. They were way past due for an IED strike, or at least an ambush. In the back of the MRAP, Gammage said, "Wow, this is the quietest this valley's ever been. Last couple times I was here we got ambushed way before anyone got this far."

Wilson whistled into the intercom and said, "Damn, Marine, you just jinxed the fuck out of us. Way to go."

"Don't be scared, soldier," Gammage answered back. "We want them to hit us. If they don't shoot, we can't shoot back and kill them."

"Touché," Wilson said. "That was a smart answer, you guys are supposed to be dumb."

Before Gammage could respond, Nunez said, "Gammage, if you shoot my gunner I'm going to write a very angry letter to your colonel. Nobody shoots him for being a smartass but us."

"Roger that, Sergeant...First Class," Gammage said. "Is it okay if I beat his ass later?"

"Of course. Be our guest."

The Marines in the lead radioed back that they had to make a short halt because the engineers were jammed up on a curve. Nunez's stick reached the engineers and saw ten or twelve ANA soldiers clustered around the front a stuck flatbed truck, all gesturing like mad and shouting orders to the driver. The two ANA trucks ahead of Nunez's MRAP pulled over and the soldiers inside them bailed out, ran to the truck, screamed orders and added to the chaos.

Nunez heard a faint crackle in the distance. "Sarge!" Wilson yelled. "Automatic gunfire down the road! Sounds like just a few guns." Ahead of them, the ANA ducked and took cover behind vehicles.

Well, here we fucking go, Nunez thought. *The fight's on.* "Alright, Wilson and Gammage, keep your fucking heads down."

"It ain't close, Sarge," Wilson said. "We're still safe."

"Well, get the fuck down if it gets close."

A calm voice came over the radio. "Overlord 6 this is Peleliu 1, contact contact contact, small arms fire from somewhere to the north." In the background ANA gunfire was audible.

"Peleliu 1 this is Overlord 6, I copy and need you to fix those fuckers and send me a grid so I can get some mortar fire onto them. The guns are hot and waiting on a target."

Peleliu 1 keyed the radio again, yelling "Tell the captain to get his fucking guys spread out and face north!" to his interpreter before speaking over the gunfire into his radio. "I copy, the fire is light and ineffective so far. My ANA think they know where's it's coming from, wait one for a grid."

Ahead of Nunez's MRAP the flatbed rocked back and forth, trying to free its wheels. Behind them dozens of vehicles were stopped on the road, and a few soldiers jumped out to piss while they had the chance. Sixty meters north of the MRAP a French mortar section set up its guns outside a small compound, stacked rounds and kicked in baseplates while riflemen maintained security.

"Overlord 6 this is Peleliu 1, stand by for grid."

"Send it."

"Grid to suspected position, India Sierra 6437, 72--"

In the background an Afghan soldier screamed something unintelligible, as the volume of gunfire tripled. From above the MRAP Wilson and Gammage yelled over each other, "Heavy fire up ahead!"

"Overlord 6 Overlord 6 this is Peleliu 1, contact east, 150 meters! They're firing from the compounds right down the road! I've got two ANA down!"

"God damn it," Nunez said. "Vlacek, drive around these motherfuckers. The lead sticks need some ass up there, let's go."

On the platoon net Klein yelled, "Jerry, move around those engineers! Hurry up!"

Nunez said, "Yeah yeah, calm down, Homie." Then he keyed the radio and said, "Already doing it, 1."

Vlacek edged around the stuck flatbed and weaved between the other vehicles in its stick. Ahead, gunners on ANA trucks fired their machine guns in a wide fan toward the mountains a kilometer away to the north. None of the gunners Nunez could see were aiming, they were just pulling the triggers and burning through belts of ammo. Somewhere on some of those mountains, French troops were in hidden positions and maybe taking fire from their Afghan allies. The other Afghan soldiers had bailed out from the pickup beds and crouched down in shallow ditches on the sides of the road.

"Wilson, Gammage, you see anything?" Nunez asked.

"Can't see shit, Sarge. ANA are running around way up ahead, but I can't see any enemy."

"I got nothing, Sergeant First Class Nunez."

"Overlord 6 this is Peleliu 1, I need some fire support on the compounds to our east, right now! The ANA are breaking contact and falling back to the west, I can't find the terp and get them to stop!"

"Peleliu 1, whatever your ANA do, hold your fucking position and adjust fire for the French! Fire support is inbound, hang tough, 1!"

"Holy fuck!" Gammage yelled. "Something just detonated on the mountain to the south!"

"What was it?" Nunez yelled back.

Wilson and Gammage both yelled "Shit!" and ducked. Nunez heard a loud *shk! shk! shk!* sound. A Milan anti-tank missile from a French position in the mountains flashed past them, high in the air on the MRAP's right side. The Milans were guided missiles fired from heavy launchers, able to hit pinpoint targets from kilometers away. Nunez watched until the missile disappeared near the front of the convoy and detonated against an unseen target.

"Peleliu 1 this is Overlord 6, give me a target sensing."

"Overlord 6 this is Peleliu 1, *huh, huh,* good effect, good effect, *huh, huh,* the fire slowed down some! Give me one more, same target!"

"Round inbound, round inbound."

Seconds later Gammage called out, "Here it comes, here it comes!"

Another round flashed by to the right, followed the same path and detonated on the same target. Nunez pulled the earphone off his left ear; the gunfire had dropped to almost nothing. Nunez's stick moved forward, cleared the engineer stick and closed the gap to the French vehicles ahead.

"Overlord this is Peleliu 1, good effect on target! I think the enemy fire stopped, I'm trying to get my ANA back here. All Peleliu elements, if you see any ANA running to the rear send them back to me."

"Peleliu 1 this is Overlord, good job, way to keep your head. What's the status on your casualties?"

"Overlord, I don't have a fucking clue. They ran off like everyone else so I guess they're not hurt too bad."

"Roger that, 1. Get your ANA together and Charlie Mike."

"Peleliu 1 copy."

Loud booms sounded in the distance to the rear as French 120mm mortars lobbed rounds toward the Taliban in the mountains who had fired on the lead troops. Peleliu 1 hadn't finished giving out the grid to that position, but Nunez figured the French had seen them and called in the mortars. He leaned forward in his seat and scanned the mountains to the north, looking for the impact. Several seconds later he saw white flashes as rounds impacted halfway up the ridgeline at the entrance to what had to be a cave.

"Good for those fuckers," Nunez muttered. But he knew the Taliban were probably well inside the cave when the rounds impacted.

Up ahead Nunez could finally see the ANA who had retreated from the ambush. One Marine and several French soldiers waved their arms and gestured at them to turn around and head back east. The Afghans stopped, milled around on the side of the road and argued with each other. Ahead of them, the firing trailed off. Nunez led his platoon closer and saw the ANA finally turn around and move east. More white flashes erupted on the mountain to the north as the French mortar crews dropped another volley onto the Taliban position.

As the *whump!* of the exploding mortar rounds echoed around them, Peleliu 1 transmitted over the radio, "This is Peleliu 1, we're Oscar Mike." On the move.

Nunez's MRAP crawled to a halt behind a VAB, and he recognized the soldiers kneeling beside it as members of the *Groupment Commando Montagne*, the battalion's Mountain Recon Platoon. The contrast between their discipline and the rabble of ANA a hundred meters ahead was striking. One of the Recon machine gunners looked at Nunez through the windshield, and the thought in the bearded, muscular young man's eyes was obvious: *Why don't these fucking ANA get out of our way and let us lead this assault?*

Gunfire rang out from the head of the column. The Mountain Recon soldiers stood up and started their move east, seconds before the VABs started inching along after them.

"Peleliu 1 this is Overlord, are you in contact again?"

"Overlord Peleliu 1, I don't think so. The ANA are firing at every compound now as they advance."

"Keep them under control, Peleliu. Don't let them hit any civilians."

"Roger that, Overlord. We don't see any civilians at all."

Vlacek rolled the MRAP forward. Behind Nunez, Wilson mumbled, "If I don't get to shoot someone today I'm going to be fucking pissed."

The column moved along for a few minutes before two quick explosions sounded from the head of the column. Heavy gunfire exploded from up front.

Alarmed, Nunez yelled, "Wilson, what was that?"

"Not sure, Sarge. It was too quiet to be an IED. Shit's hitting the fan further up."

"Overlord this is Peleliu 3! We just had an RPG fired across the road in front of us, from the south! Contact, small arms fire, from a compound to the south!"

"Where to the south, 3? Identify a target for me."

Several vehicles ahead, a French light tank lumbered across the ditch on the south side of the road and stopped in the open. The turret turned left and right as the gunner scanned compounds ahead. The turret stopped, the gun rose a few inches and the tank commander popped up above his hatch, looking east through binoculars. Two more loud booms sounded from ahead as a second RPG round zinged over the road and detonated against a compound wall.

BOOM! The French tank rocked as the gunner fired its main gun to the east. Several of the soldiers on the side of road ducked and grabbed at their ears. Nunez couldn't see the impact, but the fire up front slackened. The coaxial machine gun next to the tank's main gun fired several long bursts, then a ten-foot wide fireball exploded from the main gun again as the gunner launched another high explosive round at the Taliban.

"Peleliu 3 this is Overlord, someone talk to me."

"Overlord this is Peleliu 1, we don't know if the French hit the right compound or not, but the incoming fire stopped. Also, be advised, the ANA companies have gotten all mixed up, up here."

"Roger that Peleliu, just keep them going in the right direction, they'll sort themselves out later."

The column kept moving. Sporadic fire rang out from the front as the ANA put suppressive fire on any compound, wooded area or wall that caught their interest. Wilson and Gammage scanned everywhere, trying to find something, anything, to shoot at.

"All elements this is Overlord 6, fast movers coming in. Check your fire south of the road."

From the west, two A-10s flew high in the air over the mountains. Nunez watched as one of them circled and then dove almost straight down. Smoke bled from its nose and left a grey streak behind it. The aircraft pulled up, firing flares to its sides as the roar of its guns reached the road and echoed through the valley. Nunez saw a spot on one of the mountains erupt in white and orange flashes, heard the roar and its echo and thought: *Godzilla.*

"All elements this is Overlord, a French team in the mountains just called that four confirmed kills."

"Fuckin' badass, Sarge," Vlacek said. "You know, this is the first fuckin' time I've ever been on the attack? Every other time I been in contact, they been attackin' us. Fuck that shit, going after their asses is way better."

Nunez thought about it. When he and Wilson were in Iraq they had the same experience, every time they had been in contact it was either an IED attack or small arms fire from the enemy. Until today, Afghanistan had been the same. A lot of the active duty units had been on offensive operations against the enemy, but for the National Guard troops, the war was almost always a matter of performing some type of guard mission and waiting for the enemy to hit them. Nunez couldn't think of a single soldier in the platoon, except maybe Klein, who had actually been on the attack before this mission.

"You're fucking right this is better than waiting for them to hit us, Czech. I'd rather do this shit every day than deal with convoys and IEDs."

The firing ahead increased. Within a minute several loud booms exploded from the head of the column.

"This is Peleliu 1, we have the She Kut school in sight and we took some small arms fire from the compounds near it. We're good, the ANA are suppressing with small arms and RPGs."

"Overlord copies, advise when you start to take the school."

The column kept moving. The French Recon soldiers pushed way ahead, almost getting mixed in with the ANA. The stick behind Nunez's had also passed the engineers, who were far back. The march order hadn't completely broken down, but it was getting there. But that didn't matter much. As long as the column kept moving east, the coalition troops were winning.

Puffs of smoke popped on the side of a mountain a kilometer north of the road. "Wilson, two o'clock, halfway up the mountain! What was that?" Nunez yelled.

"Uh...fuck, all I see is smoke. What'd you see?"

Loud booms and radio traffic cut them off. "This is Peleliu 3, incoming RPG fire from the north! We just had four rounds impact on both sides of the road!"

"Roger that Peleliu, we saw it too. Stand by for fire support."

Three vehicles ahead of Nunez, a VAB with a 20mm gun traversed left, took a few seconds to identify the puffs of smoke that marked where the RPGs had been fired from, and cut loose with its slow firing cannon.

Bang! Bang! Bang! Bang! Bang!

Huge tracers lashed out and arced to a spot well above the puffs of smoke. The gunner made a correction and peppered the area with twenty rounds. Nunez hoped the gunner had just shredded some Taliban, but he knew that whoever had fired those RPGs would have to be blind and stupid to still be standing in the same spot when the VAB opened up.

The column pushed east. Peleliu 1 called out in a voice full of excitement that his ANA were assaulting the school. Nunez waited to hear an eruption of small arms fire. Nothing happened. A few minutes later, out of breath, Peleliu transmitted over the radio, "Overlord this is Peleliu 1, we took the school, we took the school! It was empty, nobody was anywhere around when we cleared it. We're consolidating on it now."

"Roger that Peleliu, fucking outstanding! Keep me advised!"

The column sped up now that most of the ANA up front were out of the way. They passed the school, which was a two story stone building with a courtyard surrounded by a high metal wall. Even without additional defenses, it was a hell of a strongpoint. The gate to the courtyard stood open and Afghan soldiers carried bales of concertina wire, boxes of ammunition and cases of water from the backs of their trucks into the courtyard. Three Marines at the gate yelled at the ANA to hurry it up.

Past the school, compounds and heavy vegetation crowded the road. If there was a good spot for an ambush, this was it. The ANA in the lead were high on adrenaline, eyes and weapons darting everywhere. The French soldiers on foot looked dead serious and well-ordered, maintaining regular intervals from each other and keeping their weapons facing outward from the road.

Peleliu 4 and a company of Afghans were in the lead now. Nunez checked the map; the assault force had already advanced an entire kilometer past the school. They were four kilometers into the valley, had already taken the first outpost, were barely a kilometer from Alasai village and so far had not suffered a single soldier killed or lost a single vehicle. The Taliban should have already detonated several IEDs, destroyed coalition vehicles and blocked the road. If they didn't do it soon, the coalition troops would be in Alasai village within minutes.

Nunez couldn't hold his tongue any longer. "Dammit, Alex, the suspense is killing me. I just know Maulawi Rahman is going to take a vehicle out any second now. I almost wish he would hurry and get it over with so I can stop expecting it."

"Just like Iraq, huh, Jerry? I had forgotten how much I miss being a designated IED target," Wilson said.

"Yup, just like Iraq, brother."

The compounds and vegetation thinned out, the column made a small curve in the road and Nunez saw Alasai village in the distance. Gunfire rang out again from the front, just a scattering of shots from due east followed by heavier return gunfire from the ANA. Peleliu 4 called out, "This Peleliu 4, we takin' some bullshit fire up heah'. Ain't nuthin', we handlin' it."

Something big exploded to the rear of Nunez's MRAP. Nunez was startled and spun his head to look out the back window but saw nothing except the MRAP behind them. Wilson and Gammage ducked below the armor as heavy gunfire tore the air behind them. Dozens of tracers flashed outward from the road, some of them ricocheted high into the air. A supercharged voice yelled on the radio, "This is Inchon 2, near ambush, north side of the road! Near ambush, north of the road! They're within a hundred meters!"

Nunez looked in the side view mirror, trying to see if any of his platoon's vehicles were in contact. He couldn't tell.

"Wilson, are our guys getting hit?"

"I don't think so Sarge, looks like it's behind us."

Nunez keyed the platoon radio. "1 this is 4, are you in contact?"

"Negative 4, it's about a hundred meters back. My gunner is suppressing to the southwest." In the background Powell's machine gun hammered rounds toward the enemy.

Nunez heard Klein again, but he was on the main net this time. "Overlord this is Colt 1, we're within 100 meters of the ambush, do you want us to back up and support Inchon?"

"Colt this is Overlord, negative, do not stop moving east! Support by fire if you can, but do not halt your move! The Taliban are just trying to distract us, my Marines can handle it."

"Colt 1 copied."

Over a dozen booms exploded behind Klein as the ANA fired RPGs into the compounds just off the road. French vehicles behind them pushed up, and 20mm gunfire was plainly audible above the rest of the battle noise.

Inchon screamed on the radio, "RPG inbound! RPG inbound!"

Gammage called it out, just before it streaked in and impacted on a compound with a huge flash of flame and dust. Not an RPG, but a French Milan missile from a team in the mountains.

"Inchon this is Overlord, that was a French Milan missile, not an RPG. How you holding up down there?"

"Shit Overlord, that one impacted less than fifty meters from us! Tell the French thanks, but they need to be careful. We're still in contact, I'll advise ASAP."

The firefight lasted less than a minute more before dying down. The vehicles in front of and behind the ambush pushed forward, stopped to wait when other vehicles halted in front of them, then rushed forward to catch up when the vehicles sped off, doing what soldiers call "the slinky".

"Inchon this is Overlord, give me a sitrep."

Inchon's situation report was better than what Nunez expected to hear. "This is Inchon 2, all Inchon elements are okay, I think we've got a few ANA wounded but I haven't heard of any KIAs. I'll advise as soon as I know for sure."

Ahead, the ANA and French had closed half the remaining distance to Alasai village. Wilson said "Hey boss, there are civilians standing at the western end of Alasai village. They're partway behind cover, but they're standing up and waving."

"That sounds like an ambush," Nunez said.

"Overlord this Peleliu 4, we gots civilians standin' around wavin' outside Alasai village. 'Bout six or eight of 'em."

"Roger, keep your eyes open."

The lead ANA closed the distance to the village. Inchon reported that he had three Afghans wounded, one seriously. They were taken by an ANA pickup to the school outpost to be treated by an Afghan army medic.

The Afghan soldiers reached Alasai village. Wilson narrated the scene as the civilian men standing at the edge of the village greeted them warmly, shook their hands and kissed their cheeks. A sarcastic Marine got on the radio and said, "Hey all, the locals just assured us that there are no Taliban in the village. We're safe!"

The ANA stopped at the edge of the village, the French and the Texans behind them kept going into the bazaar, the main hub of life in the village. The road to the district center cut to the right, but they passed it and rolled all the way through the bazaar, just as a show of force. Then they turned around, headed back through the bazaar and turned south toward the district center.

The district center was another two story stone building, but it had a stone wall around the courtyard instead of a metal one. Before they reached the district center they crossed several hundred meters of open ground, passing a three-story, red brick skeleton of a building that had been left incomplete for years. The Afghan soldiers went straight into the district center and began setting up defensive positions. The French took the red building and the area around it, and the Texas MRAPs made a loose perimeter around the district center along with several ANA and Marine vehicles. Nobody shot at them as they took the buildings south of the village.

Klein and Nunez got on the radio and ordered their soldiers to consolidate their perimeter. The men needed to stay alert, rotate positions if their drivers or gunners needed a break, take a leak if they couldn't hold it any more, break out some MREs and grab a quick bite to eat. It had been easier than they expected, but it couldn't be over already. As they settled in their positions the first engineer vehicles turned toward the district center from the bazaar, bringing the Hescos, sandbags, concertina wire, picks, shovels, hammers, stakes and everything else needed to build a combat outpost. The flatbeds were visible from the district center, being pushed forward by the trail elements of the assault force. Vehicles and dismounted soldiers were streaming into the Alasai district center now.

Nunez looked at his watch. It was nearly 11 a.m. It had taken almost six hours to reach and take the district center, but it felt like no more than an hour. Nunez didn't know where the time had gone. The Taliban had just lost the first part of the fight, and Nunez hoped Maulawi Rahman would be executed for failing to emplace IEDs in the road to stop the advance.

The radio boomed to life in Nunez's ears. "All elements, all elements, this is Overlord. The ANA are monitoring Taliban radio traffic, they report that the Taliban are massing for an assault on the district center."

CHAPTER 5

"Well, I still can't see shit. Just civilians hauling ass west out of the village."

Nunez looked through binoculars and saw the same thing Wilson did. Small groups of women and children, dressed in brightly colored clothes, walked to the west out of Alasai village. All of the villagers except the infants carried bundles on their backs, even the little girls who couldn't have been older than three. Periodically he saw an old man or cripple shuffling along with the others, but other than those there were no adult males. The information about the Taliban massing for an attack had come in over an hour earlier. The entire coalition assault force had made it to Alasai village, engineers had laid the groundwork for the new outpost and the Taliban still hadn't fired a shot.

The French began stacking sandbags at the windows of the red building they were already calling the Hotel Alasai. Two Milan anti-tank missile positions were on the roof, manned by missile crews who looked eager for the opportunity to fire at something. Bored soldiers wandered away from cover into the open, as if they didn't believe the Taliban had the gonads to shoot at them anymore. So far Klein and Nunez had managed to keep their guys from getting too sloppy, but several soldiers, including both Klein and Nunez, had gotten out of their trucks to snap a few pictures. Gammage had pulled his pack from the MRAP and headed into the district center to link up with the Marines inside.

"Hey Jerry, I just heard...okay, two bursts now. That was it, two quick bursts somewhere in the village."

Nunez asked Wilson, "Did any rounds come near you?"

"Nope, they weren't near us and I didn't see an impact."

"Roger." Then Nunez keyed the platoon radio and said, "Small arms fire in the village, two bursts so far. Don't know who they're shooting at."

"Colt One copies, we heard it too."

"Two, same traffic."

Nunez and Lattimore were on the west side of the district center, Harris and Klein on the east. To Klein's right, the east, an ANA M113 armored personnel carrier's gunner opened up with his Dushka machine gun, flinging big 12.7mm rounds, the size of American .50 caliber bullets, into the village. A few more bursts sounded in the village, and dust kicked up around the 113. The gunner fired back, and for twenty or so seconds Nunez watched as a lone Taliban and the lone ANA gunner had a personal firefight until the Taliban fighter backed down.

Half an hour passed with no more rounds being fired. A French team on a ridge called in mortars on a cave opening on the face of a mountain north of the village. The rounds made a lot of noise and smoke but the French couldn't tell if they had hit any Taliban.

"Cocksucker!" Wilson yelled. Nunez turned to see him crouching in the gunner's station. "One single round just went by, real fucking low over my head! I mean, it went right fucking by me!"

For a reason Nunez didn't understand, he didn't get excited about the near miss. "Keep your head down, dumbass. Did you see where it came from?"

"Fuck no I didn't see where it came from! It was just one round fired though, I heard the shot after it passed."

Nunez started to key the radio on the mission net and Wilson yelled out again, "Shit! He just shot at me again, closer this time!"

Nunez keyed up. "This is Colt 4, west side of the district center we're taking sniper fire and it's pretty accurate. No casualties."

Wilson had ducked his head below the edge of the armor teacup and was looking through the slit in the gun shield into the village. Nunez heard a loud, sharp *ping!* Wilson said, "That sorry fuck just hit the gun shield. He's trying to kill *me*, for no reason at all. What a fucking asshole."

Nunez had to ask himself why he was still so calm, even though one of his best friends had almost been killed three times in the last few seconds. He keyed up and said, "This is Colt 4, the sniper just hit our gun shield. We still don't know where he's at."

"Colt 4 this is Overlord, keep your gunner low and you guys find that bastard and kill him."

Nunez gave a roger, but he couldn't see anyone to kill and neither could Wilson. No more rounds were fired, and after fifteen minutes Wilson stuck his head back up above the edge of the shield, yelled out "Eat me, you sorry fuck!"

and went back to scanning for targets.

Gunfire rang out from the village. Heavy gunfire this time, long bursts from several weapons. The ANA and French fired back at unseen targets, and Nunez was a little disconcerted to see an ANA RPG gunner fired seven rounds right through the front door of a compound. He had seen women and children preparing to leave that house not more than twenty minutes earlier, but he didn't know for certain if they had left. RPG explosions smashed the doors apart, blew clouds of dust out of the windows, and set something inside the compound on fire. Nunez hoped the civilians had left, but figured he would never know.

Gunners on the MRAPs on the east side of the district center found excuses to fire, but on the west side the gunners couldn't see anything. The exchange of gunfire lasted several minutes and then the Taliban just stopped. Nobody on the coalition side could tell if they had hit anyone.

Another quiet hour followed. More civilians streamed out of the village on foot. Gunfire crackled in the village again and several guns fired back. Wilson finally spotted dust being kicked up by a Taliban fighter's weapon, at a corner on the far side of a compound.

"Hey Jerry, I see muzzle blast, other side of a compound and I can't hit it... fuck it, I'm shooting anyway."

Wilson's .50 pounded out a twelve round burst that hit the near side of the compound, nowhere near the Taliban fighter. Nunez felt better anyway, and he knew Wilson did also. The Taliban gunfire stopped for a few seconds and then started up again, but now was much heavier. Several guns fired back, including a VAB's 20mm gun. Wilson started firing into suspicious-looking windows just in case, and a Marine yelled on the radio.

"This is Peleliu 4, we jus' had an ANA hit in the stomach in heah'! Ah need the nearest corpsman to get into the district center, raht now!"

Two Marines and a Navy corpsman moved the wounded Afghan into the district center. Nunez decided to reposition the MRAP and back it up to the open district center gate so they could protect it from small arms fire. If the shit hit the fan they could back the truck straight through the gate and have good cover behind the wall.

The firing stopped. Soldiers were keyed up, looking for a firefight, but the

Taliban decided to take a break. The village and the radios stayed quiet and adrenaline wore off a little. A French VAB with a 20mm gun pushed out from behind the Hotel Alasai and took a position on its east wall, fully exposed to the village but able to deliver devastating and accurate 20mm fire from close range.

Soldiers got bored. On the platoon net, Trevino screamed in fake terror, "*Aaaaiieee!* Vla-shek! I just get heet een the deek by a RPG! The shrapnel ees poisonous, come suck eet out! Queek!"

Vlacek called back, "Fuck you, you fat Mexican! You cain't even see your dick under all that fat, how the fuck do you know you got hit there?"

As the platoon laughed and congratulated Vlacek on his first-ever good comeback, a last few groups of civilians took the opportunity to rush out of the village. Hours had passed since the warning about the assault on the district center, and nothing approaching an assault had taken place. Nunez would have loved to see the Taliban charge across open ground toward armored vehicles and massed machine guns, but it wasn't going to happen.

Nunez had to piss again. He had filled up a Gatorade bottle earlier and didn't feel like pissing into another one, so he let Vlacek and Wilson know he was getting out. He disconnected his headset, popped his door and climbed out to take a leak. After he was done he stretched and rotated his head on his shoulders, then stepped around the front of the MRAP to look west toward the setting sun.

BOOMBOOM! Bangbangbangbangbang! Adrenaline shot through Nunez's veins as twin explosions and machine gun fire ripped the air less than 100 meters away. He ducked against the MRAP's engine compartment and dashed back to his door as several more machine guns opened up in the village. He threw himself inside and slammed the door, then fumbled with his headset connector while looking outside to see what the hell that explosion had been. He spotted it, a settling cloud of dust around the 20mm VAB on the east wall of the Hotel Alasai.

"What the fuck?" Nunez yelled, out of breath. "Did Hotel Alasai just get hit by an RPG?"

"I think so Sarge, but I was lookin' the other way!" Vlacek answered.

Wilson's called out, "No, they hit the VAB! I don't know where it came from, but they hit the VAB!"

Nunez looked at the VAB. The door on the passenger side was popped open, but it looked fine.

"The fuck they did, Alex. They must have hit the building."

Everything went silent. There was no firing at all for what seemed like a long time, but couldn't have been more than fifteen seconds. Nunez told Vlacek, "This seems like a good time to implement our plan and back the fuck up into the courtyard."

"Yeah Sarge, I think you're right."

A machine gun opened up from a window on the top floor of the Hotel Alasai, sending a stream of tracers into the village bazaar. More guns joined it from other windows, then the Afghans and Marines in the district center opened up from positions on the roof. ANA trucks and personnel carriers joined in, along with some of the MRAPs, and suddenly they were in the middle of a cascade of noise and gunfire. Return fire skipped off rocks and slammed into the wall on both sides of their MRAP. Wilson pushed down on the butterfly triggers and sprayed rounds into empty windows, and ANA soldiers fired RPGs from the district center wall.

"Vlacek, back up! Back up!" Nunez ordered.

Vlacek put the MRAP in reverse and crept toward the gate. Seconds later they were all jarred and said "Shit!" in unison as the MRAP hit the wall instead of the gate.

"Czech, move up and then back up again! Hurry up! Wilson, look back and guide him in!"

Wilson screamed back, "Dude! I got shit going on up here! And that fucking VAB is on fire!" before firing a twenty round burst into the village. Nunez saw the passenger door of the VAB next to the Hotel Alasai standing wide open now, and a small fire burning inside it. Vlacek backed up and hit the wall again. Nunez looked in his side mirror and saw nothing but wall on his side, no gate. He turned forward and was about to yell an order to Vlacek when he saw four tracers rounds, spread out horizontally like four fingers, pass several feet over Wilson's head. He had never seen the Taliban use tracers before, and he knew one of them was about to get his ass kicked for not checking his belt of ammo before he fired it.

He yelled, "Vlacek, you're way too far over on this side! Pull up and move the MRAP your way!"

"Shit Sarge, I cain't even see the gate in my mirror, I only see the wall!"

Oh shit, Nunez thought. The gate was too narrow for the MRAP. They couldn't back into cover, and as he looked around he realized that other than the VAB next to the Hotel Alasai, their vehicle was the closest one to the village. That meant it was likely to take an RPG if they didn't move. He had fucked up, he had come up with the brilliant plan to back the MRAP into the courtyard but hadn't taken the time to test it out and make sure the truck would fit.

"Alex, you got something to shoot at?"

Wilson had paused between bursts. "Uh...no, not right now!"

"Okay Czech, pull up about twenty meters and then back us up around that corner of the courtyard wall," Nunez said, pointing past Vlacek to the west. "That'll at least give us cover from fire coming from the right. Let's go, hurry it up."

"Movin', Sarge." Vlacek rolled forward, stopped and threw the truck in reverse, spun the wheel hard left and started backing up.

Nunez keyed the radio and told Lattimore, "Eric, watch for our truck, we're backing around the corner of the DC! Don't shoot us, we might back right in front of you!"

"Roger that, we're a ways over from the corner, you should be clear!"

They had almost reached the corner. Wilson started firing again and Nunez craned his neck to look out the rear windows on the driver's side, making sure they weren't about to back into anyone. He snapped his head forward to look at the village, and his breath caught in his throat at what he saw.

A bright yellow ball screamed through the air toward them from the village. It looked as big as a basketball, and in the fraction of a second it was in the air in front of them Nunez had the time to recognize it as an anti-tank rocket. RPGs don't glow, but 82mm rockets do.

In Nunez's world, time slowed to almost a halt. Wilson stopped firing, Vlacek froze but didn't stop backing up. Nobody said a word. All of them watched in silence as the rocket approached, and Nunez knew that if it hit their MRAP passenger compartment, they were probably dead.

The rocket flashed by Vlacek's side of the truck at eye level, no more than ten feet from the door. An instant later the thump and roar of the explosion rang out behind the MRAP. If the Taliban gunner 300 meters away in the village had aimed maybe a quarter inch to the left when he fired, it would have hit dead center on the driver's windshield. Wilson opened up again, putting his rounds in the area where the rocket had come from. Nunez and Vlacek looked at each other, and Vlacek said, "Holy fuck, sarge. Holy fuck."

Tracers zipped into the village from all around them as the MRAP made the corner. The French at the Hotel Alasai fired two AT-4 anti-tank rockets into the village from the upper floor. Vlacek spun the wheel right to hug the wall as he backed around the corner, and once the front bumper of the MRAP was even with the corner Nunez said, "Stop here Czech, I think we're good."

Vlacek jammed on the brakes, took a deep breath and then looked out the windows. He sat upright and said, "Uh, Sarge...if he fires, it's gonna be fuckin' loud."

Nunez leaned forward and looked out Vlacek's window. A French tank was to their left, the muzzle even with Vlacek's door and maybe twenty feet away. Nunez started to give Wilson a warning, and the tank fired.

An orange flash filled the windows on the driver's side. Wilson yelled "Ow!" and dropped way down inside the turret. The inside of the MRAP instantly filled with smoke. Nunez gagged on smoke as he yelled out, "Alex, you good?"

Laughing, Wilson answered, "I'm good, boss! Hey Czech, maybe you should back us up a little!"

Vlacek backed up another ten feet. Nunez keyed the platoon radio to make sure everyone in the platoon was alright and to let Klein know that his vehicle hadn't been hit. Marines were all over the mission net, screaming orders and calling out targets. The French tank fired several more main gun rounds into the village and Nunez tried to figure out how they had missed seeing the tank behind them. Something exploded fifty meters to the rear, and a Marine called out an RPG impact at the rear of the district center. Nunez hadn't seen that one go by.

Milan anti-tank missiles exploded from Hotel Alasai's roof, impacting on compounds on the north edge of the village. Wilson screamed for more ammo and Nunez reached back, tore open a box of .50 caliber ammo and handed the belt up to him. The district center shook as ANA soldiers fired dozens of RPGs from behind the courtyard wall, and the backblasts blew out some of the windows. Wilson kept firing, the gun dropped spent shells and empty links into the truck, and Nunez handed more ammo up.

The firing from the village slowed, then stopped as darkness fell. Inside the village several compounds were on fire on the inside, but the structures remained intact. Loud booms rumbled from Firebase Walden, and blinding flares popped in the sky above Alasai village. Wilson finally got sick of being on the gun and Vlacek got hit with a bad case of the shits. Nunez got on the gun, Wilson took the wheel and Vlacek climbed out the back door of the truck to spray diarrhea in the dirt between the back wheels. Nunez looked back to see laughing ANA soldiers point at Vlacek from the roof of the district center.

Hours passed. Wilson and Vlacek fell asleep. Nunez scanned for targets and as a way to keep himself awake thought about having wild sex with his wife. Just as he began picturing it he happened to glance toward the VAB that had been hit, and saw four French soldiers carrying a body in a poncho toward the Hotel Alasai. The sex scene in his head fizzled.

Another hour faded by. Nunez thought about waking up Wilson or Vlacek to take over the gun, but Vlacek was sick and Wilson had been tensed up on the gun all day. Besides that, Nunez wanted to shoot something himself.

He looked into the village through the night vision device mounted on his helmet and saw a light moving in the village, straight to his front. He flipped the device up and looked into the village with his naked eyes, and saw nothing. He flipped the device back down and saw it again, and this time it was plain that the light was moving toward him. He was about to wake up Wilson when the radio crackled to life.

"All elements, this is Overlord. The ANA just reported that they intercepted some radio traffic, the Taliban are massing for an attack again."

Nunez looked at the light again. It was moving toward the district center, no question. But was it Taliban, or just some villager checking his compound for damage? Were there any regular villagers still left, or had they all fled?

"This is Overlord. Be advised, the Taliban attack is imminent."

Nunez keyed his radio. "Overlord, this is Colt 4. I see a light, dead center in the village, moving toward our position. I can only see it with night vision."

A Marine keyed up. "This is Peleliu 5, I see it too. I think I see another one, off to the right."

"Overlord to those units, we know we're about to be attacked, and you see lights coming toward us. Shoot."

"This is Colt 4, roger that. Watch my tracers."

Nunez leveled the .50 toward the light. The machine gun had no infra-red laser to help him aim it at night, so he was going to have to walk his tracers in. He guessed he was aiming at the right spot, and pressed the trigger. The .50 bucked and rose as the first tracers hit around where he had seen the light. The last tracers from the burst went over the village and hit the mountains two kilometers away.

Nunez's first emotion was embarrassment at his poor aim. He let off the trigger, lowered the muzzle and dumped another long burst toward the light, this time keeping the rounds in the area they were supposed to go.

Marine M240 machine guns joined in from the district center roof, then ANA machine guns let loose. French guns in the Hotel Alasai fired into the village bazaar, and the village for a few moments was bathed in streaks of red. Nunez looked for the light again, and it was gone.

"This is Overlord. The latest Taliban radio traffic is, 'Nevermind, we shall attack She Kut!'"

Wilson spoke up from the commander's seat of the MRAP. "Jesus, Jerry, you scared the fuck out of me when you started shooting. Did you just kill someone?"

Nunez ran his hand down his face. He realized that he might have fucked up again, that he should have suggested that they all hold their fire and wait for the Taliban to expose themselves. He would probably be mad at himself about that for the rest of his life.

"No Alex, I doubt I killed anyone. But I sure scared someone out there. Some Taliban might have Post Traumatic Stress Disorder now, because of me. If he's not dead, his bills for psychiatric care are gonna be outrageous. How's Czech?"

"He's okay, you woke him up too. I think you made him shit his pants."

"Fuck you Wilson, I did not shit my pants."

"Well, you must smell like that all the time then."

"Alex, quit fucking with Czech," Nunez ordered. "That's my job. Czech, you okay?"

Vlacek said in a hoarse voice, "Yeah, I'm good, Sarge. I think I'm a little dehydrated is all."

"Grab a drink, then go back to sleep."

"'Kay." Vlacek fumbled around in the commander's seat and Nunez went back to scanning the village. About a minute later Vlacek shrieked in what sounded like pure, abject terror.

"*Aaaaaaauugh!* Oh fuck! Oh my fuckin' god!"

Nunez jumped, and his hands reflexively tightened on the machine gun's grips. He ducked down into the MRAP and shouted, "What? What the fuck happened?" As he was trying to get his head down into the vehicle the insane thought occurred to him that a Taliban fighter must have snuck in through the back door of the MRAP and cut Vlacek's throat. Nunez was tired, his thinking was a little muddled, and he reached for his pistol before realizing how stupid that thought was.

He saw Wilson lean over from the driver's seat to hold Vlacek's shoulder, asking him, "Dude, what the fuck are you screaming about? What happened to you?"

Vlacek bent at the waist, holding his stomach. His right arm shot out to the door handle and he popped the door, then tore away from Wilson's grasp and stuck his head outside.

Nunez said, "God damn it Czech, what the fuck is going on?" just before Vlacek puked down the side of the vehicle. After a few dry heaves, Vlacek pulled his head back in.

"Aw, fuck, Sarge...I think...shit, I just took a drink out of your piss bottle."

Nunez and Wilson were both quiet for a second. Then they both broke into almost hysterical laughter. Nunez had to struggle to ask, "What the hell did you do that for, Czech?"

Vlacek bent at the waist again and grabbed his stomach. He mumbled, "When I'm in my seat I always keep my piss bottle on the left side of the seat and the good bottle on the right side. Now I know you don't do that. I guess I forgot what seat I was in."

Wilson was almost in tears. He said, "Don't worry Czech, we'll keep it a secret, just between the three of us." Then he keyed the radio and said to the platoon, "Guess what, everybody? Czech just took a drink from Sergeant Nunez's piss bottle! And he loved it!"

The platoon radio frequency came to life with laughter and insults. Vlacek held his head between his knees in silence. Nunez ordered him to rinse his mouth out and go back to sleep.

Wilson and Nunez traded places. The rest of the night was uneventful, except for one instance where the French opened fire on suspected Taliban in the bazaar and wound up wounding two ANA soldiers who had decided to search the bazaar without telling anyone. When the sun came up the Taliban fired a few bursts toward the district center but gave up and faded away into the Shkin valley. Later that day the villagers started returning, and dozens of them took up the ANA's offer to earn extra money by helping them to build the outpost. On the third day the civil affairs teams were out, handing out humanitarian aid packages to the locals.

On the third afternoon the Marine Colonel walked around the district center, stopped at vehicles and shook hands with the soldiers and Marines who had taken the village. Klein and Nunez took the opportunity to ask him about the estimated number of Taliban casualties.

"Well," the colonel said, "those guys are telling the locals over shortwave radio that they didn't lose anyone, and they destroyed seventeen French tanks and killed eighty-one French, American and Afghan infidels. But we still have ANA listening to their internal radio communications, and the Taliban're hurting. This morning one of them said they've counted almost thirty killed, and they've had to move a lot of guys to the Shkin valley for medical treatment. The ANA have been clearing compounds in the village and found just a few bodies, but lots of blood. Thirty's probably a good number of confirmed kills. Hopefully some of their wounded will die too."

"That's outstanding, sir," Klein said. "I'm glad we were part of this, maybe we even killed a few ourselves."

"You Texas boys are pretty good in a fight, I'm sure you got some," the Colonel said. "I was glad to have you here."

"Hey sir," Nunez said, "did the ANA hear anything on the radio about Maulawi Rahman? His call sign's Shafaq. That's the asshole we really wanted to kill."

"I know who Rahman is, trust me on that. And yes, the ANA did hear traffic about him. He was wounded and carried into the Shkin valley. That's all we heard, we don't know how bad he was hit or if any members of his cell were wounded or killed."

"Damn. Okay, thanks sir."

That same afternoon the Texas platoon said goodbye to the Marines, and rolled out of the Alasai valley back toward Firebase Pierce. No IEDs or ambushes waited for them on the route. When they rode back into the base and climbed down from their trucks the American soldiers who worked in the Tactical Operations Center or serviced the helicopters watched them with envy. The Texas soldiers were tired, dirty and unshaven. They looked just like what they were, victorious troops who had just walked into the enemy's backyard and beaten his ass senseless. The Marines, French Mountain troops and ANA had done most of the work, but that didn't take away from the fact that the Texas boys had been right there in the middle of it, had taken their chances just like everyone else and deserved to share in the glory of victory.

All of them took the opportunity to call home from the "morale phones" that night and let their families know they were okay, even if they hadn't told their families that they were going on a dangerous mission. Nunez talked to his wife and she knew from his voice that he had just been involved in something significant. She pressed him for information and he finally told her a few details, which of course made her burst into tears. He finally calmed her down and they made plans for his first night home, which was still months away. Later that night he showered, climbed into his cot and passed out in seconds, sleeping better than any night he had ever been at war.

CHAPTER 6

Nunez kicked back in a folding chair outside the little pizza restaurant on Firebase Pierce. The French, who owned the base, had contracted with an Italian company to open a pizzeria on the firebase for the troops. The Italian company hired Albanians, Nepalese and Indians to work at the pizzeria. Now a group of Texan soldiers, some white, some black, one Asian and one Jewish, sat on the patio of an Italian pizzeria on a French firebase in Afghanistan and ate real European pizza cooked by Indians and Nepalese who were supervised by Albanians. The atmosphere was like a mini United Nations, and the pizza was magnificent.

Harris finished off a slice of pizza and washed it down with lemon tea. He leaned forward across the table toward Nunez and asked, "You gonna do it today, Sergeant Nunez?"

Nunez glared at him. "Just eat your fucking pizza. I'll do it soon enough."

"It's a legit question, Jerry," Klein said. "You said you'd do it today. You're the only one who hasn't done it."

"I'm the only one who has a good reason not to."

Wilson rolled his eyes. "Jesus, Jerry, you're so full of shit your eyes are brown. I mean, Sergeant Nunez, you're full of shit. All due respect and everything, but we've talked about this before, several times. There's no reason for you not to walk over to the call center and do it."

Nunez pulled a piece of pepperoni off his pizza and flung it at Wilson, splattering grease on the sleeve of his combat shirt. "Blow me, asshole. Why would he want to talk to me? It's my fault he's down there."

Several of them spoke up at once, protesting what Nunez had just said. Lattimore spoke over them, saying, "Hey, come on Sergeant, that's a load of crap. I talked to him about that exact thing, he doesn't blame you. He even asked why you hadn't called, and I made up some bullshit about you being way too busy and having problems at home that you're always tied up with. He wants you to call and I promised him you would. Just go in there, pick up the phone and call him."

"Eric, he was following my orders that day. He did exactly what I told him to do, and he almost died because of it. If that had been me, I wouldn't want to talk to me ever again."

"He doesn't feel that way, Sergeant. You need to let him tell you that."

"He told me the same thing, Sarge," Vlacek said. "He don't blame nobody but the Taliban for what happened."

"You assholes just back off of me," Nunez said. "I'll call him when I'm ready to."

"You wan' someone to go with you, Sarge?" Harris asked. "I'll go wit' you. All of us will go wit' you. I'll even make the call and start the conversation if you need me to."

"I don't need anyone to go with me. God damn...if I call today, will you fucks leave me alone?"

"Only if he confirms it when I talk to him tomorrow," Wilson said. "If you don't do it today, we're all going to fuck with you every day until we get home."

"Well...let me finish my god damn pizza. Then I'll go."

"You better," Wilson said.

"Or else what?" Nunez growled back at Wilson.

"Or else I'll scrape some gay off Vlacek and rub it all over you. Then when you get home that hot wife of yours won't be able to turn you on, but her brother will."

"Fuck you, Wilson," Vlacek said.

"Good comeback, Czech, "Wilson shot back. "You must have worked on that one all week."

"Czech, if you kick Wilson's ass I'll call Quincy twice."

"Deal, Sarge."

"Alright. You guys leave me alone now, I'll call as soon as I'm done here."

"Gore, I want you to take Nguyen and follow Nunez to the call center," Klein said. "Then when he actually makes the call, send Nguyen back to me to confirm that he's done it."

"Roger that, Lieutenant!" Gore said, smiling.

"LT, what the fuck?" Nunez retorted. "I'm a grown fucking man. I said I'll call him and I'll call him."

"Sorry, I didn't mean to hurt your feelings, Jerry. You're right, I don't need to send Gore and Ping Nguyen to check on you. Gore, Nguyen, you have your orders."

"Fuck." Nunez dropped his pizza onto his plate. He stood up and said, "Fine, I'm going. Gore, I might even run over there just to see you try to keep up with me, you fat bastard." Then to twenty-three year old, runs-like-a-deer Nguyen he said, "And yes, Ping, I know I can't outrun you."

He walked off the patio toward the call center. After the first fifty meters he turned around and looked back to see all his soldiers on the patio watching him, including Gore and Nguyen. He turned a corner around a concrete barrier and after another seventy-five meters turned and looked back. Gore and Nguyen rushed around the corner, and when they saw him looking they stopped. Gore pointed at a mountain in the distance and they both pretended to study something on it. Nunez turned around and kept walking. When he turned to look again he saw the two soldiers jogging after him, and when they saw him Nguyen stopped and stared at his watch, Gore stuck his hands in his pockets and whistled nonchalantly while looking into the sky.

Nunez couldn't help smiling before he turned back around. Behind him he heard Gore's distinctive laugh and running footsteps in the gravel. Nunez kept walking, he wasn't far from the call center.

When Nunez walked into the plywood hut he saw three computers and two phones available. He sat in a booth and pulled his notepad out of his cargo pocket, looking for the number he had written weeks earlier. When he found it he picked up the handset, took a deep breath and dialed. Behind him Gore and Nguyen walked into the hut, and he heard Gore say, "Hey, look! There's a couple of free computers! Why don't we check our emails, Ping?"

Nguyen answered, "By golly Corporal Gore, that's a great idea!"

Without turning, Nunez reached behind his back and gave them the finger. The phone clicked in his ear, was silent for a long time and then started to ring. Nunez looked at his watch and hoped that it was too early back in Texas for anyone to answer. After three rings, Nunez told himself he'd only give it two more, then he'd hang up. Someone answered on the fourth ring.

"Hello?"

Nunez closed his eyes and took a breath. "Hello, Rodger, is that you?"

"Yeah, this is Rodger. Who's this?"

Nunez was about to answer when Quincy said, "Sergeant Nunez, is that you?"

Nunez braced himself for the hard words he knew he was going to hear, but he tried to keep his own voice and words even. "Yeah, it's me, Rodger. How you doing back there, you healing up alright? I hear you're almost ready to leave the Fisher House."

The "Fisher House" is actually a series of small housing complexes built for wounded soldiers and their families at several military bases around the country. Quincy was staying in one at Fort Sam Houston in San Antonio, Texas. He had been placed in one of the apartments as soon as he was out of the hospital and according to what everyone else in the platoon told Nunez, he was enjoying life there.

"I'm great, Sergeant, recovering real well. Damn, it's good to hear from you, I thought you'd never call."

"Yeah, I should have called a long time ago, Rodger, I'm sorry about that," Nunez said. A chair screeched on the floor behind him and he turned around to see Nguyen disappear out the door.

"That's alright Sarge, I know you're busy over there, especially since you're stuck babysitting Czech and Wilson. Life here isn't bad at all, Sergeant. I'm always busy doing rehab or group therapy or something, and there's a lot of stuff to do in San Antonio when I have free time. I've even met a girl out here on the Riverwalk, and she seems like a pretty good one. But how's everything for you?"

"Not bad, Rodger, things are a lot better since we took the Alasai. There haven't been any IED attacks in over a month. You know we wounded that sorry fuck Maulawi Rahman, and all we've heard is that he's recovering somewhere in the Shkin valley. The intel guys say they're getting conflicting reports about him. Some reports say he's nearly dead, some say he's stable but they're going to send him to Pakistan for better treatment, and one report said he's up and around except that he's got a slight limp. Did any of the guys talk to you about the Shkin valley at all?"

"They've mentioned it, but all they've known is that it's a valley that branches off from the east end of the Alasai," Quincy said. "They said Americans have never been in there, right?"

"It's not just Americans who haven't been there, nobody's been in there except the Afghans. I mean, the Russians never made it that far. Supposedly the British never went in there either, according to the local legends. The Taliban tell everyone the Shkin is their sanctuary, that no American will ever walk one meter into that valley. The Kiowa pilots have seen Taliban flags and banners in there, and they've seen groups of armed men hanging around some of the compounds. The Taliban are out in the open, they're not trying to hide at all when they're in the Shkin valley. That place is worse than Alasai was, it's their home turf."

"That's bullshit," Quincy said. "If they're armed and out in the open like that, why haven't the helicopters hit them?"

"Rules of Engagement, brother," Nunez said. "Even if the pilots see someone with a weapon, they can't engage unless the person is presenting a threat to them. If the Talibs just stand there with their rifles slung, smile and tell the helicopters to fuck off, the helicopters have to fuck off. They can't engage."

"Jesus. That's a load of shit. How many Taliban does intel think are in there?"

"They don't know, Rodger. They're intel, they only know one or two facts and the rest of it's a guess. There could be fifty Talibs in the Shkin, or maybe a few hundred. I mean, the Shkin isn't that big of a valley, I don't think there's enough villages in there to support hundreds of Taliban. But we don't know a lot about the place, you know? We have satellite photos of the valley, and the French have sent patrols to the valley entrance and gotten some good ground level pictures, but they always get shot at and don't try to push too far in. The ANA built that third outpost a kilometer east of the Alasai district center, right near the mouth of the Shkin valley, so hopefully the Taliban are kinda contained."

"Contained?" Quincy asked. "How can they be contained? Can't they just cross the mountains to get into other valleys?"

Nunez realized he was still nervous, and it was making him sound stupid. "I mean, yeah, you're right. I know the Talibs can just cross the mountains from the Shkin into other valleys, but maybe they can't carry all their IED shit with them if they do."

"Yeah, I hope they stay in there too, I know you guys have had enough of those IEDs. You know, if you guys want to keep the Taliban busy in the Shkin valley, you should have a bunch of donkeys imported into there. I mean nice donkeys, pretty ones. The Taliban will be so into screwing the donkeys they'll forget all about IEDs."

"Ha! Good plan dude, that would work," Nunez said.

"Yeah. So, how's your family, Sarge? Wife and kids good?"

"The kids are fine, Laura's okay, I think. I hope. No worry about a 'Dear John' letter so far," Nunez said. "I can't wait to get back to them."

"No problems back home?" Quincy asked.

"Nope, just the usual 'I'm pissed because you've been gone so long' from my wife."

"Huh," Quincy said. "So why'd Lattimore say you hadn't called me because you were having problems at home?"

Nunez stayed quiet for a moment. That had been more a statement than a question, and it was obvious Quincy knew Nunez had been avoiding the phone call. Nunez closed his eyes and let his head roll back a little. He exhaled and said to himself, *No use avoiding it anymore. He knows what's up and he's about to call you out.*

"Shit, Rodger...shit. Look, man, I've been wanting to call you. Really, I have. I just didn't know, uh, what to expect, you know? I mean, don't think I haven't been asking about you. Every time one of the guys talks to you, I ask how you're doing. I've been checking through battalion too, making sure you're alright. I guess...well, I know you have some pretty serious stuff you have to say to me, and I know I deserve it. I just haven't been ready to hear it."

"Sergeant Nunez," Quincy said, "what are you talking about? I do have things to say to you, but I doubt it's what you're thinking."

Nunez wasn't sure what that meant, but he didn't let it change his expectation of what he was about to hear. "Rod, call me Jerry, okay? I'm not your platoon sergeant anymore, and you're going to be a retired corporal pretty soon anyway, so just call me Jerry. Please."

"That feels weird, but I'll call you Jerry if it makes you feel better. And I'm not going to retire, I should be back on full duty early next year. I've already put in my papers to go to Officer Candidate School as soon as I get a medical release."

"No shit?" Nunez asked, surprised. "Damn Rodger, that's good to hear." To Nunez it truly was good to hear, but he also knew that someday Quincy would say to his platoon, *So back when I was an enlisted man in Afghanistan, I had this platoon sergeant who fucked up bad and almost got me killed.*

"Yeah, it feels good to me when I say it," Quincy said. "But anyway, what did you expect me to say to you, Jerry? Why have you avoided calling me?"

Nunez was prepared to hear Quincy dump a well-deserved accusation of incompetence on him, but he wasn't ready to say it about himself. Not again.

"I think you know the reason, Roger."

"No Sergeant, I really don't. I think you need to explain it to me."

God damn it, Nunez thought. *He's going to make me say it. And I have to, I can't avoid it.*

"Rod...look man, I know I fucked up that day when we got ambushed," Nunez said. "Every second since then I've looked back at it and analyzed and critiqued myself, and I've made lists of things I did wrong, or shouldn't have done, or forgot to do. And number one on that list, I sent you through that door. I ordered you to do it, and if anyone should have gone into that compound first, it was me. So I know it was my fault that you got shot...you know, that you almost got killed. And fuck, man, I did that to you after you stopped running toward the compound so you could cover me when I fell."

"Jerry, stop! Are you serious? Is this the crap you've been telling yourself these last three months?"

"Rodger, let me talk," Nunez said. "You wanted to know what's up, I'm telling you what's up. I know you're pissed at me and I don't blame you. I'd be pissed at me too."

"And I thought Vlacek was the only dumbass on our crew," Quincy said. "Why would you think that bullshit, Jerry? I mean, did I ever say anything like that? Did I ever tell any of the guys in the platoon that I thought that? I know you talk to them every time one of them talks to me, they've all told me that you're keeping up with how I'm doing. Has anyone in the platoon ever said that I was pissed at you?"

Nunez shifted in the chair. Behind him, one of the fuelers was listening to a bad rap song on the internet, and Nunez wanted to turn around and scream at him to turn that stupid shit off. That would give him a convenient excuse to cut this conversation short, or at least interrupt it.

"If Klein gave me a stupid order and I almost got killed because I followed it, I'd be pissed about it. That's how I know you're pissed at me."

"Jerry...how is it stupid for an infantryman to counterattack when the enemy attacks? The only stupid decision you could have made that day would have been to load up the KIAs and run away. Honestly, that's what I expected you to do, and not because it was you, but because that's what everyone does. That's why everyone keeps getting hit by the same assholes in the same places, because we never go after them when they attack us. But we did that day, didn't we Jerry? And so what if it didn't work, that doesn't change the fact that we did what every American unit should do when they get hit. I'm not pissed at you, Jerry. I'm pretty damn proud of what we did out there."

Nunez felt a lump form in his throat. His eyes moistened. He shut them and laid his forehead on the desk. He stayed silent a few seconds, not letting himself believe Quincy's words.

"Rodger, I'm going to beat Wilson's ass when I get back to the tent. He coached you, didn't he?"

Quincy laughed and said, "Jerry, you think I would let that doofus tell me what to say? Nobody told me what to say to you. I'm telling you what I think. I'm being honest."

"Well...I accept what you're saying, but I just can't believe it yet, you know? Maybe after I have some time to process it it'll make sense."

"Jerry, please, man," Quincy said. "I'm telling you the truth. Think about it right now, not later. I'm twenty-three years old, and I've got a fucking Bronze Star with a V and a Purple Heart. I go to these group therapy sessions to talk about my feelings with other wounded guys, and holy shit man, some of them look at me like I'm Audie Murphy. The same way I look at the guys who lost arms and legs, who were burned almost to death, who are missing parts of their brains and have one side of their head caved in. I look at those guys and I think, 'Holy cow man, these guys are awesome. These guys have to be the bravest motherfuckers on earth, to live through whatever did that to them and keep going.'"

Nunez picked his head up from the desk, opened his eyes and looked over his shoulder. The fueler was still engrossed in his song, Gore's wife was on his computer's screen but Gore was looking at Nunez. Their eyes met, and Gore nodded in a way Nunez took to mean, *Be strong.*

"And the rest of the guys here, the ones who were hit by incoming while they were crashed out in their tents or blown up while they were asleep in the back of an MRAP, they look at me the same way," Quincy said. "When I told our group that I was hit twice while charging through the door of a compound after an IED attack and ambush, they acted like I was a friggin' celebrity. Even one of the guys who lost both legs in an IED attack. Can you believe that shit? One guy in the group had a seriously fucked up arm and leg, and in front of everyone he just says he was on the firebase and got hit by incoming. After our first session we were bullshitting in the lobby and he told me that he had actually been in a portajohn jerking off when a rocket came in. Think about that, Jerry. If you were some fobbit who had been blown up while you were cranking one off in the shitter, wouldn't someone who did stuff like we did seem like a hero to you?"

A fobbit was a soldier who never left a forward operating base. Those guys would look at Quincy like he was a genuine hero, which he was. Nunez considered that, and took in what Quincy had just said: *wouldn't someone who did stuff like we did seem like a hero to you?*

Nunez shifted in his chair again, swallowed hard in an attempt to force the lump in his throat away. He twisted his head to stretch his neck, and noticed that someone had written new graffiti on the phone booth partition, in tiny letters:

Every time you masturbate, God kills a kitten. Please, think of the kittens.

Nunez couldn't hold back a laugh, and Quincy joined in. Nunez hoped Quincy hadn't thought the laugh sounded like it had a few tears thrown in. Nunez said, "Someone who did what you did is a hero to anyone, Rodger. There's a reason those guys look at you that way."

Quincy laughed again. "Jerry, I was only in Afghanistan three months. And that's been my only deployment. That day I got wounded was only my second firefight. And you remember that first one, it lasted five seconds and we never figured out where the Taliban were. Most of the guys here have deployed multiple times to Iraq and Afghanistan, and they're acting like *I'm* some kind of a tough guy?"

You are *a tough guy*, Nunez thought.

Quincy went on, saying, "Shit man, most of you guys in the platoon have deployed more than once, y'all have been in tons of shit. You get what I'm saying, Jerry? The truth is, I didn't do all that much, but I got all this recognition for it. Hey, did I ever tell you my dad was a Marine in Vietnam?"

"No, I don't remember you saying that," Nunez said.

"Yeah, my dad's a little older, my mom's his third wife. He's got five kids from before he married her, and none of them served in the military. You should have seen him when I got my Bronze Star and Purple Heart, Jerry. A general presented them to me at a little ceremony here, I was standing on crutches and everyone's cheering, and my dad's crying and looking at me like I'm really something special. And my dad was a door gunner on a Huey, he flew in and out of Hue City during the Tet Offensive. He did all kinds of heroic shit, you know? But he treats me like I'm the hero. Do you have any idea what that's like, being treated like that?"

"No, I don't. I'm glad it's happening for you though, you deserve it."

"Bullshit, Jerry. I don't deserve it any more than you guys do, or than the other guys here do. But I'm getting all this recognition, and in two years I'll be a lieutenant with a Combat Infantryman's Badge, Bronze Star and Purple Heart. And the deal is, if you had been a chickenshit, fobbit motherfucker, too scared to lead us in combat like you did, I wouldn't have any of that shit. So stop the crap about feeling guilty and making the wrong decision, Jerry. You attacked the enemy. That wasn't the wrong decision. I got wounded, and it wasn't your fault, and to tell you the truth I'm pretty fucking happy about how it turned out. So, you need to stop feeling so damn bad about it, and be proud of what we did over there, like I am. And for god's sake, quit fucking worrying about me. I'm fine, and I'm getting better. I'll have a bunch of fucking medals and some cool scars. And you know that chicks dig scars, Jerry. I'm gonna get laid like crazy because of this."

Nunez wiped his eyes. He knew there had to be a hammer somewhere in Quincy's words. He couldn't let himself relax, not if the next sentence was going to be, 'but this is what I think you fucked up on.'

"Rodger...is this all for real, or are you just trying to make me feel better?" Nunez asked. "I think the best thing is for you to tell me the truth, instead of telling me what I wanted to hear."

"Jerry, I've always been honest with you. Everything I've said is the truth. I'm doing good, I'm glad we did what we did over there and I'm proud that you were my platoon sergeant. You need to believe it, it's the truth. Hey look man, I have to run, my girl's about to get here. You stay in touch with me, and when y'all get home we're going to get together and have a party, all right?"

"All right, Rodger," Nunez said. He exhaled, thinking that the conversation was almost over, so maybe Quincy wasn't about to drop a guilt bomb on him after all. "I'm looking forward to it."

"Great, man, me too," Quincy said. "Say hi to everyone for me, and I'll be waiting for your next call."

"Roger, I swear I'll call within the week." He felt brave enough to add, "Have fun with your girl. Be careful that the sex doesn't get so wild that you reinjure yourself."

"Ha! I hope it does get that wild, Jerry. I need to jump in the shower or I might not get laid at all. See ya, brother."

"Later, Rod."

Quincy hung up. Nunez held the phone a few seconds, then put it back in its cradle. He sat in silence for a while more, then felt hands on his shoulders.

"Feel a little better, brother?" Gore asked.

"Yeah, I think I do," Nunez said.

"Good, Sarge. You needed to talk to him, I'm glad you finally did it. I'm webcamming with Deb and the kids right now, but if you need to talk, find me later. Okay?"

"Yeah, man, that's cool. Thanks."

Gore squeezed both of Nunez's shoulders, then went back to his computer. Nunez got up and walked out of the hut. He felt a little shaky, a little dizzy. He hadn't expected Quincy to say the things he had said, and the surprise was difficult to take for someone accustomed to facing hard words and harder realities. Nunez knew he had to let some of his barrier down, allow himself to accept Quincy's words.

He thought back to an incident in Iraq. One night his convoy had been stopped on Route Tampa, south of Baghdad, waiting for another convoy going the opposite direction to make a turn behind them. Nunez was in his humvee at the back of his team's convoy, bored to tears and struggling to stay awake by asking his crew stupid questions about TV shows. Wilson was on the gun and had just offered his opinion to the question *Who is the biggest slut to ever appear on reality TV?* when one of the trucks in the other convoy was blown apart by an IED twenty-five meters behind Nunez's humvee.

Wilson shrieked like a ten year old girl and dropped out of the turret onto the seat below him. Shrapnel rained down onto Nunez's humvee. And the screaming started.

Nunez and the driver screamed at Wilson to look at them and confirm he was okay, Wilson screamed to leave him alone as he jumped back to his feet and manned his gun, other soldiers on his team screamed at Nunez to make sure his truck hadn't been hit, soldiers from the other convoy screamed that a truck had been hit and was on fire. When the pandemonium died down Nunez found that Wilson hadn't been hit, the shrapnel all over his humvee was just small pebbles that had been blasted into the air, the truck that had been blown apart was an empty 18-wheeler, and its American civilian driver had escaped with nothing worse than embarrassment at the load of crap he had dropped into his underwear.

Nunez had quit smoking three months before that IED attack. When he found out nobody had been hurt he took a cigarette from his driver and had the best smoke of his life, wallowing in the relief of surviving such a close call. Looking back, Nunez realized that what he felt then was a fraction of the relief he felt after finally talking to Quincy.

The sky was darker now, and Nunez headed back toward the platoon's tent. He turned over the things Quincy had said to him and compared them to what he had been telling himself the last several months. Had he been too hard on himself, the way he always was when he was on the street as a cop and made a mistake under pressure? Or would any reasonable leader in a combat situation feel the same way he felt about his decisions? There were plenty of officers and senior sergeants who wouldn't have thought twice about it, would have brushed off any doubts about their own actions and put themselves in for medals the same day of the ambush. Whatever his faults, he wasn't one of those guys.

Ahead of him Durrand walked out from between two conex storage boxes, heading in the direction of the Tactical Operations Center. Durrand was walking quickly and cursing, and Nunez called out to him, "Hey Durrand, what's up? Your commander tell you you have to shave or something?"

Durrand stopped and looked at him, eyes full of anger. "Funny, asshole. I thought you would have taken this more seriously, but I guess you're not too fucking worried about it."

Nunez was puzzled. He had never seen Durrand angry before, the man had never been anything but friendly toward him.

"Dude, what's your problem? I would have taken what more seriously?"

Durrand's eyes rose in surprise. "You mean you haven't heard?"

"Apparently not. Heard what?"

"The French just got hit by an IED on the way to Bagram, about twelve kilometers from here. Catastrophic loss. A VAB got blown onto its side, the fucking fuel ignited and the whole thing is still burning. Right now they think they have one dead and maybe three critical. We're still getting more information, but it's fucking bad, Jerry."

Nunez felt the color drain from his face. "Aw, son of a bitch," Nunez said. "Nothing ever happens between here and Bagram, what the fuck? What Taliban are operating over there?"

"It just happened a few minutes ago, we don't know much. But when the IED blew and the French were crawling out of it on fire, the Taliban hit them with AKs and at least one PK machine gun and killed one of the French guys. What does that tell you?"

"Oh, god damn," Nunez said, imagining the horror the French must have experienced. First the IED strike, then heart-stopping terror as the fuel turned the passenger compartment into a raging fireball. And for those who did somehow find a way to climb past the flaming, writhing bodies of their friends, avoid snagging their equipment on the fittings or edges of the narrow top hatches, and kick their way out of the flaming steel box full of their dying comrades, instead of safety they found machine gun rounds tearing them apart.

"Durrand, please do not tell me fucking Shafaq and his group of assholes are back in action."

"We won't know that one way or the other for a while," Durrand said. "But yeah, that's what I'm thinking."

"Fucking shit." Nunez shook his head and wished for a cigarette. "I'm going to go get the guys together and let them know, and see if there's anything we can do right now. I'll find you later for an update."

"Roger that, I'll keep you in the loop."

Nunez went to the TOC and found the French were doing everything that needed to be done, there was nothing the Texas soldiers could do. A French quick reaction platoon had headed to the IED site as soon as the first reports had come in, the casualties were being treated and evacuated, there was no way for Nunez's platoon to help. He went back to the tent and told his soldiers that they might want to be there when the QRF returned.

Hours passed before the QRF rolled back through the gate in clouds of dust and exhaust fumes, and the Texas soldiers stood in silence as the VABs parked and the men clambered out. The French were quiet as they dragged their packs out of the vehicles and cleared their weapons in the clearing barrels. Nunez recognized a friend of his, waited until he had cleared his weapon and approached him, asking quietly, "Alain, how are you?"

The Frenchman turned to him, shook his head slowly and took a deep breath. He pulled a pack of cigarettes from a pocket, drew one out and stuck it between his lips. When he flicked a lighter and held it to the end of the cigarette, Nunez saw that his face was smoke-blackened except for the areas around his eyes that his goggles had protected. Alain wore ragged green combat gloves with the forefingers and thumbs cut off. The gloves were stained with blood. He took a drag on the cigarette and turned to lean against a VAB.

"Jerry...my god. *Mon dieu, mon dieu.* It is terrible, terrible."

"I know it must have been bad, Alain, and I know you lost a friend. I'm sorry."

Alain shook his head. "No, Jerry. We lose two friend. One shoot, one die by burned."

"God damn it," Nunez said, feeling himself redden with anger. "I'm sorry man, we heard only one had died."

"That is not all," Alain said. "Another one will be die, I think. He burned so bad, Jerry. He stuck in the VAB, when he get out he in complete flame. We arrive before the *helico* land to get him, and he cry so loud. He say me, 'Please kill me, please kill me, Alain'."

Alain took another drag on the cigarette, and Nunez saw the track of a single tear in the glow. It was strange to see a man like him crying. Alain was handsome and muscular, the collar of his faded camouflage jacket turned up, body armor covered with magazines and grenades, helmet chinstrap hanging loose, FAMAS carbine on his chest. When Nunez was a kid and imagined himself as a soldier, he wanted to look the way Alain did right then. And this man, who was the picture of what a combat soldier should be, was in tears.

"I hate say this, Jerry, but...I wish he die. His body is just, just destroy. His face, his both hands...everything. I wish he had die when the IED explode, and I wish he die now, he die soon. I hate say you this, Jerry. He is my friend, for many year. We serve together in Africa, in Guyana, and here. I am friend with his wife, I meet his mother and father. And I want he should die. Because he in so many pain."

Alain took another drag. Nunez stood in front of him, saw the agony in his eyes, and didn't know what to say. He took a step forward and put his hand on Alain's shoulder, and Alain looked back at him, left the cigarette in his mouth and reached to Nunez. They gave each other a half handshake, half hug. Alain held it for a moment, then said, "I must go, Jerry. I see you later, you come to the tent for food tomorrow, *bien*?"

"That sounds good, Alain. Tell your men that we are here if they need anything, okay?"

"I tell them, Jerry. See you tomorrow."

They parted ways. On the way back to their tent Nunez's men spoke quietly, discussing how bad it must have been for the French who were inside the vehicle when it was hit. Klein pronounced, "We need to go back into the Alasai, or into the Shpee or Shkin valleys, wherever these cocksuckers are, and kill them all." His soldiers agreed out loud. Nunez hoped that would happen, and happen soon.

Durrand stood outside the tent waiting for them. "Another French soldier just died in the hospital in Bagram. The French are fucking pissed, they're already talking about mounting another operation to go after these guys in the Alasai. I keep telling them that Shafaq's been in the Shkin valley lately, and that's where the operation needs to be, not in the Alasai. The French intel major says the same thing."

"Jesus," Klein said. "I don't blame the French for being pissed, I just hope they stay pissed enough to actually pull this operation off. You think it'll happen? The mountain troops are only here another month before they get replaced."

"Yeah, I know. It's going to be hard to get it done that quick, but lieutenant, you haven't seen how furious those guys in the TOC are. I mean it, those guys are about to lose their fucking minds about this. If I were you, I would start prepping your guys for it. I'm willing to bet that within a couple of weeks, you guys are going to be rolling into one huge ass fight in the Shkin valley."

CHAPTER 7

Durrand had gotten it wrong. More than two months had passed, and there was still no plan for an operation into the Shkin valley. The commander of the French Mountain troops had tried like hell to get a mission planned and approved so that it would take place before his battalion was due to rotate out, but his best efforts hadn't been able to overcome the natural inertia and inefficiency inherent in every military force in the world.

When the French Marines came in to replace the Mountain troops a month after the IED attack, the frustration felt by the outgoing Mountain troops was palpable all over Firebase Pierce. The Mountain troops wanted revenge and thought they would have the chance to get it before they left. They had the will and the drive to do it, they were all motivated by an intense desire to make the enemy suffer in the same way the French had suffered. Nunez didn't believe a man among them would have backed away from the opportunity to walk into the Shkin valley and kill as many enemy as they could find.

Instead they had loaded up their gear and rolled or flown out of Pierce, gone to Kabul, then boarded a plane to Cyprus. A few days later Alain emailed Nunez to say that they were back in France. Still angry, still frustrated, still feeling the conflict between pride in their service and their victories, and bitter sadness at their losses. The glory would fade, the bitterness would find a hole to hide in and stay there forever.

The French Marines did their best to aggressively patrol the valleys of Kapisa province. Their commander had his Marines on foot in the villages, learning the terrain, getting accustomed to the Afghan people's patterns of life, learning what was normal and what wasn't. What they found to be normal was rifle and machine gun fire coming at his Marines at least once every patrol, from hidden positions hundreds of meters away. Not once did the Taliban ever hit anyone, not once could the Marines determine where the fire came from, not once did they ever see an actual Taliban fighter.

One morning during the fifth week of their six month deployment, a company of French Marines rolled out of Firebase Pierce in company strength, supported by a light tank, one Afghan Army infantry platoon and the four MRAPs of Nunez's platoon. One Georgia National Guard soldier, wearing the lightning bolt and double striped patch of the 48th Brigade Combat Team, was in the French company commander's vehicle. His battalion was new in country, about to take over the Afghan Army embedded training team mission from the outgoing US Marine unit. He was there to act as a liaison between the US Marines with the ANA, and the French Marines in front of them.

The mission was to distribute food and school supplies to the villagers of the Ghayne valley, check the area around Ghayne village for suspected caches of ammunition and explosives, and ask the villagers if they knew anything about Maulawi Rahman and his cell. Nobody who had any firsthand experience with Afghans in their villages expected anyone to give any real information, but they had to make the show of trying anyway.

The convoy of French, Afghan and American vehicles headed south over the river and into the Kohi bazaar. The vehicles made the turn east into the Afghanya valley and travelled almost its full length, passed the villages of Bataan and Maidani and the small compound that served as an Afghan army outpost on the main road outside of Bahadurkhel village. Afghan soldiers from the outpost lined the road for 500 meters east and west of their compound to provide some security for the patrol. The soldiers on the road were from a well disciplined platoon and were properly spaced, had their eyes and weapons facing outward from the road and looked ready for a fight. Their platoon leader, a lieutenant named Sikander, walked up and down the road checking on his men and communicating with his command by radio just as he was supposed to.

The Afghan soldiers still around the compound were a different story. As Nunez's platoon passed the compound they saw Afghans standing around the doors smoking and eating *naan* bread, some with weapons and some without, and other half-dressed soldiers lazing on the decks of two old Russian armored personnel carriers inside the outpost's tiny perimeter.

Nunez's platoon was at the rear of the convoy behind the ANA, who were behind the French. Just after Nunez's platoon passed the last ANA soldier standing on the road east of the outpost they heard the Georgia soldier with the French

94

commander report on the radio, "Razor 1 this is Cadillac, we're makin' the turn south into the Ghayne. Nuthin' to report up here, it's all good."

"Razor 1 copied."

Over a kilometer ahead, dismounted French Marines and engineers walking point for the convoy turned south off the Afghanya valley road, followed by the lead French vehicles. The road was curved and the view of the Texas soldiers was obstructed by trees and compounds. The French kept pushing into the Ghayne without meeting any resistance.

Nunez's MRAP made a curve and he could see Afghanya village a few hundred meters ahead, identifiable by the Afghan National Police outpost on the road and the scattering of Afghan policemen milling around near it. As Vlacek drove through the checkpoint the soldiers saw two VABs stopped forty meters off the road, the French mortar gunners unhooking their towed mortar systems from the backs of the vehicles. If there was a contact, the French could call on 120mm mortars from Firebase Pierce and 81mm mortars from the police checkpoint.

"Razor 1 this is Cadillac. The French just called a halt. I ain't sure what's up, but the French are all excited on the radio."

The US Marine lieutenant further to the rear with the ANA asked, "Cadillac this is Razor 1, what's the French mission commander saying?"

"Razor, he's talking on two different radios right now and writing down a bunch of crap. I'll ask him when he's free."

The long line of ANA pickups ahead of Nunez's platoon came to a slow halt. The soldiers packed into the beds of the trucks didn't look horribly interested in what was happening, and Nunez hoped that was a good sign. If the ANA were nervous, then everyone needed to be nervous. But the opposite wasn't always true. Afghans could look relaxed even when they knew they were about to get hit.

"Razor 1 Razor 1, this is Cadillac! The Captain here just told me the French engineers found a buried IED, about a hundred fifty meters ahead! They're settin' up a cordon around it now!"

"Razor 1 copies, do the French need some more ass up there? We can push up if they need us."

"Uh...hang on, I gotta wait til he's done on the radio again and I'll ask him."

Above Nunez on the gun, Wilson said, "Well, holy cow. We finally found one before it went off. Suck on that shit, Maulawi Rahman."

"Razor 1 this is Cadillac, the French said don't move up. They're settin' out a big perimeter with their infantry, they said they'll let us know if they need ANA support."

Ahead of Nunez's MRAP the ANA soldiers climbed out of their trucks and set security. Some of them wore full body armor and helmets, some had only helmets, and Nunez saw one young soldier with no armor, no helmet, green bandanna tied around his head, carrying an RPG launcher with a single round loaded. That was it. No rifle, no extra ammunition, no radio, no water, just an RPG launcher with one round ready to go. The soldier laughed and slapped hands with other soldiers, and looked like he was in a great mood.

"I wonder if this is Mowee-wowee Rahman's work, or if this is a group of amateurs," Nunez said. "I would think Rahman's guys are better than this. And they always have an ambush set, but there hasn't been any fire and they've had enough time to do it. I think this one's someone else's work."

Quiet minutes passed. On the radio, the Georgia soldier said, "Hey Razor, be advised, the French just found the triggerman's hide, wires and a car battery. They said it's about a hundred meters west of the road. We're waiting on a grid."

Nunez looked into the distance toward the Ghayne valley. "Hey Alex, that triggerman's site should be at around our 2:00 o'clock, six or seven hundred meters away, not real far from the base of that one mountain to our south. Keep an eye that way."

"Roger that boss. I can't see shit through all the trees, but I'll watch what I can."

Quiet on the radio, quiet in the villages. Soldiers bullshitted and made fun of each other, some Afghan soldiers walked to the MRAPs and tried to make conversation with the gunners and truck commanders. None of the Texans could understand a word any of the ANA said, until one approached Wilson, made a "give it to me" gesture and said "American sex magazine?" Wilson laughed and shook his head, and the Afghans gave up and went back to their trucks.

Klein keyed up on the platoon radio frequency. "Colts this is Colt 1, is anyone else seeing the locals starting to disappear from the fields? I swear we saw a lot more people out here a few minutes ago."

"Hey Jerry, yeah, Homie's right," Wilson said. "The locals are fucking off. I can see a few groups walking toward compounds right now."

"Aw, shit." Nunez keyed the mike on the mission radio. "Razor and Cadillac this is Colt 4, the locals are starting to disappear back here. Pass that on to the French and the ANA, the shit might be about to hit the fan."

"Razor copies."

"Cadillac's got it. We don't see a fuckin' soul here in Ghayne. I don't think anyone was in here when we started into the valley."

Nunez looked into the fields. He saw one old woman herding three children into the door of a compound a few hundred meters away. Not another soul was visible anywhere. The ANA soldier with the bandanna kneeled by the side of the road looking southward, no longer laughing. The rest of the Afghan soldiers looked tense and paid close attention to the villages to the south, toward the Ghayne valley. As Nunez watched, the ANA took cover behind their vehicles or in the shallow ditches on the south side of the road.

"Colt 1 this is Colt 4, be advised, the ANA are gettin' all jacked up, up front."

"Roger that. Harris, make damn sure your gunner keeps his eyes to the rear."

"Colt 2 roger."

Nunez yawned and rubbed his face. He was tired, it had been an early morning and he hadn't slept well. He rarely slept well while deployed. He had been frustrated for months at the American and French troops' seeming inability to hit back at the enemy who hit them whenever they wanted to. He drank way too much caffeine, didn't exercise enough and couldn't remember the last time he had taken a solid dump. Whenever he looked in a mirror he saw a little more grey in his hair, a little darker shadow to the creases on his face.

He felt old and worn out, because of what he knew would happen. They were about to get hit, again, by Taliban they couldn't see, who would have the initiative like they almost always did. Nunez had found combat to be exhilarating for the most part, and like almost every American combat soldier he wanted to get into a good fight. But he was tired of the enemy always having the upper hand.

Wilson stretched in the turret and groaned, then said, "Hey guys, what's the bet we're not going to be able to get into this one either?"

Twin explosions sounded in the distance, followed by heavy gunfire. Adrenaline shot through Nunez's veins, but he kept his composure. His men weren't in any danger yet. The radio stayed silent for what seemed like a long time as everyone waited for an update from the Georgia soldier with the French. The ANA all ducked lower behind cover, but there didn't seem to be any fire coming toward the soldiers and vehicles on the Afghanya valley road.

"This is Cadillac, contact contact contact! They're firin' on us from that mountain and from compounds at the bottom of it, small arms and RPGs!...Holy fuck! We got guys down! We got some guys...*shit, we need fuckin' help!*"

Tense communication on the radio, but nobody moved forward. Minutes passed, and the ANA in front of the Texas platoon were still in their positions, none of them mounted back up in their trucks. Klein keyed the radio and said, "Razor this is Colt 1, are you guys pushing up?"

The Marine with the ANA sounded exasperated as he keyed the radio and said, "Colt this is Razor, I'm trying to get them to move up, their fucking commander told them to stay where they are! Wait one, I'll get back to you."

The sounds of combat ahead intensified. The French fired mortars from their position at the police checkpoint and Wilson said, "Hey Sarge, the French are hitting the top of that mountain to the south."

"Can you see anything on it?" Nunez asked.

"Nope," Wilson answered as he looked through binoculars. "There's no vegetation on it, it's just a bunch of big ass rocks."

"Well, fuck it. Shoot at it, just make sure you don't put any rounds low where you can't see their impact."

"Roger." Wilson opened up with short bursts, causing the ANA in front of them to cringe. Nunez keyed up and said on the platoon net, "Colts this is Colt 4, we're hitting the top of the mountain that the French mortars are hitting. If you fire on it make sure you keep your rounds high, don't drop any into the wooded areas that we can't see into."

"4 this is 1, can you push past these fuckers? We need to get up there and help out the French."

"We've got ANA trucks all over the road, give me a minute to try to get them out of the way."

The road they were on was narrow, and the MRAPs wouldn't be able to get around the ANA trucks unless they were pushed way to one side. Nunez popped his door, stood up and yelled at the Afghan soldiers, "Hey, move this truck! Move the fucking truck out of the way!"

The ANA soldiers nearest the truck either gave blank stares or yelled back in Pashto or Dari. Nunez and the ANA couldn't understand each other at all. Nunez disconnected his headset and jumped out of the truck, yelling and gesturing to the ANA to move the truck. They yelled and gestured back. He ran to the driver's door to tell the driver to move. The cab was empty. He jumped inside to move the truck himself. The keys weren't in the ignition. He got back out of the truck and made motions like turning a key, yelling, "Who's got the fucking keys to the truck?"

The ANA yelled and gestured and pointed toward the Ghayne. Nunez couldn't tell what the fuck they were trying to say. Cursing out loud, he stomped back to his MRAP.

"1 this is 4, the truck in front of us is blocking the road and I can't find the fucking keys. We can push it out of the way if you want us to."

"Roger that, do it."

On the mission net the Georgia soldier yelled over the gunfire, "This is Cadillac, we're tryin' to back out toward Afghanya! This is a real fuckin' small road, tell the ANA not to jam the fuckin' road or we won't be able to get out! Razor, did you get that?"

"Razor copied, what the status on your casualties?"

"I think we got two KIA and one wounded, they're still tryin' to get 'em back here!"

"Okay, tell the French we're pushing up a dismounted element directly south from here through the villages toward that mountain. Then we're going to move toward the Ghayne so we can hit the Taliban from two directions. Tell them to watch for us. You copy, Cadillac?"

"Okay, I copied! I'll tell them!"

Klein was on the mission net right away. "Razor, you want some more ass with you for that dismounted element?"

"Roger, send me anyone you got."

"Roger, all TCs, dismounts and the medic meet me up front at 4's truck."

Nunez, Harris, Klein, Lattimore, Lyons, Trevino, Nguyen and Doc Poole met up at the lead MRAP and moved up the ANA column to meet Razor. Razor was a bulky, black haired, thirty-something Marine Staff Sergeant named Poston. Poston had eleven ANA and one interpreter with him and after taking all of two minutes to lay out a plan with Klein, the nineteen of them headed south into the fields in a column.

The roar of machine gun fire and explosions rang out far to the left of the little column as it moved out. They crossed furrowed fields, having to drop down from some fields onto others five feet lower. Whenever the ANA came to a compound they broke from the column, split into pairs and flowed around the compounds like water without anyone giving a command. The difference between the Americans, trained in traditional tactics, and the ANA, who were natural, tribal fighters, was never more apparent than when they were on a mixed patrol.

As they moved across the countryside the distinct blasts of tank main gun and RPG fire shook the air several hundred meters away. The soldiers in the patrol could see nothing through the dense vegetation and scattered compounds to their east. Every time they crossed an open area the ANA and Americans set a few soldiers in a line kneeling and facing east, able to give some protection to the soldiers with no cover in the field.

Nunez and his soldiers looked everywhere as they moved, walking at a crouch with their weapons at the ready in front of them, fingers off the triggers and thumbs on the safeties. At one point they had a short halt while the ANA pushed forward to clear one compound away from any others, and Klein said to Nunez, "You know, every fucking Afghan out here is watching us, calling their Taliban friends and family members on cell phones and telling them, 'Hey, there's a bunch of Americans and ANA headed toward you. You might want to go ahead and kill them.'"

The patrol took almost twenty minutes to make the 800 meters and stop at a deep ravine at the base of the mountain. Cadillac got on the radio several more times to tell everyone that the French had recovered their casualties but now had a VAB stuck in the mud off the road. A few minutes later he was on the radio again, telling Razor that the French air controllers were trying to get helicopter support but the available Kiowas and Apaches were tied up supporting a larger engagement west of Bagram. The helicopters would head to Kapisa as soon as they could. The patrol cleared another compound just short of the ravine and set up in the compound's courtyard, and Razor got on the radio.

"Cadillac this is Razor 1, tell the French we're about to start pushing east next to the ravine. We'll advise when we have them in sight. Tell them check their fire to the west and try not to shoot my ANA this time."

"Cadillac copies, Cadillac copies, stand by."

Razor walked to Klein and Nunez and said, "We're real likely to get ambushed on the way in there. The ANA are going to stay in the lead, they see shit way before we do. If we get hit bad and pinned down out there, we kick a compound door in, strongpoint it and scream for help like little girls. That plan sound good to you two?"

"Well," Klein said, "in officer school they taught us to make a five paragraph operations order with annexes every mission. But 'Go that way, kill the enemy, if we get hit bad take a compound and scream like a bitch' sounds like a good plan to me. We're ready."

"Cadillac this is Razor 1, tell the French we're at the base of the mountain and about to push east toward them."

Nunez looked at his soldiers. All were a little out of breath, a little sweaty, a little nervous. They knew that within minutes they would be taking cover behind compounds, mud berms and rock walls as bullets and RPGs screamed at them. They couldn't say for certain what the ANA would do if their patrol took casualties or if the incoming fire got heavy; a good group of ANA would hold their ground to the end, a bad group might retreat on their own or just disappear into a compound without telling a soul. If they got hit before they were in visual contact with the French, they couldn't rely on the French to support them with direct fire weapons. Not only that, the French might accidentally fire in their direction. If the ANA gunners on their trucks on the Afghanya valley road got spooked they might just fire blind toward the mountain, putting the patrol at risk of taking friendly fire from two directions. Without air cover, the patrol would be moving blind and probably under the eyes of Taliban informants watching from their compounds. No doubt, this little mission of theirs could go way wrong, way quick.

Razor said something to his interpreter, who repeated it to the ANA soldiers. The ANA soldiers climbed over the courtyard wall and kept their eyes to the east while the Americans followed them, then started toward the raging firefight out of view in the Ghayne.

"Razor 1 this is Cadillac, halt your move, halt your move! The French don't want you moving this way, they say we're going to have a friendly fire incident! Razor, you copy? They've recovered their casualties and their stuck vehicle and they're startin' to pull back!"

"Well, mother-fucker," Poston said. "This is bullshit." Then he keyed his radio and said, "Roger, I copy, we're halting our move." Behind him the Americans groaned as one. Nunez turned and looked at Klein, then shook his head. Klein spat to the side and muttered, "Jesus, what a fucking waste of time. Why are we even here?"

They took less time getting back than they took getting to the ravine. The fire slackened and dropped off to nothing as they moved through the fields, and by the time they got back to the road the MRAPs and ANA trucks were already turned around. The first VABs out of the Ghayne had linked up with troops holding the road. Dismounted French troops walked beside the vehicles.

Most of the dirty and angry-looking French Marines glared at the ANA and made an obvious effort not to give dirty looks to the Americans. Nunez was surprised to see a few of the others laughing and smiling, shaking hands with Americans as they came back to the road.

Nunez climbed back into his MRAP and reattached the Velcro strap for his headset. As soon as he was connected Wilson asked, "So boss, let me guess... fatal case of blue balls?"

"Fuck yes," Nunez said. "Man, I think I'm going to have to get Doc to give me a hand job tonight or I'll go fucking insane. This sucks, man. We should have gone up that ravine and hit those fucks, not just let them ambush us. Maybe I would have even shot Maulawi Rahman right square in the back."

"Next time, boss," Wilson said. "Next time."

The ride back was uneventful. The MRAPs were already parked by the time the first VAB hit the gate, Nunez and Klein waited by the motor pool to talk to whoever Cadillac was. They spotted him easily, the only soldier in bright green digital camouflage among the French dark green and black woodland pattern. He wasn't shaking as he climbed out of the VAB's back doors, but with the look he had on his face, he might as well have been.

"Hey, Cadillac," Klein said. "You got a minute? We need to know what the fuck happened up there."

The Georgia soldier slung his patrol pack over one shoulder and walked toward them. He was blond and blue eyed, average height but stocky, built like a football player. He had Staff Sergeant rank and a nametape with "Gowens" on his body armor.

"Yeah, I got a minute. Who are you guys?" Then, looking at the Texas 36th Infantry division "T-patch" on their sleeves, he asked, "Are you guys Colt?"

"Yeah, we are," Nunez said. "So what was the deal up there? We heard when y'all found the IED, what was it?"

"I don't know for sure, I never seen it," Gowens said. "They said it was somethin' buried in the road, attached to a wire. They said most of the wire was buried, but they had part of it hidden in some high grass or somethin' and one of them engineers who pushed out on the side of the road walked through the grass and tripped over it. I mean, I think that's what they said, I don't speak French and they don't speak Georgia."

"Damn, that's a lucky break," Klein said. "How'd the ambush start?"

"Shit, lieutenant...after they found that IED everyone was all hinked up, you know? They kicked out a cordon around it, then pushed a bunch of dismounts forward to look for the hide site and set up a perimeter. Right after that they found the hide. It was only like a hundred meters from the road, in one of them fields that's dropped down lower than the one next to it. They were pushin' out from there when the ambush started."

Gowens took a breath and searched his gear for his hydration hose. He sucked down a long drink of water before saying, "Man, I was watchin' them guys when they got hit. I was stickin' up out the back of the captain's VAB lookin' through bino's, and when the first RPG rounds got fired I seen that one squad drop and start puttin' down suppressive fire. Then one section jumped up and bounded back toward this one little rock wall, like we do in trainin', you know? I was lookin' right at that one Marine when he got hit by a PK machine gun. I mean, I swear to fuckin' god I seen the god damn rounds go right through him, one came out his stomach and one musta' hit him in the back next to his plate. It came out, like right here, right under his arm. He dropped like fuckin' that," Gowens said, snapping his fingers, "and then them other two Marines turned back and grabbed him and that god damn PK nailed them too. I couldn't see them when they fell, they were all on the other side of that rock wall. If I couldn'ta heard all that fuckin' screamin', I woulda' thought they were all dead."

Gowens took another drink and spit some water into his hand, then rubbed it in his face and hair. Klein and Nunez stayed quiet, giving him the time he needed to get his thoughts together. Then Gowens said, in a quieter voice than before, "Holy shit, man. If every mission's gonna be like this one, it's gonna be a rough fuckin' year."

A shout caught their attention. "Nunez! Lieutenant Klein! Hey, you guys alright?" When they looked toward the noise they saw Durrand walk toward them, holding a notepad.

"We're good, Durrand," Nunez said. "Gowens here had some close calls, but he's good too. You get any news about this IED?"

"I got some new stuff," Durrand said. "It's not confirmed or anything, but we've received several reports that it was Maulawi Rahman in the Ghayne." He held up his hands and said, "I know, I know, we already knew that. But there's some real important new shit today, these reports today say that he was in command of the IED cell and a hundred fighters from the Shkin valley. This is the first we've heard about him being in command of anyone but his own cell."

"When did that happen?" Nunez asked. "Did he get a promotion or something?"

"In effect, yes he did. He scored a lot of cool points with the Taliban for all the IED attacks he carried out, and then they made a big fucking deal out of all the supposed heroic bullshit he did in the Alasai. He's kind of a legend now. They say he survived the Special Forces raid in Uzbin, even though we know he was nowhere near the compound the SF team hit. Then he blew up dozens of coalition vehicles, then was wounded while bravely rescuing a wounded fighter in the

Alasai or some other bullshit, then survived wounds that would have killed any ordinary fighter, then he recovered, which proves he has Allah's special blessing, then he went back to blowing up coalition vehicles and killing infidels. And he still prays five times a day like a good Muslim should. He's pretty much a golden boy, he walks on Afghan water."

"Yeah, well, who gives a fuck?" Nunez asked. "They can keep building him up, it'll just be that much better when we kill his fucking ass. So you're getting reports he has a hundred fighters, how many does he really have?"

"I guess you're familiar with Afghan math," Durrand said. "Well, this time we can't do the usual divide by five method."

Gowens gave Durrand a curious look, and Durrand said, "Afghan math is what you do every time an Afghan tells you anything with numbers. If a local tells me, 'there are fifty RPG rounds in a compound in Tagab', I divide by five and say, 'okay, there's ten.' These fucking guys exaggerate everything. But this time, I think that at best we can divide by two. The shit that happened today wasn't done by just a handful of Taliban. I was in the operations center keeping track of the whole fight, and with all the places the French were taking fire from, there had to be at least fifty Talibs out there. And they were good. They were in prepared positions, they made coordinated attacks with different weapon systems from multiple locations, they fought almost like professionals today. That's a bad thing, Nunez. These aren't chickenshit little trash talkers who fling a few rounds, run away and brag to everyone that they killed a hundred Americans. These guys want to fight, they're pretty good at it, and Rahman's a pretty good leader. They only killed one French Marine today, but it wasn't for lack of trying."

"One? I thought it was two," Klein said.

"No, it was one," Gowens replied. "One dead, two seriously fucked up."

"So, what's next then?" Klein asked. "How do we get these fuckers?"

"This is the next step," Durrand said. "Apaches and Kiowas will fly around the Ghayne today, looking for the fighters to cross back over the mountains to the Shkin valley. The fighters and Rahman aren't stupid, they'll hang out in compounds drinking hot tea and poking each other in the ass until the helicopters go away. Then they'll go back to the Shkin, get in bed with their wives and have mandatory sex to make some more Taliban. The next morning they're all rested up waiting for orders to conduct the next IED attack. That's what's next for them," Durrand said. "For us, I don't know. We'll be pissed off for a few weeks, and someone in Bagram will schedule a staff meeting to take place in a month or so, and a bunch of officers will watch power point presentations and discuss how we need to hand out more humanitarian aid to the locals to get them on our side. Then they'll all pull out their counterinsurgency manuals and remind each other that you can't kill your way to victory in this war, and they'll talk about the one single war in the history of the world where being nice to the enemy worked and show how it's proof that we need to be friends and not fight with the Afghans. Then Rahman will blow up another French or American vehicle and kill a bunch of us and it'll start all over again."

"Don't be such a douche, Durrand," Klein said. "For real, what's next?"

Durrand shook his head. "I don't know what's next, lieutenant. For real. If there was any justice in the world, we'd head for the Shkin valley, figure out where Rahman is and kill him and all his friends. If shit happens the way it usually happens, we'll just talk a lot about what needs to happen and then never get anything done."

"We got something done in the Alasai," Klein said.

"Roger that, sir, you're right, you did. But you don't know how many teeth we had to pull and fobbit officers we had to jerk off to convince them to let it happen. I don't know that anyone in the chain of command is up to letting it happen again."

"Well, I'm gonna be hopeful, Durrand. I don't think the French are going to just sit here and wait for this shit to happen again. I think we're going to mount an operation into the Shkin, and we're going to flatten the fucking place. It'll be our own little Fallujah, right here in Kapisa province." Then to Gowens Klein said, "Hey brother, come with us and grab some pizza. You look like you need it. My treat. Durrand, you're invited too, but you pay your own way, douchebag."

CHAPTER 8

The American officers, vehicle commanders and two English-speaking French officers crowded into a tent inside the eastern Alasai combat outpost. They sat in a semicircle around the American colonel, call sign Navajo, who was in charge of the mission. A large map covered with a plastic sheet and marked with colored pins and lines was mounted on an easel behind him. The colonel had already gone over the specifics of the mission, the basic "who's doing what, when they're doing it, and where they're doing it". The soldiers and Marines in the room had at least a basic idea of what they were supposed to do the next day. Those who were still confused would get it straight later, when they went over the plan again with their own platoons or teams.

For this mission ten soldiers from Nunez's platoon had been attached to a Georgia unit to give them badly needed manpower. Three Georgia platoons would take part in the major push into the Shkin valley. They were the new Embedded Training Team for the Afghan National Army battalion taking part in this operation. The vehicles Nunez's men were riding in were crewed by Georgia troops, so the Texas soldiers would be able to get out and fight on foot like real grunts were supposed to. A few U.S. Marines were also embedded with the Georgia troops, men who were being assigned to a new embedded training team and needed the experience of working with the ANA in a large operation. For Nunez and his men, this was going to be as close to a pure infantry fight as they would ever see in their lives.

The army colonel paced back and forth in front of the men, held a laser pointer in one hand and a plastic cup in the other. He spit tobacco juice into the cup, then took a look around the room. "We won't go over the details any more. You know the basic plan, and I know you'll carry it out. We all know what we have to do tomorrow."

He gave the men a hard look. "Listen, I know what everyone's thinking," he said. "I've thought it myself. 'This son of a bitch Rahman always holds all the cards. He always hits us first, his intel is better than ours. After all this damn time, we still don't know what he looks like. We don't even know how old he is. We could have seen him on the road a thousand times and not known it.' And you're all right, you've all made the correct assessment. He does know we're coming.

"He's in charge of as many as two hundred and fifty fighters in the Shkin. The Taliban aren't going to make the same mistakes they made in the Alasai, because this time Rahman calls the shots. Tomorrow we can expect IEDs to be in place and waiting for us. We can expect dozens of fighters to launch coordinated attacks like they did in Ghayne. We can expect casualties, maybe more than the ones and twos we've had in the past. We might see Rahman and not even know it, so he could get away. If you're worried about what's going to happen tomorrow, good. You should be worried."

The colonel spit into the cup again. Nunez looked at Klein and raised an eyebrow. Klein gave him the same look in return. They were smart enough to be a little scared about what could happen the next day. They had already talked about it in private, away from their platoon.

"But you men keep this in mind when you step off tomorrow," the colonel said. "Every single worry we have has been addressed. If there are IEDs on the road, our dismounted ANA infantry will find them before the vehicles push into the valley. If there are prepared positions, we have dedicated helicopter and A-10 support to find and destroy them." Nodding to the French Marine officers, he said, "If the helicopters and A-10s have to pull off and some smartass Taliban says 'They're gone, we can come back out and shoot again,' French sniper and Milan missile teams in overwatch positions in the mountains will hit them from above. Those tough French motherfuckers are walking into the mountains tonight, carrying those heavy .50 caliber sniper rifles and Milan systems with them. They'll be in place when we need them."

The colonel spit again. "If we take fire from positions we can't identify, give an area and we'll hit it with mortars. If you see people who look like civilians leaving the valley, remember that the ANA are going to stop every last person who tries to walk out, and they'll be identify and photograph them. If they catch someone who they don't believe is from around here, they'll detain him until we say they can release him. And we don't even need to worry about the ANA catch-

108

ing Rahman, because we all know he isn't going to try to escape. He's too proud for that. He's the Taliban's hero, so he'll stand and fight. He'll be in one of those compounds directing his boys, and we'll figure out where he is."

Heads nodded in agreement throughout the room. The soldiers and Marines had been told that Rahman was bragging about how many Americans he was going to kill in the Shkin valley, they knew he would be there when the fight started. The colonel was counting on Rahman's pride being too great for him to back away from a fight.

The colonel said, "Now, we all know the Rules of Engagement. If we take fire from a compound, even if we know Rahman is in there, we can't just destroy it with air strikes or indirect fire. You men on the ground, you have to push all the way to that compound, get the ANA in there and clear it. They have their own ROE, which is no rules at all. And when they find Rahman inside one of those compounds, make sure they bring him back out to us. Trust your ANA to pick out who's who, they can identify the head motherfucker in charge even if we can't. They can bring him out alive and in one piece, they can bring him out alive with no arms or legs and his guts hanging out, they can bring him out dead with a bullet through his face, or they can bring him out dead and in little bitty burned pieces. They can even bring out just his head if they want. But they have to bring him out, not leave him inside where they find him."

Another spit into the cup, another turn in front of the assembled men. "To-morrow, we *will* push into that valley. Hopefully we'll get all three kilometers in there, maybe we won't get that far. But we'll get into that valley that those bas-tards swear we'll never set one foot in. We *will* kill any and all Taliban who fire on us. And if at all possible, we will kill Rahman. If we push three kilometers to the end of the valley, we'll piss on the walls of all the compounds and then turn around and come back out. If everything goes wrong and we get stopped cold somewhere in that valley, we take the nearest compounds, make a strongpoint and hold it overnight. Those bastards will go insane if we hold ground in that valley that they've told all their people we can't even enter. They *will* come to force us out. Well, fuck them. We'll let them come to us, and we'll kill them all. When we pull out of there the day after tomorrow, we leave hundreds of dead Taliban behind us and more importantly we leave the message, 'We'll come in here whenever the fuck we feel like it, and kill anyone who tries to fight.'"

Another spit into the cup. The colonel pointed toward Klein and Nunez, who sat next to Lieutenant Spicer and Sergeant First Class Sardinea from the Georgia National Guard. "You Georgia and Texas boys in the Quick Reaction Force are going to have your hands full. You men are going to roll in to who knows what situation, maybe a kilometer into the valley, maybe three kilometers into the valley. Whatever you find, wherever you are, just get there and follow the basics. Security, fire superiority, and communication. And if it helps, keep in mind that these Taliban are all Yankees from northern Afghanistan, so you rebels from down south get to win the war against them this time."

There was a ripple of laughter in the room. None came from the two French officers, who traded puzzled looks as the colonel paused and gave a slight smile.

"Men, remember that the goal of this mission isn't to establish combat outposts in the valley. The goal isn't to hold ground permanently. The goal isn't even to hold a fucking peace and love meeting with the village elders in the valley, even though that's what we told the higher-ups in Bagram so they'd sign off on this thing. This mission has two goals. First, we kill all the Taliban we can. Second, we kill Rahman. For me, there is no other reason for what we're doing tomorrow. We always beg for the chance to get out there and kill the enemy, to do what every fucking soldier and Marine who's ever been here has dreamed of doing. Tomorrow that dream comes true. Tomorrow our only job is to kill the enemy. We all want to do that, we know how to do that, we're ready to do that. It's going to be a good day."

The colonel tossed the spit cup into a trash can, then stuck his index finger between his teeth and lower gums and scraped out the remaining tobacco. Nunez thought he was about to dismiss the group of men. Everyone had a lot of last minute planning to do, last minute equipment and weapons checks before they stepped off the next day. Instead of releasing them, the colonel said, "You know what the locals say about us? They say we don't have the will to stay here and win this fight. They say we're like the Russians, and the British before them. That we'll get tired of this, we don't have the strength to accept losses. That we'll quit, because they're better than us, braver than us, tougher than us. That we don't have the resolve to win this war. Anyone buy that bullshit? Anyone here think the Talibs are better than us? No, we don't believe that. And after tomorrow, the locals won't believe it anymore either."

The colonel stopped pacing and gave all the men in the room a hard stare. "Tomorrow we show them what we Americans and our French brothers are really made of. Tomorrow we do to the Taliban what they've been doing to us. Tomorrow...tomorrow is proof of our resolve."

The colonel walked to the door of the small briefing room, turned and looked at all the men. "I know you have a lot to do, I won't keep you any longer. Get back to your soldiers and Marines, make sure you all get some sleep. My last order to you tonight, I want to shake every man's hand as you leave. Good night, warriors. I'll see you in the morning."

The soldiers and Marines rose as one, making small talk as they walked to the door. The colonel shook their hands as they left, gave words of concern and encouragement, called most of them by name and made note of which names he still needed to learn. The men filed out into the dark and went back to their unit's areas on the small outpost. The other eight soldiers from Nunez's platoon were all still awake, hanging out with the Georgia soldiers at the fighting positions on the eastern perimeter.

"Well Lieutenant, got anythin' new?" Harris asked.

"Nothing new. The Georgia boys and Marines with the ANA walk from here into the Shkin tomorrow and clear the road so the trucks can come in afterward. We wait on the perimeter until they call for the QRF. There's no question, at some point they'll call us. When they call us, we load up into the Georgia platoon's vehicles and roll to wherever they need us. When we get there we dismount, figure out what the fuck is going on, maintain security, put fire on the enemy and communicate with the outpost. Personally, I think we're going to wind up holding a couple of compounds overnight. If that happens, it's one hundred percent alert, all night. Everyone needs to quit fucking off and get some sleep tonight. Tomorrow's going to be a busy day."

CHAPTER 9

The American soldiers hunched behind the thick perimeter wall of the combat outpost. Taliban fighters sprayed random rounds from the Alasai valley but so far hadn't managed to hit anywhere near where they were aiming. The gunfire had been light and sporadic so far this morning, but the start time for the push into the Shkin valley had almost arrived. They knew the fire would get more intense as soon as the first troops walked out of the base and reached the mouth of the Shkin. Afghan soldiers, contemptuous of their own lives as usual, lounged around in the open or on the backs of BMP armored personnel carriers parked outside the perimeter, daring the Taliban to shoot them.

The firing had started over an hour earlier, before dawn. Nervous American soldiers whose pre-battle nerves allowed them only a few hours of sleep during the night were already awake. Two Apache helicopters arrived over the valley as soon as the sun was up, swooped and dove toward suspected enemy positions but never fired a shot. Nobody in the Alasai valley, not the soldiers at the outpost or the pilots in the air, could spot a single enemy fighter anywhere. When the Apaches arrived, the Taliban hid their rifles and acted like every other civilian in the area, or just sat under trees that were too thick for the helicopters to see through and waited for them to leave.

For almost thirty minutes the soldiers watched as the Apaches flew over the valley, took fire from unknown positions, circled back to look for a target, and then got shot at again. One Taliban fighter had the guts to fire an RPG that burst well above the Apaches, but even then nobody spotted any backblast that revealed the fighter's position. All around the outpost, soldiers squinted through rifle scopes, tank sights or Milan missile launcher optics, but could not see anything resembling a Taliban fighter anywhere in the valley. The Apaches were finally called off by the French Air Controllers. The controllers told the pilots to stay just out of earshot and wait to be directed in on specific targets. The infantrymen about to push into the valley would need helicopter support, real soon.

Another burst of fire rang out from somewhere in the valley, and a few seconds later Wilson muttered "Fuck, I still can't see a damn thing," as he peered through the scope of an M14 rifle. "I mean, I don't see anything at all. No people, no cows, no camels, no goats, no dogs, nothing. I have no idea where the hell they're firing at us from."

"Mahnd if Ah take a look through that thang?" one of the Georgia National Guard soldiers asked Wilson. Wilson nodded and sidestepped away from his firing position. The Georgia soldier looked through the scope for a couple of minutes and gave up. He couldn't see anything either.

The mouth of the Shkin valley was visible through trees several hundred meters away, but the soldiers couldn't see into it. They had studied the maps enough to know that the Shkin valley itself was a terrain nightmare for an attacking force, a dream to defenders. The valley was much narrower than the others they had been in before, with high ground close in on both sides of the narrow valley road. In other valleys the mountains were far enough from the road that the troops only had to worry about long range harassment fire coming from them, but in the Shkin they would be within RPG range of Taliban fighters in the high ground to their left and right. For the infantry attacking into the valley on foot, life was going to suck. For the Quick Reaction Force that would ride into the battle in MRAPs down the narrow, possibly mined road with Taliban fighters ready to rain RPGs and heavy machine gun fire on them from both sides, it might suck worse.

The previous night neither Nunez nor Klein could force themselves to sleep. After an hour of trying they got up and went to the outpost gate. Small teams of French Marines were using the cover of darkness to push out on foot and occupy positions on the high ground, Nunez and Klein shook hands with them and wished them good luck.

The French were loaded down with weapons and gear. The Milan missiles some of the Marines carried weighed about thirty-five pounds, as did the launcher. The .50 caliber sniper rifles weighed almost forty pounds each, and were strapped down inside specially designed backpacks that were full of all the other equipment the snipers needed to carry. In addition to all that weight the snipers also carried carbines up front, in case they were ambushed on the way to their position.

One of the snipers, a short dark Marine with an intense, focused look on his face, carried his huge rifle on his back and a twenty pound machine gun up front. Nunez thought that the small French Marine had to be carrying at least his own weight in weapons and gear. He would be lugging all that weight up a mountain, and then might have to run down the mountain under fire with all of it, if the operation went wrong in the morning. But the French Marines had established their positions without incident, and now that the sun was up they called in to the command post to report they couldn't see anything either.

Afghan and French runners jogged back and forth from the command post, relaying information to the Georgia soldiers and their ANA platoons spread out in the open center of the outpost. The outpost was only about fifty meters across, just a small square of Hesco barriers housing a few tents, topped with sandbagged machine gun positions spaced twenty meters apart. The ANA had Dushka 12.7 mm heavy machine guns at several of the positions, and between the Dushkas there were PK machine guns. A lip around the inside of the perimeter allowed riflemen to jump onto the wall between the gun positions and fire their AKs.

The outpost sat on elevated ground, with steep slopes to the north and east. Close behind the outpost to the south was a chain of mountains, with several ANA positions strung along their crests. Outside the perimeter French light wheeled tanks and armored personnel carriers faced the valleys. A few Afghan Army vehicles were dispersed among them. French 81mm mortar teams had dug their weapons into a shallow pit, ready to provide close-in indirect fire support. The four MRAPs of the QRF were staged inside the outpost along with the ANA pickup trucks.

Nunez checked his watch. Almost 7 a.m. His soldiers were ready, their weapons on them but body armor and helmets staged next to the MRAPs. In the center of the outpost the Georgia troops gave instructions to the Afghan officers, who barked orders to their troops. The first company lined up in platoons at the outpost gate, standing by for orders from their own colonel to move out.

Inside the command post, French Marine officers sat at desks monitoring computers designed for use in the field and listened to reports coming in from the array of radios around them. The ANA colonel stood by one of the desks, waiting for the French ground commander to tell him when to start the advance. Seven a.m. arrived but the order didn't come, delayed until the French were prepared to fire on what they thought could be Taliban positions in the mountains.

Without warning, the mortar teams dropped the first rounds into their weapons, the heavy steel bombs making their distinctive *thoonk!* sound as they were launched from the tubes. To their west they heard the sounds of 120mm mortars being fired from several kilometers away. Inside the outpost the first ANA platoon tightened up against the gate, waiting on the order to move. Taliban fighters in the Alasai ceased fire and took cover in case the mortar rounds were coming for them.

Gore was the first to stand back up from behind the compound wall after the mortar fire, long before the rounds came back down onto their targets. He looked over his M240B machine gun and said , "I hope the mortars make some Taliban fighters run. C'mon, gimme something to shoot at." The rest of the Texas and Georgia soldiers jumped up in ones and twos. Several of them pulled cameras from their pockets and tried to get them started before the rounds landed. The sound of the 120mm impacts in the Shkin valley rumbled and echoed from the northeast back toward them, violent and reassuring.

The ANA battalion commander ran from the command post to the assembled platoons at the gate, screaming and gesturing madly the way Afghans always do when they're excited. When the first platoon started moving out of the gate, several of the Georgia soldiers on the perimeter turned and yelled out to the two Georgia soldiers, their friends, who were walking out with that platoon.

"Hey Ellis! Hooah, get some, motherfucker!"

"Woowhee! Do it, dawgs! Yeehah!"

The Georgia soldiers raised their fists and rebel-yelled back to the soldiers on the wall, just as the mortar crews fired a second volley. The lone Marine with the platoon was a very young looking artillery forward observer. He stayed quiet, slapping the magazine of his M16A4 as he sauntered out with the Georgia boys. French infantrymen outside the gate yelled *"Bon chance!"* Some of them undoubtedly wished they were going with the Americans into the teeth of the enemy.

The second platoon started out the gate, to the same shouts and wishes of luck. The lead ANA platoon came into Nunez's view. The ANA were tense and crouched, not walking in their peculiar, jaunty manner like they normally did.

The Georgia troops and their Marine, on the other hand, swaggered into battle with their heads held high. One of the Georgia boys let his right hand swing down for a moment, and Nunez saw him flick ashes from a cigarette, as if he was just strolling through the countryside.

Nunez marveled at their calm. The Marine could be accused of being so well trained and combat hardened that he could walk nonchalantly into what he knew would be the biggest fight of his life. But the Georgia boys were Guardsmen. In civilian life they were full time students, grocery store managers, construction workers, cops, rodeo clowns or who knew what. They were not professional soldiers and yet there they were, seven thousand miles from home in a hostile foreign land, advancing into an ambush and firefight they could likely be carried out of dead. Nunez watched the two Georgia soldiers and their Marine, and wondered how many people back home appreciated the bravery those three American warriors were showing.

The second volley of mortars landed in the valley north of the outpost. After the echoes of the mortar impacts subsided the few Taliban fighters in the Alasai sprayed short bursts in the general direction of the exposed platoons on the road and hit nothing at all, not even drawing a flinch, as far as Nunez could tell. Wilson stayed down on the scope and Gore swiveled his machine gun side to side, scanning everywhere, ready to fire on anything that looked like a threat. The rest of the Texas platoon searched through binoculars or scopes on their carbines but saw nothing.

The lead platoons disappeared behind compounds and vegetation while the next two platoons readied themselves at the gate. The road from the outpost to the Shkin valley wound haphazardly through sparse villages, doglegged, turned back on itself and followed a path that made no sense at all until you took geography into account. It took the soldiers on a kilometer and a half track to reach a point no more than seven hundred meters straight line distance from where Nunez stood.

An Afghan runner stepped out from the command post and yelled to the troops in the outpost. The next two platoons were being ordered out, earlier than planned. Four Georgia troops with their single Marine followed the Afghans out the gate. No gunfire rang out as they made their way down the road toward the Shkin. The Guard soldiers on the perimeter wall watched as they made the curve, covering their move but seeing no enemy.

A loud, deep gunshot emanated from the Shpee valley, distorted by the terrain and wind but still identifiable as a .50 caliber. Another followed it seconds later.

"French snipers hitting something?" Powell asked Klein.

"Probably so. I'm going to walk into the CP so I can listen in on what's happening out there. I'll yell if it's anything interesting."

Klein climbed down off the wall and walked to the command post. Lyons huddled close to Nunez, Gore and Wilson, looking nervous as hell. Specialist Manny Lyons, only twenty-one years old, rail thin and on his first deployment, had been assigned as Gore's assistant M240B gunner for this operation, something he had never done before. Nunez knew that no matter how calm he tried to look, he was scared of getting killed, or even worse, of screwing something up. To their left Harris, Doc Poole, Powell, Vlacek and Nguyen knelt in a circle with two of the Georgia soldiers, wargaming who would do what if the shit hit the fan. Nunez and Klein had already done that for hours on end with the Georgia platoon leader and platoon sergeant, and Nunez thought that for him to do it any more would just weigh down his thought process.

The Georgia lieutenant, Spicer, was in command. If he went down, Klein took over. If Klein went down, the Georgia platoon sergeant, Sardinea, took over. If he went down, it went to Nunez. If both lieutenants and both platoon sergeants went down, well, they were just flat out having a bad day, and whichever staff sergeant had enough nuts to take the reins would be in command.

Klein stepped out from the command post and called out, "The snipers just whacked two insurgents in the Shkin, trying to set up a Dushka! One KIA, one wounded! South side of the valley on a mountain, waiting on a grid!"

"Roger!" Nunez called back. Then to Gore, he said, "It's gonna kinda suck if they get a Duskha up there in the mountains to fire down on us. I'm not sure, but golly, I don't think our body armor can stop a 12.7."

Gore smiled, turned his face from his machine gun and pulled out a dog tag-shaped silver medallion on a chain. "Don't worry Sarge, I've got the 'Armor of

God'! Nothing can get through this!"

"Me too. I'm fucking bulletproof," Wilson said. Nunez reached out and picked up the medallion. He knew what was on it but still got a laugh every time he saw one. On one side was an etched crucifix surrounded by the words "Put on the Armor of God!" On the back was an engraving of a medieval knight with each part of his armor identified by an arrow with a description: "Breastplate of Righteousness," "Helmet of truth," "Loins girt with Strength." The loins thing gave Nunez the biggest laugh, because he always thought of loins as testicles.

"Strong nuts," Nunez said to Gore. "Good deal, you'll need them today, Eli. Too bad you don't have two of these medallions, you could tie one to each wrist and block bullets with them like Wonder Woman."

Gore laughed and then mimicked Wonder Woman standing calmly in a hail of gunfire, throwing his wrists out in random positions, making "*Tink! Tink! Tink! Tink!*" noises to simulate the bullet impacts. Gore stood under a tiny American flag attached to the end of an old radio antenna, sticking up ten feet above the Hesco wall. Nunez again wished he had a camera on him, so he could have proof that when his thirty-five year old, married father of five kids, graying former mechanic-turned-grunt was about to carry his machine gun into a huge shitstorm in a forgotten and worthless valley, he had stood under an American flag and danced like a cartoon heroine.

He thought back to Quincy on the day of the IED attack, remembered how Quincy had slowed to a walk in the open under fire so he could give Nunez cover fire. Quincy had been dignity and strength under pressure, Gore was prancing around and laughing like a moron before battle. Both actions were displays of bravery.

"How's your ammo loadout, Eli?" Nunez asked.

"I'm carrying a hundred round belt on the gun, and I have four hundred more rounds in my pack. Lyons has another four hundred, Nguyen and Vlacek have another hundred rounds apiece. 1100 rounds on us, before anyone would need to get into another ammo can."

"Okay," Nunez said. "You and Lyons break off a hundred rounds each and give them to me and Homie. I don't want you two guys overloading yourself with ammo, that much is heavy as shit and you're going to be loaded down with the gun already. Hooah?"

"Hooah Sarge. Don't worry about me being able to move, I took some extra steroids this morning." Then in a much louder voice he added, "That, and Vlacek swallowed last night, so I'm all refreshed today. He's great Sarge, he does this little trick with those buck teeth that just drives me kuh-*razy*, you know?"

"Hey, fuck you, Gore! God dang faggit! I'll beat yer ass!" Vlacek yelled from his circle.

Gore yelled back, "Awwww, sorry, Czech. I didn't mean to give away your special man-pleasin' secrets!"

Vlacek muttered something under his breath and turned away. Gore smiled, winked at Nunez and said, "He wants me."

A few more minutes passed, quiet except for the occasional crackle of gunfire in the Alasai. Once the soldiers heard a single round zing high over their heads, prompting one of the black Georgia troops to cringe in mock terror and scream "They's shootin', they's shootin'!", which drew tension-breaking laughter. The command post stayed calm, no reports of attacks on the ANA platoons or the Marines in the mountains. Klein stepped out of the command post again and called to the soldiers on the wall, "Hey! The first two platoons are at the mouth of the Shkin valley! The first village is about 800 meters ahead of them!"

"Roger!" Nunez called back. At the gate, two soldiers with heavy Dixie accents yelled to their friends as they moved out with their ANA platoon.

"Headin' out, boys! We gon' get some o' dem motherfuckers fo' y'all!"

"Next time y'all see me, Ah'm gonna have me a god dang Taliban tied to the hood o' mah truck! Hooah!"

Soldiers on the wall stood and cheered, some of them raised fists and bellowed victoriously. Two Marines were with this platoon, and instead of staying quiet like their predecessors had done also yelled with bravado.

"Semper fucking Fi! Let's do this shit!"

"Ooh rah, motherfuckers!"

The soldiers whistled and yelled back, "Semper Fi! Get some, Marines!" as the fifth ANA platoon left the gate. On the wall, Georgia boys slapped each other on the backs, reassured themselves that their friends would come back from this operation alive and well.

Another .50 caliber round was fired in the Shkin valley. Nunez hoped the snipers had just wasted another Taliban trying to stage for the ambush. A few bursts of fire answered the .50 caliber shot, not worrying Nunez, who thought it was probably just frustrated Taliban fighters shooting blind toward the sound of the sniper's rifle. The fire stopped after a few seconds, and Gore looked toward Nunez, smiled and said "Looks like they just got another one. Good on 'em."

A long burst rang out from the valley. A second weapon joined in, and then the valley exploded with sound as dozens of weapons opened on full automatic. Three pairs of dual explosions punctured the wall of noise, the sounds of RPGs being fired and then exploding on impact. The remaining platoons waiting to leave the gate jumped to their feet and readied themselves to push out. On the road outside the outpost, the platoon that had last left the gate ran past the east wall, the soldiers huffing under the weight of their gear. The two Marines had moved to the front of the platoon.

After nearly a full minute of gunfire, Klein ran out of the command post. "The first platoons just got hit, hard! Just inside the Shkin, they say the fire is coming from the mountains to the north, not sure exactly where yet!"

"Roger!" Nunez yelled back. Then to Gore he said, "Fuck, they got hit already? They just got into the fucking valley." Wilson tapped him on the shoulder and asked, "Hey boss, should we mount up now?"

Nunez thought about it, looked through his scope toward the platoon that was just disappearing around the first curve toward the Shkin valley. He was about to tell him yes and then give the order for his soldiers to head to the MRAPs when they heard the explosion of an RPG being fired in Alasai village. The round whooshed about fifty feet over the top of the perimeter wall, air-burst with a loud boom and left a blackish-brown ball of smoke in the air well behind the outpost. French and Afghans returned fire into the village. A few rounds of small arms fire whacked into the north wall, making the soldiers duck as they popped off return fire. Lieutenant Spicer and Sardinea ran toward the pandemonium of radio calls and screaming officers. Nunez knew both of them were hoping like hell they weren't about to hear that some of their friends had just been killed.

Something small and sharp slapped into Nunez's left side, making him exclaim "Shit!" and jump in surprise. He reached for the stinging spot on his ribs, almost expecting to see blood when he looked at his hand. Instead, he saw Klein standing outside the command post, about to throw another rock at him.

"Jerry!", Klein yelled over the gunfire. Nunez heard him say "Tell the guys..." before the noise drowned out his words.

"What? I can't fucking hear you!"

"I SAID TELL THE GUYS TO MOUNT THE FUCK UP!" Klein yelled back.

Soldiers on the wall heard him and scrambled to climb down and get to the MRAPs. Nunez tried to yell to the others, then gave up and ran over to them, slapped their shoulders and yelled in their ears to mount up. The soldiers ran along the wall and down sandbag steps to the bare dirt floor of the outpost toward the vehicles. Klein was already there, throwing his body armor over his head.

"What's the deal, what happened?" Nunez asked as he hoisted his own gear.

"The first platoon got nailed pretty good, they lost at least one ANA killed and a couple wounded, and when they tried to get to cover they got hit from another direction. They had to run up a hill to this wooded hollow, it was the nearest cover. They're pinned down now, and the ETT guys are screaming on the radio that the backup platoons won't move up and support them. It sounds like the Georgia boys and Marines in the Alasai are leaving their platoons and moving up on their own."

"Fuck. Okay, got it. I'm gonna go check and make sure we have everyone."

"Hey, one more thing!" Klein said. "The ANA are listening to the Taliban on the radio again, they heard someone called Shafaq giving orders. The ANA said there might be more than one Shafaq, so we don't know if it's Rahman or not."

"It's Rahman," Nunez said.

"Yeah, I know."

Nunez finished getting his gear straight and then gave quick situation updates to the soldiers as he accounted for each of the ten men from his platoon. All of them were there, geared up and ready to climb into their assigned MRAPs for the ride into the firefight.

Spicer and Sardinea ran toward the vehicles from the command post, screaming "Mount up!" Nunez got into his MRAP with Gore and Lyons. He and Klein were in separate vehicles from each other and from the Georgia lieutenant and platoon sergeant. No use losing two senior leaders in one IED strike.

Nunez closed the back door of the MRAP and locked it, then yanked one of the headsets from a bungee cord and pulled it on. Across the vehicle from Nunez, Gore and Lyons wiped off their machine gun with rags. The lone Georgia soldier in the back of the MRAP, Specialist Ruttan, sat in the seat closest to the gunner, checking to make sure the ammo cans stacked around the driver's feet were staged how he wanted them. 7.62mm ammo by his right foot, spare M4 magazines, grenades and pop flares by his left foot.

The QRF vehicles were on their own radio frequency but also monitored the frequency being used by the soldiers with the ANA platoons heading into the Shkin valley. Nunez got the headset turned on and the volume turned up, listened to the frantic voices in the valley communicating in barely controlled screams, a crushing roar of gunfire and explosions in the background.

"Red 3 this is Red 4, where the fuck did you go? Ah cain't see shit from back here!"

"Break break break! This is Chosin 3, we're trying to get to you! Tell your ANA not to fire to their rear!"

"Chosin 3 this is Red 4, stop where you're at, stop where you're at! Mah ANA are firin' all over the fuckin' place, gimme a dang minute to get 'em under control!"

"Tarawa 43 this is Red 1, where's that god damn helicopter support you said was inbound?"

"Break, god damn it! This is Red 2, someone tell me if that's a fuckin' American or an ANA layin' out there on the side o' this hill! Ah ain't seen him, but the ANA are sayin' someone's down out there!"

Nunez thought, *Oh, shit.* Nobody else in the back of the MRAP had a headset on so they hadn't heard the call. Nunez kept quiet, waiting for more information. At that moment the soldiers felt like they were the attackers, they were the ones about to bring the fight to the Taliban. If they knew an American was down, they might mentally switch to the defensive. He didn't want to tell them that an American might be dead, didn't want to risk demoralizing them until he had to.

The MRAPs crept toward the gate. Before they got there, six ANA pickups sped out the gate. ANA soldiers stood on the running boards of two of the trucks and yelled toward other Afghan soldiers inside the compound. MRAP commanders tried to talk to each other over the radio, their conversation nearly incomprehensible against the screams of the soldiers and Marines in the valley.

The air cleared long enough for Nunez to hear Lieutenant Spicer say to Sardinea, "Why the fuck ain't Captain Najibullah goin' out with his guys? That son of a bitch always acts so tough, why's he stayin' back?"

"Couldn't tell ya, lieutenant, but Ah bet that's a bad sign, if he's too chicken-shit to leave the wire and get in the middle o' this thang."

"Can anybody get their eyes on that soldier back down the hill?" a soldier in the Shkin valley yelled. "We cain't see him from our position. All our ANA are accounted for, it ain't one of us."

"Red 3 this is Red 4, where are you? Tommy, where you at?"

The MRAPs accelerated out of the gate. The gunner on Nunez's vehicle swiveled his turret to keep his weapon pointed toward the Alasai valley but held his fire. Spicer strained his voice calling out orders to the other three truck commanders over the chatter and sounds of battle on the ETT frequency. Nunez tried to keep track of it all but at this point still didn't know what their specific mission was, or if there was in fact an American casualty. There were so many moving pieces, and it was all happening so damn fast.

Klein jumped on the radio during a quiet moment and asked Spicer what their mission was. He responded in a loud but calm voice, trying his best to make sure Klein could hear him over the other radio traffic while speaking as fast as he could.

"Colt 1 this is Cherokee 1, all the ANA platoons except for the first two took cover in compounds before they got to the Shkin. Their trainers ditched them and headed toward the first two platoons. Break...I think the first two platoons took a few ANA killed and wounded, but we're not sure exactly how many yet. Our mission right now is to get to the first two platoons and help them get this shit under control. I think the ANA trucks that headed out are going to pick up their own casualties, but I don't know for sure. There might be an American down also. Break...bottom line, we'll figure it out when we get there."

"Colt 1 roger."

Spicer seemed to have a good handle on the situation, and hearing his no-

nonsense summary of what was happening made Nunez feel a little better. They were still heading into a horrible, fucked-up mess, but at least they knew the basics about what they would find when they got there. Nunez started organizing his thoughts; he had to cut the mission into individual tasks, simple steps that they could deal with one at a time. If he tried to figure out how to handle the entire situation, it would overwhelm him.

First thing, Nunez thought. *As soon as we dismount, get the guys behind cover. First thing, get to cover.*

The MRAPs wound down the road as fast as they could, which was just about at crawling speed. Klein's MRAP was second in line, Nunez's third. Nunez searched in every direction for muzzle flashes, smoke, puffs of dust, civilians running, any possible sign of the enemy. He saw nothing. The platoon had to come to a stop several times, waiting for the lead MRAP to negotiate tight turns or drive through deep ruts.

Second thing, make sure we've got fire superiority before we move, Nunez told himself. *Give the gunners a minute to suppress anything that looks danger-ous.*

"Red 4, God dangit...Ah think that's Red 3 layin' out there. He ain't here with me, and mah terp's tellin' me he got hit as we was gittin' our asses up this hill. Ah got four o' mah ANA down over here and we're still takin' rounds, Ah cain't get to him raht now. Can any o' y'all tell me if he's alive?"

"Red 4, this is Chosin 43," one of the Marines said. "I got eyes on your man, and it doesn't look good. We've got three ANA with the three of us, that's all, and it's going to be a motherfucker to get up that hill to him. Rounds are still landing around him. Copy?"

"Aww, son of a bitch...Red 4 copy."

Nunez's face tightened. He did not relish the thought of dealing with another dead or wounded American soldier. But he was the platoon sergeant. It was his job to recover casualties, no one else bore that responsibility.

Okay, we know there's a casualty. Third step, organize a team to recover him.

He took a breath and steeled himself for it, then keyed the mike and said, "Cherokee 1 this is Colt 4, when we dismount I'll get a team together and re-cover the casualty. Copy?"

Spicer gave a terse "Roger that" in reply. Nunez would have to tell the rest of the soldiers what was going on now, he couldn't avoid it any longer. He pulled one earphone off and said to Lyons and Gore, "Hey. One American's down, maybe KIA. We're going to get him. Got it?"

"Got it, Sergeant," Gore said. Nunez turned to look at Ruttan, whose face looked a little paler than it had been before. Ruttan asked, "Sergeant, did they say who it is?"

"Someone called him Tommy, I think. His call sign is Red 3."

Ruttan's eyes dropped. "Aww, fuck man. It's Ellis. Damn, I hope he's okay."

Nunez reached out and grabbed his arm. "If he's alive that's great. If not, we Charlie Mike. No matter what we find when we get there, we do our jobs, find Rahman and kill him. There will be time to cry later, if we have to. Hooah?"

Ruttan looked back and wiped his eyes. "Roger. Hooah, Sergeant."

The MRAPs passed ANA soldiers clustered around a compound pulling security for themselves but not doing much else. Several of the Afghans gestured toward the Shkin and argued with a single ANA soldier. Nunez got the impression it was an argument between Afghan enlisted soldiers who wanted to get into the fight and their platoon leader who ordered them to stay put. More ANA soldiers occupied another compound several hundred meters closer to the Shkin. They directed their weapons toward the valley but didn't show any desire to move toward their fellow soldiers.

The road curved right, the MRAPs passed through thick woods and suddenly the vehicles were facing northeast, down the long, straight mouth of the Shkin valley. Nunez couldn't see much from the back of the vehicle, but this part of the valley looked bare of compounds. The lead vehicle slowed so that Spicer could brief everyone on the situation.

"Okay, everyone listen up. We've got about 300 meters of open ground to our left, then it's all mountains. The French are somewhere in those mountains, so watch your fucking fire if you have to shoot that way. There's a low hill up ahead to the right, with, uh, two compounds on top. Just west of the compounds there's a wooded area on the hill, I think that's where our guys are. Look on the slope for Ellis, I think he's on the side of the hill someplace."

"Cherokee 1 Cherokee 1, this is Red 4. You hear me, Lance?" the ETT sergeant in charge of the first two platoons asked, on Spicer's radio frequency.

"I hear you Derek, tell me what you need."

The ETT sergeant's voice was like a marathon runner at mile twenty, a combination of weariness and adrenaline. "Okay, your trucks are about 400 meters to our west. Look to your left front, there's a wooded area at the base of the mountains. The first ambush came from there. On the road to your front you see that little wooded area to the left of the road, Ah think Ah got two or three dead ANA in there. To your right there's them two compounds on the hill, Ah think we're taking rounds from there too. About 200 meters past them two compounds there's kinda a low mountain, I'm pretty sure we took rounds from there. Break... there's a couple o' compounds way down the valley, like another 500 meters from where we are, and we maht be getting shot at from those. We're in a depression in the wooded area west o' the compounds, on the crest o' the hill. You got all that, you oriented?"

"Roger that Derek, I got it," Spicer replied. "What do you need us to do?"

"First thing, suppress that treeline to your left at the base of the mountains. Second, hit the two compounds on the hill. We're less than a hundred meters from the compounds, so watch your rounds, 'specially if you're firing grenades at 'em. Third, once you're suppressing them targets, Ah need your dismounts to get to Red 3 and get his ass to cover. We'll figure from there what's next."

"Roger. Where are the other ETT's that had to leave their platoons?"

"Man, Ah wish Ah knew," the sergeant sighed. "One o' the Marines and two of our guys are somewhere to our west, but Ah don't know where the other ones are at. They were talkin' to us until about five minutes ago, Ah haven't heard shit on the radio from them since then, so tell me if you see 'em. Copy?"

"Copy and moving. Hang in there brother, us and the Texas boys are all over this, we'll be there in a few." Then, to his own vehicles, Spicer said, "This is Cherokee 1, we're gonna hit the treeline to the north with our Mark 19. Cherokee 2 and 3, you guys hit the compounds on the hill with your crew-serves, and control your fire. Cherokee 4, stay oriented west to cover our rear."

A few tense, quiet seconds followed, then Spicer yelled into the radio, "Gunners, open fire now! Follow me!"

The first three vehicles' gunners opened up on command, spraying 40mm grenades into the wooded area to the left front and a mix of .50 caliber and 7.62mm toward the compounds on the hill to the right side of the road. Spicer's driver raced to cover the four hundred meters to the base of the hill where the ANA had taken cover. Nunez turned in his seat and craned his neck to look for the American casualty. He saw an explosion as an Afghan soldier fired an RPG from the wooded hollow to the right. Nunez spun his head and caught sight of it in his peripheral vision just as it streaked into the woods on their left. Tracers screamed into the treeline around the RPG's explosion. The gunner on Nunez's MRAP dumped dozens of rounds toward the compounds on the hill ahead. Tracer rounds bounced off the walls and streaked straight upwards.

A voice screamed on the radio, "Get ready to dismount! We're almost there!"

Step one. Get to cover, get to cover, get to cover.

Nunez stood up and unlocked the handle on the MRAP's back door, ready to hit the button that operated the door's hydraulic system. Gore and Lyons stacked behind him. Ruttan jumped up and forced his way behind Lyons.

Explosions rang out from the woods to the left as French mortar rounds punched through the tree branches. Smoke and shards of steel and rock blasted outwards from the explosions. Nunez saw a thick tree branch fly out from the woods, spinning and on fire. Spent shells and links rained down from the turret, the empty links making a *ting!* sound when they hit metal.

Step two, give the gunners time to suppress.

A voice came over the radio, yelling above the din of the battle. "Cherokee, this is Navajo! Be advised, the ANA confirm Rahman is in the valley directing the fight! He just said he can see American vehicles approaching! Cherokee, do you copy?"

The driver hit a bump. The soldiers in the back rocked sideways, and Lyons fell onto a seat. Ruttan and Gore yanked him back to his feet and he grabbed Gore's shoulder for support. Ruttan grabbed Lyons' shoulder to steady him, and Gore reached up to grab Nunez's shoulder, just like they did when they were stacked to clear a building. Nunez turned back and saw them crouched and tense, weapons muzzle down, breathing deep, ready for the rush out the door. Gore looked into Nunez's eyes and whispered what Nunez knew was a prayer. Above them the gunner burned through the last of a belt of 7.62 ammunition, then screamed "Reloading! Reloading!" as he jammed the end of another belt onto the weapon's feed tray.

Step three, get the casualty.

Nunez's heart felt like it was pounding out of his chest. It wasn't from fear, or at least he didn't think it was. He took a deep breath and let it out, then hit the forward assist on his carbine. He turned back toward the door, covered the red "door open" button with his hand and noticed his hand was shaking. That had never happened before. He opened and closed his hand twice, trying to force the shaking to stop.

They were almost there. He shut his eyes and took another deep breath, trying to bring his heart rate back down. In the two seconds his eyes were closed he saw his wife and children, back home in Houston. He never let himself think about his family when he was going into battle. Nunez had to focus on what he was doing, he didn't need the distraction. He opened his eyes and made himself think of something else. The only thought that entered his mind was, *Damn, this is going to suck.*

Nunez's vehicle jammed to a stop, jarring everyone in the back again. Over the headset, Spicer yelled "Dismount! Dismount! Stay on the right side of the fucking vehicles!"

Nunez ripped the headset off and punched the button. The door swung open, letting in blinding sunlight and the roar of gunfire louder than anything he had ever heard. Gore screamed "Hooah!" in his ear and Nunez launched himself out the door, into the light and noise.

CHAPTER 10

Gore was already out the door and on Nunez's ass as Nunez hooked left to find cover. Nunez dropped into a small ravine on the right side of the road and pointed his carbine toward the treeline. He thought about firing a few rounds to cover the other soldiers' exit, but with the Mark 19 on the lead vehicle firing grenades into the treeline non-stop, his own piddly little 5.56mm carbine rounds would just be wasted ammo. Lyons and Ruttan bailed out of the truck and ran around to use the vehicle for cover.

Nunez listened through all the other noise and did not hear rounds snapping by. Incoming rounds are easy to distinguish, their sharp zinging sounds are different than the deep booms of outgoing crew served weapons fire. Lyons, Gore and Ruttan dropped into the ravine on Nunez's right and got themselves together, along with dismounts from other vehicles. The treeline where the fire had been coming from before they arrived was about 300 meters from the road. Nunez looked at it through his scope for several seconds and saw nothing. No enemy, no muzzle flashes, no RPG backblasts, nothing. He rolled onto his back to check out the other side of the road.

Not forty meters from where Nunez lay, a pair of boots jutted out from a rockpile about halfway up the hill. That was all he could see, just a pair of tan, army-issue boots. The boots faced the bottom of the hill, toes toward the ground, looking to Nunez like the soldier they belonged to was laying face down in a hollow on the hill. Past him was the crest of the hill and the wooded depression where the ETT soldiers and the ANA had taken cover.

"Gore! Lyons! Listen up!" Nunez yelled, pointing toward the feet. "I'm going to get some guys together to get to that soldier, right there! I need you two to find a good position where you can put fire into that first compound. Hooah?"

"Hooah!" they yelled back in unison.

"Ruttan! Get ready, me and you and a couple others are going to get your soldier!"

Ruttan nodded, looking sick and scared as he stared toward the downed soldier. He stood up and ran to Nunez. Nunez led him toward the last vehicle in line and grabbed Vlacek and Powell from their spot.

"You guys come with me, we're going to get that soldier. The vehicles are suppressing the treeline and the compounds, and Gore is going to put more fire on the first compound, so we should be okay. When we get to him, Ruttan and Czech, you two guys pull security while me and Powell grab the guy and drag him down the hill, back to this spot we're standing on. Got it?"

They nodded and rogered. Nunez told them to stay where they were, then ran back to Gore and Lyons.

"Have y'all picked out a spot to set up yet?"

"Roger!" Gore yelled. "Twenty meters up the side of the hill, there's a little crevice with big rocks around it that'll give us cover from the treeline. I might have to get up on my knees to be able to hit the compound, but it'll work."

"Good deal," Nunez said. "Get ready to move, I'll tell you when. And listen, once you get there, stay put. I mean, if you get there and it turns out the spot sucks and doesn't give you any cover, find another spot. But once you're set, stay the fuck there and lay down cover fire. I'll move you as soon as I can."

As they called out "Hooah!" Nunez keyed the shoulder microphone. "Colt 1 this is Colt 4, I have enough guys together, we're going to get that soldier on the side of the hill. He's real close. Do you copy?"

"This is Colt 1, I copied," Klein said. "Need anything from me?"

"Negative, just make sure the gunners keep suppressing the treeline and compounds. We're going to get the casualty back here to the last MRAP and assess."

"Roger, make your move."

To Gore and Lyons, Nunez yelled "Go! Go!" and ran back toward the last MRAP. Lyons was young, thin and fast, but Gore was a little overweight and out of shape. They moved up the hill slow enough to make Nunez worry that they would attract the attention of every Taliban in the valley. Nunez returned to the small rescue team he had just put together, and looked back to see a few scattered bursts of dirt on the hill. The nearest was no closer than twenty meters from Gore and Lyons.

The two soldiers reached the spot Gore had picked out and flopped down onto the safe side of the rocks. Gore lifted the M240's muzzle high into the air before lowering it toward the first compound. Within seconds they were firing bursts into a compound window.

As soon as their machine gun fire began hammering at its target, Nunez yelled "Let's go!" and started up the hill. Forty meters uphill with fifty or sixty pounds of gear is not a short distance. The soldiers were sweating and struggling before they made the first twenty meters. On the crest of the hill, the fire coming from the ANA and ETT soldiers intensified as they tried to cover the movement of the four soldiers in the open.

A round slapped into the dirt several feet to Nunez's left, between him and Powell. Another round blazed over his head and hit the rocks. Ruttan yelled "Oh fuck, they're shooting at us! Fuck!" Vlacek turned sideways and fired several bursts back toward the treeline hundreds of meters away.

"Czech! Don't shoot, just run! You won't hit shit anyway, just run!" Nunez yelled. Vlacek turned to his front and ran. Several more rounds landed in a random pattern around the soldiers. Nunez knew that some Talib with a machine gun had just gotten a decent bead on them. They were within ten meters now, and Nunez could see the downed soldier in a deep depression surrounded by torso sized rocks. He hoped it was big enough for all of them to dive into.

They closed several more meters and were almost on the soldier when they heard a loud explosion across the valley behind them. Powell yelled "RPG!" and dropped onto the rocks. Nunez and Vlacek did the same, but Ruttan screamed "Fuck!" and kept running. An RPG round exploded in a loud, dirty ball of smoke and dust forty meters away from Nunez. Machine guns at the crest of the hill increased their rate of fire, sending tracers lashing over the soldiers' heads into the treeline across the valley.

Ruttan reached the lip of the depression and dropped inside as Nunez, Powell and Vlacek jumped to their feet and charged the last few meters to the depression. They reached it as another RPG was fired from across the valley. The second round went all the way over the crest of the hill, as if the RPG gunner had been shooting at something in the air over their heads.

Nunez and his two soldiers dropped into the depression. Nunez landed on Ruttan and Vlacek fell onto the casualty's back. The fallen soldier in the crater had a single, ragged hole in the upper back of his body armor, in the soft Kevlar barely an inch above the solid armor plate. The solid plate could stop a rifle or machine gun round, but soft armor couldn't.

There was enough room for the five soldiers in the depression, but just barely. The four soldiers who had just made the run up the hill heaved, puffed and sucked water from their Camelbaks, trying to recover from the sprint up the hill. Ruttan scooted forward on his chest and reached out to the casualty, slapped him softly on the shoulder and said, "Ellis...Hey Tommy, it's Rick. Come on man, look at me. I know you're okay, look at me."

Nunez rolled to Ellis. Ellis' head was twisted to the side, one arm pinned under his body and his weapon thrown just forward of his head. Powell slid toward him and picked up his wrist, feeling for a pulse. After a few seconds he forced his hand between Ellis' helmet and shoulder, straining to get his fingers onto the carotid artery. Nunez knew that if he managed to find it, he wouldn't feel anything. Ellis was dead.

Powell tried for several more seconds before he got onto his knees and forced Ellis onto his side. Ellis' head lolled toward the dirt and his arms hung forward, limp and heavy. A large bloodstain covered the top of his chest to the bottom of his nose, his eyes were half open and dull yellow. Powell held him in a half turned position and felt for his carotid again, then lowered him back onto his face and wiped blood from his glove onto his thigh. Nunez was already keying the mike when Powell looked at him and shook his head.

"Cherokee 1 this is Colt 4, your soldier is confirmed KIA."

"God damn it. Roger," Spicer replied. "Nunez, we're going to switch our radios to the other guys' frequency so we can all talk to each other on the same net. Have all your people switch now."

"Roger," Nunez responded. Only Nunez, Klein, Powell and Harris had radios, and as Nunez pulled his radio from its pouch he heard everyone acknowledging the frequency change. As soon as Nunez switched to the other ETT channel he heard a near-frantic exchange between two southern-accented voices.

"Red 4, how the fuck do they know he's dead? They got a god damn medic with them?"

"Red 2 this is 4, they're right there in that hole with him, they checked him, he's dead. We ain't gonna get nobody killed to recover a KIA, we'll wait until air cover shows up and move him then. Got that?"

"Red 4 Red 2, that's bullshit! He might still be alive and nobody can do shit for him out here. We need to get him back, right now!"

Nunez keyed his mike. "This is Colt 4. I'm with your casualty, he's KIA. My soldiers know what they're doing, we checked your man and he's KIA. Trust me."

There was silence on the net for several seconds, until a pissed off voice came on the radio and said "Red 2 roger."

From the west Nunez heard the sound of helicopters. He turned onto his back again, searched for them but saw nothing. He noticed for the first time that because of a slight rise between the depression and the crest, the soldiers on top of the hill were unable to see where their casualty had fallen. That explained why they hadn't tried to get him, and why they had been asking where he was even though he was in plain sight on the side of the hill below them.

Incredibly loud gunfire exploded from the air to the west. Nunez still couldn't see the aircraft, so he rolled back over to see what they were shooting at. Across the valley rocks just above the treeline exploded into a random burst of brilliant white flashes as 30mm guns from two Apache helicopters tore into them. The pilots adjusted their fire and put the next burst into the treeline itself, sending leaves and small branches into a shower of debris above the trees. A Hellfire missile shrieked off one helicopter's rail, flashed over the road and exploded out of sight in dense vegetation. A second missile impacted fifty meters to the right of the first, spraying rocks in a fan. 30mm fire picked up again as pilots fired into the trees. Across the valley in the mountains, Nunez heard the distinct sound of one .50 caliber round being fired, from an invisible location on the mountainside.

Without warning Wilson and Nguyen bounded over the rocks and landed on top of the soldiers in the depression. Nunez yelled "Ow!" as Wilson's knee dropped hard onto the back of Nunez's right thigh and Nguyen stepped on his calf.

"Sorry boss," Wilson said, breathless. "Let's get this casualty down now, while the air strike is still going. Come on, help me out."

Soldiers got to their knees and grabbed whatever handhold they could find on the dead man's gear. Powell reached out and grabbed Nunez's arm to stop him.

"Not you Sarge," Powell said. "You go ahead and get up there and figure out what the fuck is going on. We'll get the casualty down the hill."

Nunez nodded, then said "Alright, but Wilson, you come with me. You'll do better with your M14 from up there instead of on the road."

Wilson smiled and said "Cool." Powell and the others lifted the dead soldier as Nunez and Wilson climbed out of the depression and trudged toward the crest of the hill. Gunfire from the Apaches kept hammering from the west, and as Nunez got clear of the depression he finally saw the evil-looking helicopters several hundred meters from their target. Breaths of smoke drifted from their noses in intermittent strings as their guns fired.

Nunez had to stop for a few seconds to bend down and catch his breath. He turned to see Powell and Ruttan bound as fast as they could, dragging the dead soldier headfirst and on his back down the hill. Nguyen and Vlacek ran alongside to provide cover. Tracers still streaked from the crest of the hill. As Nunez and Wilson approached the crest of the hill Nunez waved his right arm over his head and yelled, "Friendlies coming up, friendlies coming up!"

A voice on the crest echoed "Cease fire, cease fire, friendlies comin' up!"

Fire from above trickled to a stop, giving Nunez and Wilson the chance to dash the last several meters up the hill. Rifles and machine guns poked out from the rocks and trees at the edge of the big depressed area, and two Georgia soldiers stepped out from the trees to wave Nunez and Wilson in. The Texas soldiers staggered into the trees and dropped below the uneven edge of the depression. Before falling onto his back, Nunez looked back down the hill to make sure Powell and his small group had gotten the dead Georgia soldier back to the road. He took an extra second to make sure Gore and Lyons were still working their machine gun toward the compounds.

The ANA soldiers who were spread out along the trees using tree trunks and rocks for cover opened fire again, and Nunez saw one Georgia soldier rest his back comfortably against a rock, lean to his right and fire his SAW around the side of another large rock. To the west the Apaches' fire stopped, and the noise of the rotors began to fade. The sound of aircraft was replaced by another intense exchange of gunfire in the Alasai. The firefight ended with sounds of eight or ten explosions in a row. Nunez had no idea if the explosions were RPGs, tank rounds, BMP main gun fire, mortars or what.

One of the Georgia soldiers who had waved Nunez in knelt next to him and asked, "Which one o' the Texas guys are ya?"

"Nunez," he answered, out of breath. "Colt 4...the platoon sergeant."

"Ah'm Guidry, the ETT sergeant in charge," the man said, extending his hand. "Thanks for gettin' our guy, Ah appreciate that."

"Yeah, no problem," Nunez said as he got his breathing under control and shook Guidry's hand. Wilson reached out and shook his hand also, then asked "Okay, so we got the Taliban positions suppressed, and we recovered your casualty, so now what? And do you know where Lieutenant Klein is?"

"Shit, man," Guidry answered. "If Klein's with Spicer and Sardinea, they're up there," he said, pointing toward the side of the depression facing the two compounds to the east. "As far as a plan goes, well...raht now Ah think we just need to stay put and figure out where the fuck all our guys are at."

"Colt 4 this is Colt 1, what's your sitrep?" Klein asked on the radio.

"Colt 1 this is Colt 4, me and Wilson are up here on the crest," Nunez answered. "Gore and Lyons are in a covered position laying rounds on the compounds, the other guys who went with me up the hill got the KIA and took him back to the vehicles. I'm not sure where everyone else is right now, me and Red 4 are trying to get a handle on everything."

"Roger. I'm with Cherokee 1 on the east side of the depression, meet me here when you can."

Nunez rogered, then looked into the trees to the east and listened to gunfire blasting toward Taliban positions to their east and north. The depression they were in held two ANA platoons, a handful of American soldiers plus at least one Marine. Another Marine and two more Georgia soldiers were somewhere west, making their way to the depression.

Nunez tried to figure out how many ETT's and Marines were missing. *Five platoons with two Georgia guys each left the gate,* he thought. *There was one Marine with the lead two platoons. So on the hill there should be four ETT soldiers and one Marine...no, one of the ETT soldiers is dead. So, four live Ameri-*

cans on the hill before the QRF arrived. That meant there should be six more Georgia soldiers with...god damn, how many Marines total had there been?

"Guidry, you got ten Georgia soldiers total with the five platoons that left the gate, right? And how many Marines total?"

"Yeah, ten o' mah guys and four Marines left the outpost," Guidry said. "Ah got three o' mah guys here with me, includin' Ellis, you know, the dead one, plus one Marine. We been tryin' to figure out where the next four guys and their Marine are at. Ah got their grid, but I ain't plotted it yet. Ah know they're about 300 meters someplace to the west, but they got pinned down. And Ah ain't got a clue where mah last two guys with them last two Marines are. We been calling back to the CP, they been tryin' to order them last ANA platoons out the gate but the chickenshit ANA colonel won't let 'em go."

"Okay," Nunez said. "Let's make a plan. Check this out, what do you think about taking that first compound and setting up in there? We'll have better cover in there, and better fields of fire. We can leave an ANA squad with a couple of Americans here to watch for the other ETT's coming from the west. Sound good?"

Guidry rubbed his chin in consideration. "Yeah, that makes sense. It beats just sittin' here gettin' shot at, anyways. Let's get to Spicer and run it past him."

"Hooah. Let's go," Nunez said, rising to his feet. Wilson jumped to his feet as well, and the three of them worked their way through the trees and brush toward the east. As they wound their way toward Spicer, Nunez saw an ANA medic kneel over two wounded Afghan soldiers. One Afghan was propped against a tree, both legs bandaged and an IV in his forearm, talking to the medic in a calm voice. The other soldier looked nearly dead, motionless with his head wrapped in bloody bandages. Nunez knew he was alive only because he breathed in rasping, gurgly moans as they passed. Several feet east of the wounded they jogged past a dead ANA soldier, sprawled on his back with his old Russian helmet placed over his face. His camouflage uniform shirt was punctured and dark red.

Nunez keyed his mike. "Colt 1 Golf this is Colt 4, what's your location?"

"Colt 4 this is Colt 1 Golf," Powell answered. "We're behind cover in the woods on the left side of the road. We found two dead ANA here and three wounded. We're in a good spot, so we're suppressing from here and treating the wounded."

"Roger. Who do you have with you?"

"Czech, Nguyen, Harris and Doc. Doc's got his hands full right now, two of the ANA are fuuucked up. Who's with you?"

Relieved, Nunez answered "I've got Wilson and Klein, plus Gore and Lyons in a position on the side of the hill. We're accounted for."

"Roger."

The trees thinned, the sound of gunfire increased and a couple of rounds zipped through the treetops as they reached Spicer's and Klein's position. Spicer peered through binoculars around the side of a rock toward the first compound, barely a hundred meters away. Klein and the Marine forward observer bent over a map. Sardinea was nowhere to be seen.

"Hey, Lieutenant! Noon-ez here has an idea Ah think maht be purty good."

Spicer turned away from the compound and scuttled over to the map. "What'd you come up with, Nunez?" he asked.

Next to the map, Nunez drew a rough sketch of the mouth of the Shkin valley in the dirt. "Okay, we're here, the bad guys are here and here, and maybe here, right? So right now we have enemy shooting at us from different angles, we've lost guys and we're on the defensive. I think we need to push forward into this first compound and clear it. We can make that our tactical command post and casualty collection point. And you," Nunez said, pointing toward the Marine forward observer, "you'll have better observation so you can call in supporting arms. At the very least, if we take that compound it gives us two angles on the Taliban across the valley. The way we are right now, we're just in one big group and we're not really doing much. We can leave a squad of ANA with two ETT's here in this low ground so they can link up with your other guys that are coming from the Alasai. And if Rahman is right here in one of these two compounds, we kill him and the fight's pretty much over right then. What do y'all think?"

Klein spoke first. "That's all good, except for the casualty collection point being in the compound. There's one dead ANA here and two wounded, and one of those wounded is gonna die. It's gonna be fucking hard to move them to that compound, so the CCP should stay here. We'll need to leave more than one squad with them, that's for sure."

Spicer agreed, saying "That sounds like a decent plan to me. I don't like sitting in one spot taking casualties, we need to maneuver on those fucks."

The Marine said "Hang on," then jumped to his feet and looked to the south for a few seconds. He got back down and drew another small hill in the dirt, showing high ground within a couple hundred meters of where they were sitting.

"Right there," the Marine said, pointing south, "there's a little hill, smaller than this one we're on, with a compound on top. It's actually not even a compound, it's just a walled courtyard. Let's call it compound three. If we can get an ANA squad to compound three they can use it as a support by fire position and suppress the Taliban on that little mountain east of these two compounds in front of us. We'll call those compounds one and two, number one's this first one that's close to us. We'll have to clear compound one first," he said, pointing to their east, "and then send a squad to the south after we get some suppressive fire on compound two. Once the ANA squad's got compound three clear they can cover us and we can take compound two. Make sense?"

"Crystal clear," Nunez said, surprised at the young Marine's ability to throw a plan together so quickly.

"Not really," Spicer said. "Say it again."

"Alright. Compound one," the Marine corporal said, jabbing his finger onto the circle that represented the compound closest to them. "Compound two," poking the second compound next to it. "Compound three," moving his finger to indicate the compound on the hill immediately to their south. "First thing, we take compound one. Second, we suppress compound two. Third, we take compound three. Fourth, we take compound two. I don't think there's anything left to clear after that, so we sit tight, waste millions of motherfuckers when they attack us tonight and then pull back in the morning, just like the plan says. Make sense now?"

"I got it," Klein said. "Jerry, you clear on that?"

"I'm clear," Nunez said. "I need to get a look at this hill to our south, I haven't seen it yet. And I'll need to pull Gore and Lyons in so they can support us. But I'm clear."

"I'm good," said Spicer. "I think we should get some mortar fire onto that treeline across the valley while we're doing it though."

"We can't," the Marine said. "That target's already been hit so it's a lower priority now. Besides that, A-10's are on the way in from Bagram, they won't fire mortars if there are aircraft in their impact area. And we can't get the A-10's to fire on targets here either, I already tried but the French have them on a possible anti-aircraft gun in the Shpee valley, you know, over those mountains. If they have anything left after they hit that target, hopefully we can get them over here."

"Well, fuck," Spicer said.

"Hang on, Ah really don't get this plan," Guidry said. "Ah know it sounds simple, but damn, Ah'm just kinda wore out from all the shit that's happened already. Hell, Ah ain't even sure how many ANA Ah lost so far. Tell you boys what, y'all just tell me what to do and what the ANA need to do, Ah'll just follow along and make it happen."

Across the valley two .50 caliber weapons fired almost simultaneously. Nunez couldn't see through the vegetation to the mountains across the valley, but he heard ANA increase their fire for a few seconds. He hoped they weren't shooting at French snipers.

"Guidry, how about you stay here in this low ground with two ANA squads," Spicer said. "You can make sure they're maintaining security and treating the casualties, and make contact with the other guys walking in from the west. We'll take the other compounds and then have you move up. I'll get Sergeant Sardinea to stay with you. Cool?"

Guidry nodded, his face red and sweaty. "Yeah. Yes sir, that might be best. Don't be scared to call me though, Ah can come runnin' if you guys need the help."

"We know," Spicer said. "You've done a good job in a bad situation, we know you'll come when we need you to. Right now just get your two squads set up here, and most important, get the other ETT's and Marines in without getting them shot by the ANA. Hooah?"

"Hooah sir. Ah'm gonna head back toward the west edge of the woods, see if Ah can spot them boys comin' in."

"Roger. I'll have Sardinea meet you there."

Guidry got up and walked back through the woods. Nunez was impressed;

Lieutenant Spicer had recognized that one of his soldiers was becoming overwhelmed, not breaking but at least bending. Spicer had given him something vital to do but at the same time took the weight of responsibility for the rest of the advance off his shoulders. In truth Guidry had been relieved of his command on the spot. But in his mind and in the eyes of his fellow soldiers Guidry had simply been given something different but equally important to do. After this fight, he wouldn't have to feel guilty about letting anyone down or being unable to do his job. As Guidry disappeared into the trees, Spicer pointed at his back and said, "That's a good man, right there."

The soldiers prepared for the assault. Guidry and Sardinea managed to guide in most of the missing embedded trainers, and reestablished contact with the others. All the while, ANA maintained a base of fire from the hill. Nunez ran to Gore and Lyons and led them up the hill to the depression. As they made it back they heard the roar of an A-10 and the low *rrriiiiiiipppp* sound of its 30mm gun firing into the Shpee valley. The echo rumbled back at them and Nunez saw Godzilla again, above the mountains of northeastern Afghanistan.

The Afghan soldiers were ready to take compound one. They would lead the charge, followed by Americans. Interpreters translated orders from the ETT soldiers to the Afghan lieutenants and sergeants, who staged their soldiers behind rocks and trees near compound one. The Marine forward observer called for an A-10 to fire a burst into the treeline across the valley, to ensure the Taliban would keep their heads down as ANA made the hundred meter move across the open crest of the hill.

Everyone who was going to make the assault crept to the edge of the depression, tense and ready. The A-10 roared in toward the valley from the west, nosed up and then dove almost vertical toward Taliban positions inside the treeline. The roar of its one long burst tore the air around the soldiers below. Flashes of orange and white exploded in the trees across the valley, and the ANA charged toward compound one.

CHAPTER 11

Nunez and Wilson stuck their heads up as the ANA ran toward compound one. Other Afghans opened up toward the compound to provide cover fire. They peppered the blank wall facing them they weren't doing any good as far as Nunez could tell. He hoped ANA wouldn't get mowed down by Taliban fighters waiting inside as they ran through the gate.

The A-10 stopped firing and pulled up, firing off flares to its sides. The treeline across the valley was now a mass of dust and smoke covered by waves of reverberating echoes from the explosions. Nunez hoped there were dozens of Taliban under the trees, torn to shreds.

The first Afghans reached the wall of the compound, flattened against it and lifted their weapons over the wall to spray rounds into the courtyard. That was the signal for the Americans to move up. Nunez was first out of the depression, leading the Texas and Georgia troops in a sprint toward the compound. More ANA reached the compound. Some of them also ran to the wall and fired blindly over it, but Nunez was shocked to see about ten of them plus one interpreter run straight through the open gate without so much as slowing down.

Gunfire erupted inside the compound, several weapons fired on automatic at once. The Afghans on the wall slowed their fire but didn't stop. Just before he reached the wall, Nunez heard a single round tear through the air in front of him. Several more went low over their heads, and he heard a Marine behind him exclaim "Motherfucker! That was close!"

He ignored the fire, ran until he hit the wall to the left of the door and spun around. He snapped his head to the side, looked across the valley for the source of the fire. Klein tripped and fell hard against the wall on the other side of the gate, cursed and grabbed his right shoulder. Nunez could barely hear himself over the gunfire as he got on the radio to scream for the MRAPs to suppress the treeline again.

"Cherokee gunners, hit the treeline on the north side of the valley, hit the treeline on the north side of the valley, we're taking rounds up here at the compound!"

The Mark 19 gunner in the lead MRAP spun his turret and dumped almost an entire belt of thirty-two 40mm grenades into the treeline. The .50 caliber gunner also turned and opened fire, but the M240B gunner in the third MRAP kept his weapon aimed at the two compounds on top of the hill. Several ANA who had stayed in the depression on the hill opened up toward Taliban who had somehow managed to survive all the gunfire plus two airstrikes.

Spicer and another Georgia soldier charged past Nunez and Wilson and ran through the gate. The two Marines followed them, and Klein screamed to the Afghans, "Cease fire, cease fire!" Two interpreters who had moved up to the wall screamed to the ANA and got them to stop firing. Klein turned in the direction they had come from and yelled back to Gore and Lyons.

"Machine gun team, move up to the wall! Machine gun up to the wall!"

On the other side of the valley the sound of a .50 caliber rang out from the mountain above the treeline, as a sniper fired toward a target Nunez couldn't see. Seconds later more gunfire rumbled from across the valley, but this time Nunez could clearly distinguish that it came from the crest of the mountain and not the treeline. Then Nunez heard a loud boom as a dust cloud exploded near the crest. A second later another dirty blackish explosion erupted from a spot about fifty meters below the crest of the mountain.

Nunez figured it out. Taliban had gotten onto the crest above the snipers' position and were firing down on them. There was nothing the ANA or the Guard soldiers could do because the Taliban and the French were too close together. The MRAPs wouldn't be able to fire their crew served weapons toward the crest without possibly hitting friendlies. The distinctive sound of a light machine gun chattered from the snipers' position as one of the French Marines, maybe the intense little sniper Nunez had seen the night before, opened up on the Taliban above them on the mountain.

Wilson slapped Nunez on the chest. "Come on, let's get in there! Let's go!"

Nunez ran through the gate with Wilson at his back. Two or three ANA stood at the open doors to each room and fired as fast as they could through the doorways. Most of the rooms were in a row on the left side of the compound. The compound's courtyard consisted mostly of stepped terraces leading down the hill to the south.

The compound was one story, with a single row of rooms along the north wall. The east wall was high enough to give good cover to soldiers inside the compound. One distinguishing feature of the compound was that it had a small room on its roof that was accessible by a stairwell located in the middle of the row of rooms. Gore and Lyons would be able to do some good work from up there.

Klein pushed Gore and Lyons through the gate. The weight of their machine gun, spare barrel and ammo made them stagger. Firing inside the compound stopped, and several ANA yelled to the interpreter who had run into the court-yard behind Nunez.

"They say the compound is clear!," the interpreter yelled to Spicer.

"Yeah, sure it is," Spicer said to the Georgia soldier who had come in with him. "We need to get into every room and make sure they didn't miss anything."

The Marines joined them and confirmed that every room had been cleared. Not a single enemy or civilian, living or dead, was anywhere inside. Spent shells were everywhere, but with all the rounds the ANA had expended, there was no way to determine if the Taliban had even been inside.

Spicer ordered his Afghans on the east wall to start suppressing so the desig-nated squad could take compound number three. Interpreters repeated the orders to the ANA. Several Afghans yelled and gestured in protest, and an interpreter told Spicer, "They say they are almost out of ammunition, so they cannot provide cover for the other squad."

"Son of a bitch," Spicer growled. "Tell them to redistribute ammo, you know, share their ammo so every has the same amount. Then tell them to keep their AKs on semi, and just fire one round every five seconds or so. They don't have to empty a fucking mag every time they pull the trigger."

The interpreter relayed orders, and eventually got the ANA lined up on the east wall as they passed ammunition among themselves. Wilson found a long metal box to stand on and a shallow notch to rest his rifle at the top of the wall. He kept his head low as he scanned through his scope toward the next compound.

Several minutes passed before the ANA were ready to provide cover so that compound three could be cleared. During the time it took to organize, the last two Georgia soldiers and last two Marines finally staggered into the depression at the crest of the hill and collapsed, exhausted from the kilometer-long escape and evasion they had just made.

Nunez ran up the stairs to the room on the roof, took a few seconds to assess, then ran back down and told Gore and Lyons to follow him up. Once they were in the room, Nunez told Gore, "Set up your 240 here, facing out this window to the east. You're going to have the best view of anyone here, make sure you hose the fuck out of that compound and keep hosing it until the ANA get inside. Control your rate of fire, it's probably going to be a while before they're ready to make the assault. Remember, right now they're going to take the compound to the south first, before they take the next one to the east. Got all that?"

"Got it, Sarge," Gore answered.

"How y'all doing on ammo?" Nunez asked.

"Eight hundred rounds or so, I think. While you were up on the hill Powell ran out and gave us more ammo, so we're good."

"Awesome," Nunez said. "Stay low, make sure you keep an eye on the mountains across the valley in case they start shooting this way again. And same deal as before, if you need to go because the Talibs are shooting the fuck out of this place go ahead and move, but otherwise, stay here. I'll come back for you when it's time to move. If you need ammo, Lyons, it's your job to do whatever the fuck you have to do to keep that gun fed. Got that?"

"I got it, Sarge," Lyons said, nervous as hell. "I'm all over it."

"Word," Gore said, then smiled and held his palm out to Jerry. "Gimme five."

Nunez slapped his palm. "Y'all have fun. Laters." He ran back down the stairs. An Afghan lieutenant yelled orders in the courtyard and the ANA opened up toward the next compound to the east. Gore opened fire from the roof with the M240. Nunez ran to the east wall, jumped on the box next to Wilson and stuck his head up.

The next compound was close, and was bigger than the one they were in. The wall of the compound that faced them was solid, the gate somewhere on one of the other walls. If there was no gate on the south side, the only relatively safe side, they were going to have a huge problem getting anyone inside it. Automatic

146

fire rattled, coming from inside the compound walls.

Behind Nunez, one of the Georgia soldiers yelled "Now! Get 'em goin'!" into his radio. Nunez ducked his head back below the edge of the wall and looked south toward compound three. Several seconds passed before he saw twelve ANA soldiers, running flat out as hard as they could in nothing resembling a formation, heads down and limbs flying as they charged down the slope toward the next hill. No Americans were with them, which was a good thing, because nobody in the world moved up and down hills as fast as Afghans. The squad of soldiers sprinted to the bottom of the slope, ran across a dirt road and then started up the hill to the south without slowing. Fire from compound two to the east increased but Nunez didn't see any rounds land near the squad as they bounded up the hill to the south. They made it into the courtyard and set up in a line along the low wall, then opened fire on compound two. One of them fired an RPG that exploded against the south wall.

Nunez jumped down from the wall and ran up the stairs to the 240 team. They were hitting the second floor of the compounds with short bursts. Gore had the gun's bipod still folded under the barrel, weapon resting on the window ledge and muzzle sticking out the window. He stood in a fighter's stance, feet spread a little wider than shoulder width, cheek glued to the machine gun's stock, right hand on the pistol grip and left hand under the stock for stability. Lyons stood to Gore's left, held his carbine out the window with his right hand and fed a belt of ammunition over his weapon with his left.

"Hey! You guys see anything?" Nunez yelled.

"I think we had muzzle blast coming from the second floor!" Gore yelled back. "I'm putting rounds in the windows, but there's another part of the room that doesn't have a window facing this way, it's probably got one facing south! I can't see shit on the first floor or in the courtyard!"

"Alright, keep it up!" Nunez ran back down the stairs, looking for Klein and Spicer. He found them in the room next to the stairs, hunched over a map with the Marine forward observer. The Marine jumped to his feet to look out a window, then knelt and plotted something on the map.

Nunez dropped to his knees next to Klein. "Hey Homie, I think compound two only has a couple of Taliban in it. There's not much firing from there and

Gore says he hasn't seen anything except for muzzle blast from the second floor. The ANA have compound three already. I can't tell where the gate to that courtyard is, but there isn't any way to get into compound two from this side. If the ANA in compound three have a radio we need to ask them if they can see a gate on the south side."

Klein asked Spicer, "You guys have commo with that squad at compound three?"

Spicer looked back at him with a weird look on his face. "Did he just call you 'Homie'?"

"Yeah, he did," Klein answered. "Homie D. Klown. For Henry D. Klein. I'll explain later. Can your terps talk to that ANA squad?"

"Fuck, I don't know," Spicer said. "Lemme find out."

The Marine spoke up. "I think we need to hit compound two with something to soften it up, but I don't know what we can use. We're way too close for mortars or a fixed wing aircraft strike. Maybe if we could get an Apache in here that would work, but on the supporting arms net they're saying the Apaches aren't coming back until they refuel and rearm. Not only that, but I don't even know if they'll authorize an air strike on a compound, not unless we have positive ID on enemy inside and are sure there aren't any civilians with them. We can't say yes to either one of those things right now."

"What about the French hitting it with a Milan missile?" Nunez asked.

"Don't know shit about the Milans," the Marine answered. "Will they work?"

"They'll work, dude. Trust me," Nunez answered. "We just have to find out if the French have any Milan teams in range. And they're insane about avoiding friendly fire, we're going to have to mark this compound with something so they know which one they're supposed to be shooting at."

"Alright, I'll request it. I'm sure it'll take a while, hang on."

The request took several minutes, but the French were enthusiastic about the idea. They had a Milan team across the valley that hadn't had an opportunity to fire a shot all day. The Marine relayed the target compound grid and fired a green star cluster into the air. The French confirmed that they knew which compound to hit and which ones held friendlies.

The ANA in compound three reported there was a gate on the south side of compound two. An ANA platoon would clear the compound as soon as the French hit it. Then everyone would stay where they were, maintain security and wait for more ammo. At some point they would also have to evacuate the dead soldiers, but that would have to wait until later.

Things were quiet in compound one for several minutes while preparations for the assault were completed. Gore fired only sporadically, conserving ammo for the night. Then the Marine forward observer stepped into the courtyard and yelled out, "Get ready, missiles inbound within a minute!"

The soldiers tensed up. Across the valley something boomed, then they heard a strange *shk!shk!shk!* that got louder. The sound turned into a steady tearing sound before a blurry black mass streaked into the second floor of compound two in a thunderous explosion. Dirt and mud-brick fragments flew through the air and the compound's courtyard filled with thick dust. A second boom sounded in the valley, then the same odd stuttering sound repeated as another missile tore the air and blasted a hole in the north wall of compound two. ANA at compound three fired a volley of RPGs. Some impacted on courtyard walls and a few cleared the walls to explode inside. The Americans cheered, and the ANA platoon that had staged outside compound one rose to their feet and ran toward compound two.

Nunez ran back upstairs to Gore and Lyons, who had stopped firing so they could listen for any gunfire coming from the smoking compound in front of them. Nunez looked over their shoulders and saw that compound two was still and silent. A few ANA fired single shots of cover fire, but it looked like the Taliban inside compound two had either run or been hit. Nunez figured they had somehow escaped before the missiles hit.

"Hey Sarge, think we just wasted Rahman?" Gore asked hopefully.

"I fucking hope so, Eli," Nunez said. "I hope they find his face on one side of the compound and his nutsack on the other side."

The ANA platoon reached the southwest corner of compound two, stacked there briefly and then crept in a line along the south wall. Nunez lost sight of them. If they got hit on the way in, about the only thing Gore's M240 could do to support them would be to fire on the wrecked second floor.

The radio came to life. "Cherokees, Cherokees, this is Navajo. Be advised,

Rahman just told one of his fighters to come to his compound and get more ammunition. We know he's inside a compound, and we're guessing it's not the one that just got hit. How copy?"

Gunfire crackled to the east. Nunez and the gun team searched for the source but saw nothing. Within seconds the fire intensified, then became a roar as Taliban in caves and crevices on the small mountain east of compound two opened fire on the ANA platoon trying to force their way into compound two.

Gore pulled the trigger and sprayed rounds over the compound toward the face of the mountain. The Afghans in compound three launched a barrage of machine gun and RPG fire toward the hidden positions on the hillside. They received heavy and accurate return fire that made them duck but didn't stop their cover fire.

Screams came from the exposed platoon at compound two as enemy rounds hit soldiers scrambling back to cover. Nunez watched as the first ANA troops stumbled back around the corner. Two of them limped and one held his side. Seconds later several more soldiers dragged the limp body of one of their men around the corner. A few more soldiers trickled around and dropped to the ground along the west wall.

Nunez made a count. Several Afghan soldiers hadn't made it back. He had to gather another team and go get them.

CHAPTER 12

Rounds thudded against the wall of the small room. Nunez and the machine gun team ducked back from the window. In the courtyard below, the Marine forward observer ran to the box Wilson was standing on, jumped onto it and looked toward the Taliban positions with binoculars. Wilson scanned through his scope and shouted that he still couldn't see a damn thing.

Gunfire rang out from across the valley again as the Taliban opened up on the ANA and coalition soldiers clustered in and around compounds one and two. The sound of individual .50 caliber rounds added to the noise as the French Marine snipers engaged targets below. From the east there were several booms as Taliban fired RPGs from distant compounds. Their rounds exploded somewhere Nunez couldn't see. He looked across the valley to the MRAPs, saw their weapons fire like mad into the treeline.

"I'm heading down, stay low!" Nunez yelled to Gore and Lyons as he ran down the stairs to the forward observer. Wilson methodically fired his rifle, one round into any spot he saw that looked like it might be a Taliban position, while the forward observer read grid coordinates into his radio.

The Marine finished his radio traffic and Nunez asked, "What you got?"

"I have 120's on the way to hit the side of that little mountain. I don't have any real targets for them, it's just an immediate suppression mission. I wish I knew where the fuck the Taliban are shooting from, but I can't see shit. Things were different in Helmand, it was desert so the Taliban were easier to spot. This heavy woods bullshit sucks, I can't see a fucking thing. You know, I haven't seen a single Taliban this whole time?"

"Welcome to my world," Nunez said. "You know where Klein and Spicer are?"

Before the Marine answered, several rounds zipped through the air high over their heads, coming from the north across the valley. Nobody in the compound ducked.

"Yeah, they went outside to see how many ANA got hit when they tried to get into compound two," the Marine said. "I think there's a good number of dead or wounded still laying out there."

"Yeah," Nunez agreed, "I think so too."

Rounds from the east sliced the air above them, low enough to make them duck this time. Gore's M240 stopped, then fired a long burst. Nunez saw tracers arc high into the air from the machine gun position before it stopped firing again for several seconds. When the fire resumed, it was much heavier. The gun team fired twenty round bursts instead of six to ten round bursts like they were supposed to.

Without taking his eye from his scope, Wilson said "Sounds like someone got the shit scared out of them. Fags."

Klein and Spicer ran into courtyard. Klein called out to Nunez, "Jerry! Get your ass out here, we have a bunch of ANA down and we need to get them to cover!"

"Moving!" Nunez yelled back, then turned to run toward the gate. Behind him, Wilson yelled "Right behind you!" and jumped from the wall to follow. As he ran out the gate, Nunez was surprised to see dozens of Afghan soldiers sprint up the hill from the dirt road at the base of the hill. All twelve ANA pickup trucks were there, scattered on the sides of the road.

"When did these fucking guys get here?" Nunez asked Spicer.

"Just now. We didn't know shit about it until they showed up."

The radio crackled. "Cherokee this is Navajo, we have an update on Rahman."

Spicer's hand flashed to his handset. "This is Cherokee, send it!"

"Cherokee this is Navajo, it's not real clear from the translation, but we think Rahman is in one of the compounds due east of you, not the ones you're hitting now. He keeps saying something about the American tanks that were coming right at him, and about how far they are. We think he's talking about your MRAPs driving toward him earlier. If he's in the group of compounds we think he's in, that puts him within 500 meters of your position. How copy?"

"Cherokee copies, Cherokee copies! Can we get some fucking air or indirect fire onto those compounds?"

"Hey, Nunez! Did you hear that last traffic?" Klein shouted. Nunez was about to answer when the Marine forward observer yelled "Fast movers coming in! Fast movers coming in!" A fast mover was a fixed wing attack aircraft, on the way to hit something in the valley.

Nunez turned back and yelled, "What's he going to hit?"

Something flashed by to the left, barely catching Nunez's peripheral vision. He jerked his head up to see two fighter jets flash down the length of the valley from the west. They nosed up before the roar of their engines crushed out all other sound. Almost all the men in the compounds, Afghan and American, threw themselves to the ground. The two aircraft pulled up from the valley and barrel-rolled as they shot straight up. Nunez recognized them as French Rafale fighters. Nothing exploded in their wake, but the Taliban seemed to stop firing immediately.

"Hey!" Nunez yelled to the forward observer. "Why didn't they hit anything?"

"It was just a show of force, they haven't gotten permission to drop anything yet!" the Marine yelled back. "They're getting out of the way so the 120's can fire on the mountain!"

"Son of a bitch," Nunez muttered. He thought about it and decided they were too close to the Taliban for the Rafales to drop bombs.

Soldiers on the hill got back to their feet and searched the sky for more aircraft. Loud explosions rumbled from the west as French 120's fired from the Alasai valley. Nunez ran to the compound's south wall and looked toward compound two. Two ANA soldiers lay sprawled on rocks outside the gate and two more crouched in a shallow depression ten meters away.

Without waiting for the mortar rounds to impact, several ANA soldiers ran toward compound two. Some of them knelt in the open and sprayed rounds toward the mountain. Others scooped up dead and wounded and ran in clusters back to the pickups. Faster than any American unit could have done it, the ANA recovered their casualties and had them back to the vehicles.

Newly arrived Afghan soldiers ran around the positions, yelling orders. ANA soldiers who had been in the fight all morning looked at each other in confusion, then in ones and twos ran down the hill to the trucks. Flashes and smoke erupted from the mountain to the east as 120mm mortars impacted on its slope. The trickle of ANA leaving their positions increased to a waterfall as word spread among the Afghan soldiers.

Spicer ran into the open, looking down the hill. "What the fuck?" he nearly shrieked. "Why are those motherfuckers leaving?"

Another group of four ANA with an interpreter ran out of the compound, not down the hill but looking for Spicer. The ANA jabbered and gestured toward the trucks while the interpreter yelled "They have been ordered to leave! Their commander has ordered them back to the outpost!"

"That sorry fuck!" Spicer yelled. "Son of a bitch!" He got on his radio and called back to the outpost.

Nunez heard confirmation on the radio. The ANA battalion commander had ordered his men to completely withdraw from the Shkin valley. As Spicer spoke into the radio, the interpreter stood way too close to him and yelled "These men say they will not leave without the Americans! They will stay here until you are ready to leave with them!"

"God damn," Spicer said. "Everyone get out of the open, let's get back in this compound and figure out what the hell we do now."

Below him on the road, overloaded ANA trucks turned around and crept back toward the Alasai on creaking springs with dismounted ANA soldiers running alongside. As the Americans headed back into the compound, a voice called out from Nunez's radio.

"Colt 4 this is Colt 1 Golf!"

"This is Colt 4, go ahead!" Nunez said back to Powell.

"Are you getting this shit? Two ANA trucks are here picking up their casualties, they're telling the terp that everyone's pulling out!"

"Yeah, we just got that. Y'all stand by down there, we're getting this figured out. But it's confirmed, the ANA up here are buggin' out too."

"Fuck. Roger. We're not leaving, are we?"

"Fuck no we're not leaving!" Nunez yelled into the radio. "Rahman is in one of those fucking compounds to the east, and we're going to get some fire support on him! Hold your position!"

Inside the room on the roof, Lyons called out in what sounded like panic.

"Sergeant Nunez! Lieutenant Klein! I need ammo, I need ammo! Hurry!"

Wilson ran past Nunez toward his old spot on the wall. American soldiers and Marines ran in through the gate behind Nunez as he made his way up the stairs. Nunez yelled, "Gore, control your rate of fire!" As his head rose above floor level into the room Nunez stopped, eyes wide, stunned at what he saw.

Gore lay in a crumpled pile on the floor in a huge pool of blood. Lyons fired the M240 out the window. His body shook and tears ran down his face.

"Sarge, I need you to get ammo from Gore's patrol pack! Hurry, I'm almost out!"

Nunez threw himself into the room and knelt in the pool of blood, then pulled Gore's body as straight as he could in the small room. When he got Gore onto his back and turned his head, Nunez saw that Gore had been hit just under his lower left jaw. The round had blown open the side of his neck.

Nunez knelt next to Gore for several seconds, looking at his friend, and drew a complete blank. He held his hands over Gore as if he was praying over a sacrifice, but in reality he was just trying to force himself to think clearly. He had trained on how to assess a casualty many times, had just done it in real life a little while before, and now he didn't have a clue what to do. Gore wasn't moving, didn't look like he was breathing, and his eyes were half open and dull. He looked like every dead body Nunez had ever seen.

Nunez covered his mouth with his left hand, eyes wide as he tried to figure out what to do. Lyons fired long bursts toward the enemy and screamed, "Sergeant Nunez, please! I need ammo! Come on, hurry!"

Gore's patrol pack hung open on his back. Nunez forced himself to act. He dug out one belt and tossed it to Lyons. Lyons laid it over the edge of the windowsill and opened fire again, ready to reload the gun as soon as he finished firing the last few rounds he had left.

"God damn it! When did this happen?" Nunez yelled at Lyons over the sound of the 240.

"A little while ago Sarge, fuck, I don't know! It was before the planes came by!"

Nunez popped the buckle on Gore's helmet and pulled it off, holding the back of Gore's head so it wouldn't hit the floor. Gore's graying crew cut was smeared with blood on the left side of his head. His blue eyes were still, his lips parted. Nunez pulled his own helmet off and ran his hand over his head, not realizing he was smearing Gore's blood through his own hair.

Check his pulse, dumbass, Nunez told himself. He put his fingers on Gore's neck. There was no pulse on the carotid artery on the right side. He turned his head and put his ear to Gore's mouth, feeling for breath. There was none.

Halfheartedly Nunez reached for Gore's first aid kit, thinking that he should put a bandage on Gore's neck to stop the bleeding. When he touched the first aid kit he stopped, looking at Gore's wound again. *What bleeding are you going to stop? He's not bleeding anymore.* He pulled his hand back to his side, fighting himself in silence. One side of him wanted to do something, anything, to treat Gore's wound. The other side knew there was no reason to waste his time on first aid. His friend Eli Gore was dead.

As Lyons' gunfire hammered above his head and spent brass and links rained down onto them, he touched his forehead to Gore's forehead and whispered, "I'm sorry, Eli. I'm sorry." Then he sat back up, took a long breath and put his hand on Gore's forehead for a few seconds. He took another breath and shook off his emotions. His time to mourn would come later. He had a job to do right now.

Nunez put his helmet back on and dug through Gore's pack again. He pulled out two more belts of ammo and laid them over the windowsill next to Lyons, telling him, "Stay here, I'll be back."

He ran back down the steps and yelled to the group of soldiers and Marines huddled outside a room, "Hey! Gore's KIA, I need someone up here with Lyons on the gun!"

Everyone reacted. Wilson looked back toward Nunez with a painful grimace on his face, then turned back to cover the east. Klein shook his head and got on the radio to tell the soldiers in the MRAPs about the casualty. Two of the Marines ran to the stairwell, followed by a Georgia soldier. As the three of them ran up the stairs, Guidry walked up and put his hand on Nunez's shoulder. "Damn. Ah'm sorry, man. Really."

Nunez nodded and walked back to the stairs. Lyons came down as the Georgia soldier opened fire with the M240. Nunez took Lyons by the arm and led him into the room by the bottom of the stairs, told him to sit down and drink some water. Lyons still shook, and Nunez noticed something he had missed before.

Flecks of blood and bits of flesh were spattered up and down Lyons' right side, from helmet to waist.

As Lyons sat back against the wall he said, nearly sobbing, "I'm sorry, Sergeant Nunez. I didn't know what to do. I didn't mean to let Gore die. I'm sorry, I...I just didn't know what to do. He was shooting and then he got hit and his head jerked back and he just stood there, and he stopped shooting, and blood was pouring out...then he pulled the trigger again and he fell, and he was still shooting 'til he hit the floor. When he fell I picked up the gun and kept shooting, 'cause I didn't know what else to do." He shook his head and shut his eyes. "I'm sorry, Sarge. I'm sorry."

Nunez squatted in front of Lyons and put both hands on his shoulders. "Manny, you didn't let Gore die. You did your job up there, you should be proud. Gore could have been inside the best emergency room in the world when he got hit, and it wouldn't have mattered. He couldn't have survived that wound." Nunez didn't know if that was true, but he hoped Lyons would believe it. "You did a brave thing, Manny. You held that position by yourself and kept killing the enemy. You took over the gun, just like you were supposed to. You understand that?"

Tears ran down Lyons' cheeks, but he did his best to keep from breaking down. He said, "Sarge, I never even saw any Taliban. I don't think I killed any."

"That's alright, Manny. You put a shitload of rounds on their positions. You got some of them. Now I need you to take a break, get yourself back together and then get back out here with us. We'll need you on the 240 tonight, and I know you'll be there for us. Stay here and chill out for a minute, alright? I'll come back and get you."

"Roger, Sergeant. I'll be okay. I'll be ready for tonight."

Nunez nodded to Lyons, squeezed his shoulders and stood up to leave. Lyons sucked some water from his Camelbak and dug a pack of cigarettes out of his cargo pocket with shaking hands. Nunez saw that the tears had stopped, and the shaking wasn't as bad as before. Lyons pulled a lighter from the cigarette pack, lit the cigarette in his mouth and took a long drag. It seemed to calm him immediately. *He'll be okay,* Nunez thought.

Nunez walked back out of the room, in time to see two Marines struggle to carry Gore down the stairs, feet first and face down. Above them the Georgia

157

soldier fired the machine gun at a slow and steady rate. The two Marines reached the bottom of the stairs and arms reached out from American and Afghan soldiers who were waiting to help.

The Marine dropped Gore's feet onto the floor and soldiers helped to lift Gore's body to an almost upright position before lowering him onto his back. The toe of Gore's right boot caught a crevice in the floor and his leg folded underneath him, making him look awkward and contorted. Nunez struggled for several seconds to free his foot and lay his leg out straight, unreasonably concerned with making Gore more comfortable. The soldiers stood above Gore in silence for several seconds, then one of the Marines mumbled and made the sign of the cross. Nunez grabbed two soldiers and they moved Gore into a room, away from Lyons.

Klein asked, "Anyone have a poncho?"

Nobody responded, until one of the Marines said, "I don't have a poncho, but I got an air recognition panel."

"Okay, that'll work."

The Marine pulled a bright orange panel from his patrol pack, unfolded it and handed one end to Klein. The two of them pulled it open and laid it over Gore's body. When they stood up, one of the Georgia soldiers knelt down by Gore's feet and pulled a combat knife from his body armor. All the soldiers in Nunez's platoon had one dog tag laced into a boot, in case they were killed and the tag around their neck was lost. The Georgia soldier cut the laces holding the dog tag on Gore's boot.

Nunez asked, "What are you doing?"

"I'm cutting out his dog tag so I can give it to you," the soldier answered.

Nunez couldn't remember ever having been told to collect dog tags from the dead. He asked the Georgia soldier, "Why?"

The soldier turned back to Nunez and asked, "Ain't we supposed to?"

Nobody said anything. The Georgia soldier pulled out the dog tag and handed it to Nunez, who held it close and read it.

GORE, ELIJAH P.

U.S. ARMY

A POS

CATHOLIC

Nunez squeezed the dog tag in his fist, then put it into his sleeve pocket. He had no idea what the rules said he was supposed to do with it, but he knew without question he would never give it to anyone except Gore's family.

Spicer said, "Alright, here's what's up. We stay right here, all of us in this compound overnight. We leave the MRAPs on the road with three guys in each one, so they can take turns on the gun. Everyone else, ANA and American, stays here. The Taliban will hit us tonight, and we'll kill shitloads of them."

"What about our two KIAs?" Klein asked.

"They stay with us. I don't see any reason to send them out now."

"Okay," Klein said. "That might freak the guys out in whatever MRAP they put Ellis in, but yeah, that makes sense." He turned to Nunez and said, "Switch Lyons out with someone else as the 240 gunner. I'll probably put him in the driver's seat of an MRAP for the night, so he can get a break."

Nunez shook his head, still looking down at Gore. "No, lieutenant. Lyons stays on the 240. He already thinks he let Gore die, if we take the gun from him he'll feel like we don't trust him anymore. If we don't want him to break down and be fucked up for the rest of the deployment and probably the rest of his life, we leave him on the gun."

Klein looked at Nunez in surprise. Nunez looked away from Gore back at him. After the two held a staring contest for what seemed like a long time, Klein finally said, "Alright, that's fine. We'll get one of the Marines to be his A-gunner and keep an eye on him."

The echo of the last volley of mortar rounds faded. The valley seemed quiet and empty now that the ANA had gone. Klein got on the radio to organize their defense and ordered the soldiers and Marines from the wooded area at the top of the hill to come inside the compound.

Nunez made a perimeter check, making sure nobody was wounded, dehydrated or out of ammunition. As he checked each man he reassured them, and himself, "We're good, brother. We're good, and we're going to hold here and waste every last one of those shitbags who tries to hit us tonight. We lost a couple of guys, but we're going to win this fight. That cocksucker Rahman is here somewhere, and we're going to kill him."

Nunez stopped at the east wall to check on Wilson. The Marine forward observer moved to the wall next to Wilson and pulled a map from his cargo pocket. He looked through his compass and checked his GPS, then wrote on the map. Wilson asked him what he was doing.

"We keep hearing reports that your guy Rahman is in one of the compounds to the east. I'm working up grids to those compounds, so if they approve some heavy fire support I'll be able to direct it in. I'm thinking maybe the Milans might be the best choice, the French don't seem to have much concern with the rules of engagement if they blow away compounds with those."

Nunez said, "Yeah, the Milans should work. And Wilson, we'll call in flares all night, so you'll have plenty of chances to get confirmed kills with that rifle. It's gonna be a good night, brother." Nunez wasn't just spouting bullshit, he meant it. He felt nothing but joy at the thought of holding a position against a determined enemy attack overnight.

"Yeah, it will be, Jerry," Wilson responded. "We're going to get revenge for Gore. And Ellis."

The young Marine interrupted, "Wow. I'll never get used to you army guys calling your supervisors by their first names."

"I know," Nunez said. "We shouldn't. But me and Wilson have deployed together twice, and we're friends back home too. He's been to my house, he knows my family. It's hard to keep that whole 'Me sergeant first class, you sergeant' thing we're supposed to."

"I'm practically his son," Wilson smirked.

"Well, I guess that's cool, Sergeant First Class Nunez. My platoon sergeant would bayonet me in the nuts if I did that. Hey, can you let the lieutenant know, I'll have the grids to those compounds east of us in a couple of minutes."

"Roger, I'll tell him."

Nunez walked back to Spicer and Klein. Just before Nunez reached him, Spicer received a radio call and turned away from the other soldiers to answer. Nunez turned instead to Klein, asked how he thought they should set up their defenses.

A few seconds later Spicer said, "Fuck that! We're here, we're strongpointing this compound like we're supposed to! Don't tell me that shit, we're doing exactly what the fucking mission plan said!" Nunez turned his radio up, but didn't hear anything. Spicer had switched to another channel, maybe the command net. Nunez figured that someone back at the outpost didn't have a good understanding of what was going on and had criticized Spicer.

Spicer returned a minute later, spitting angrily into his mike. "Yeah roger, I fucking heard you. Wilco." Then to the soldiers and Marines in the compound, he said, "They just pulled us out. The ANA battalion commander ordered a complete withdrawal. The French will pull back as soon as it's dark, and Navajo doesn't want us out here alone. We need to get back to the outpost."

Soldiers and Marines in the courtyard looked at him in disbelief, but nobody said a word. Klein opened his mouth to speak, then stopped and looked off toward the mountains. Nunez held his tongue for as long as he could, which was no more than five seconds.

Almost in a rage, he exploded, "That's fucking bullshit, Lieutenant! We stay here and follow the fucking plan like we're supposed to! Didn't they hear that Rahman is within 500 fucking meters of us, right fucking now? If we leave, he gets away. We're not going anywhere!"

Spicer looked like he was about to explode right back at Nunez. "Yes, I know what the fucking plan says. I know Rahman is out there. I argued it with Navajo, and it didn't work. Trust me, I don't want to leave either. But that's the order."

"Leave then," Nunez said. "Take the Georgia guys and go. We're staying."

"Check yourself, Sergeant Nunez!" Klein yelled. "Check yourself! That's the order, and we're following it!"

Motherfucker, Nunez thought. He spun and faced away from Spicer. His hands started shaking again and he balled them into tense fists. *I don't believe this shit,* he thought. *Jesus fucking Christ, I don't believe this shit. Why the fuck are we even here? Why did we do this? We're supposed to hold the fucking ground overnight and kill these fucks, not run away.*

Behind him he heard Spicer say to everyone, "Hey, I'm sorry, it ain't my call. If it was up to me, we'd stay. I don't want us to have just lost two guys, for nothing."

Nunez opened and closed his hands, closed his eyes, breathed deeply. When he opened his eyes he found himself looking at the room Gore had been killed in. He had put Gore there, had helped lead them all into this fight, had known and accepted the risks. He could accept suffering losses. What he couldn't accept was this decision, to pull out before the fight was won.

When he calmed a bit and turned back to Klein, he saw his lieutenant staring at Gore's body. "Well," Klein said, "it would have been nice if we had gotten this withdrawal order about thirty minutes ago."

"Yeah, it would have," Spicer agreed. "I'm sorry, brother. I almost told Navajo to go fuck himself. And he's the fucking colonel. Really bro, I'm sorry."

The Marine forward observer looked at his watch and said, "Well, that's nice of those bastards to order us out now. At least we'll be back in time for lunch."

The withdrawal of the Americans and the few remaining Afghans took almost half an hour. Mortar fire covered their movement down the hill to the MRAPs. The Taliban left them alone for most of the evacuation, fired a few bursts to harass them but didn't hit anything or anyone. The Taliban knew they had won, there was no reason to provoke a firefight and maybe lose any more of their fighters than they already had.

Final insults came in the form of two RPGs the Taliban fired just as soldiers were climbing in the back of the MRAPs. Men hit the dirt after Spicer yelled "RPG!", waited to hear the round tear past the vehicles and got back to their feet. Nunez muttered curses under his breath as the round went over, and swore to himself that no matter what the Taliban did he wouldn't hit the deck again. Then he had to drop into the thick dust with everyone else again as another RPG was fired from straight down the road. It exploded against the side of the hill they had just climbed down.

Nunez popped up from the road and aimed his carbine east, looking for a target. He saw nothing. Everyone else scrambled to get into the vehicles while Nunez scanned like mad through his scope. *Show yourselves, you cocksuckers,* he thought. *Give me one fucking shot. Stick your head up so you can see if you hit anything. Stand so you can fire another RPG round. Bound from one tree to another. Shoot at me so I can see your muzzle blast. Give me a fucking target.*

Behind Nunez, Wilson yelled out, "Sergeant Nunez, come on!" Nunez ignored him and kept scanning. He flipped his selector to burst and told himself, *If I don't see a target in five seconds, I'm going to dump a magazine just for the hell of it.*

"Jerry!" Wilson screamed. "Get in the fucking truck! Please!"

Nunez bit down hard and bared his teeth. He put his finger on the trigger, took another look through the scope at nothing.

I'm putting my Joes in danger. I have to move.

Nunez straightened his finger, flipped his selector back to safe and bounded to the back door of the MRAP. The driver was already moving as Nunez clambered up the steps through the doorway. The MRAPs rolled back toward the Alasai.

The soldiers and one Marine in Nunez's vehicle rode in a stunned silence, except for Lyons. Lyons smoked and talked to himself, saying "Fuck this place, fuck these people. I hate this fucking country. I hate it. God damn these people, I hate them all." The lone Afghan interpreter sitting in the back of the vehicle didn't react at all to Lyons' words, or maybe he just didn't understand.

The vehicles wound back down the road and finally rolled into the outpost gate. Soldiers and Marines poured out of the vehicles as if they were big, armored clown cars. Gunners and drivers stayed inside to throw empty ammo cans and piles of spent shells and links out the back doors. Nunez was disgusted to see Afghan soldiers run to the vehicles and scoop up brass, stuffing as much as they could hold into their pockets and helmets, desperate to make some money from it.

Several French Marines helped put Gore's and Ellis' bodies onto litters, carried them toward the command post and covered them with French camouflage ponchos. The Georgia and Texas soldiers accounted for all their troops and reloaded their magazines, just in case the Taliban attacked the outpost again. Nunez didn't have to reload. He hadn't seen a single Taliban fighter or fired a single shot, not once.

Apaches flew over the valley, air cover for a single Blackhawk helicopter that landed behind the outpost to pick up some ANA wounded. When the helicopter touched down a mixed group of ANA and French Marines carried two litters with wounded Afghan soldiers to it, then a French Marine ran back to the outpost and yelled in English, "Send one of the American dead!"

The Georgia troops reached Ellis first, lifted his litter and rushed to the landing zone. Nunez went out after them, hoping the helicopter would have enough room for Gore. The Georgia soldiers reached the Blackhawk and helped the door gunners load the litter inside. Nunez stood almost nose to nose with one of the door gunners, held up one finger and yelled, "One more? One more?" over the deafening stutter of the rotors just above their heads.

The gunner looked into the helicopter's fuselage, then turned and screamed into Nunez's ear, "One more! Hurry up!"

Nunez ran back to the outpost, yelling at his men to get Gore to the helicopter. Wilson, Powell, Doc Poole and Nguyen each grabbed a handle of the litter and rushed out of the outpost to the LZ. Nunez was surprised to see Lyons coming after them. The door gunners waved them over, and they struggled to get the litter onto the helicopter. Lyons was crying again, and Nunez saw him grab Gore's hand as the litter slid across the helicopter's floor.

A door gunner waved them away as he spoke into the microphone in his helmet. Wilson grabbed Nunez's shoulder as the Texas soldiers turned and jogged away from their friend's body. They had just seen his face for the last time.

The sound of the helicopter's engine increased in pitch and volume. The soldiers ducked as the Blackhawk kicked up a hurricane of dust and swirling dirt. Nunez sprinted, his body armor strained his lower back and the world in front of him bounced with each step he ran. He squeezed his eyes shut as the dirt and rocks slapped his back and whirled around to his face. The Blackhawk roared low to the west, the sound faded and the dirt no longer stung Nunez's face. They reached the gate and French Marines were there, guiding them behind the cover of Hesco walls.

There was no more fire outside the outpost. The Texas soldiers stopped running. Some of them dropped to one knee to rest, others bent at the waist, breathing as deeply as they could. Nunez went to a knee with his head down and dropped his carbine into the dirt. He tore his helmet off and threw it to the side before flopping back to rest against a Hesco. Lyons walked into the outpost, away from everyone else.

Wilson wiped his forehead and sat back against the wall next to Nunez. Powell collapsed against the other side, put one arm on Nunez's shoulder as he drank the last bit of water in his Camelbak. A French Marine walked up and offered them bottles of Gatorade. Nunez took one, but felt like he didn't even have the strength to open it.

Wilson looked at him. "Sarge, you have blood on your head. You okay?"

Nunez wiped his head and saw a mix of blood, dirt and oil on his fingetips. "I'm okay, Alex," he said quietly. "It's not my blood."

Wilson was quiet for a second. Then he said, "Jerry, what the fuck just happened? I mean...did we just lose?"

Nunez asked himself the same question. He looked around at the outpost, watched the Georgia troops load boxes of ammunition into their vehicles in preparation for the ride back out of the Alasai valley. The command post was a madhouse of activity. Afghan soldiers clustered in different spots around the outpost, pulled off bloodstained camouflage jackets, treated minor wounds and wiped down their weapons. He took a look at his own gloves, pants and boots. They were smeared with Gore's blood.

The mission had gone wrong, but he and his soldiers had held together. Nobody had been a coward, nobody had fallen apart. He didn't feel like he had just been beaten. Or at least, he didn't feel like he had been beaten by the enemy.

"We didn't lose, Alex," Nunez said. "Eli didn't lose. We did exactly what we were supposed to do. Somebody in charge chickened the fuck out and didn't let us beat the Taliban like we could have. Maybe someone on our side lost, but it wasn't us."

CHAPTER 13

The last weeks of the deployment passed. A few patrols, one brief exchange of gunfire, no casualties, not much interest from either side. The battalion chaplain and his assistant flew to Pierce to conduct Gore's Fallen Comrade ceremony. Gore's extra boots were set in an empty spot on the firebase, the bayonet he never used was mounted on his carbine and jammed into the dirt behind the boots. Another helmet, not the bloodstained helmet Gore had died wearing, was placed atop the carbine. The chaplain's assistant had made a new set of dog tags for Gore, and they were hung on the carbine's grip.

Soldiers stood in formation while a few words were read, a few prayers recited. Each man walked to the boots and carbine to say his personal goodbye. Lyons and Powell walked up together and knelt before the dusty little memorial. Lyons was in tears before his knees touched the dirt, and Powell had to hold him up.

Nunez stood in the platoon sergeant's spot behind the formation, not reciting any prayer, not bowing his head. When his turn to approach the memorial came, all he could do was whisper "You deserved better" to the boots and helmet Gore never wore, the carbine Gore didn't carry, the dog tags Gore never saw.

When the formation broke, the rest of the soldiers clustered together, exchanged hugs and told stories of Gore's jokes and laughter and bravery.

"Remember when Powell saw the picture of Gore's family on his computer and asked him if the red-haired black Chinese kid was his?" Doc Poole asked Harris.

"Yeah, I remembuh," Harris said, laughing. "Gore said, 'You mean the one my wife named Mohammed junior? Yeah, he's mine, why do you ask?'"

Behind them Vlacek sobbed to Lyons, "I called him a God dang faggot the day he died. Shit, man, I hope he knows I didn't mean it."

Lyons didn't respond. Lattimore said, "He knows you didn't mean it, Czech." Nunez saw Lattimore look right at Lyons and say, "He doesn't blame any of us for anything that happened in that valley."

He doesn't have to, Nunez thought. *I'll do that for him. And it's not Lyons who deserves any blame.* Then he walked past his soldiers and went to the perimeter to be by himself.

****

Durrand met with Klein and Nunez in his office one night to update them on new information about the Shkin valley battle.

"Yeah, Rahman was in the compounds where you guys thought he was," Durrand said, frowning. "That sorry fuck didn't get a scratch during the fight. Now he's been promoted again, he's one of the senior Taliban commanders in Kapisa province. He'll ride the glory of his win against us in the Shkin valley for years."

Klein muttered, "Son of a bitch" and rolled his eyes. Nunez said nothing. Klein asked, "So how many Talibs did we kill in there? With all the small arms fire, mortars and air support, we had to have killed at least a few. I know the snipers hit some too."

Durrand perked up a little. "Oh yeah, you guys killed some, no question. At first we thought it was only ten or so, but within the last couple of days we've gotten reports that it was closer to twenty-five."

Klein and Nunez looked at each other. Nunez turned away, and Klein asked a question Nunez didn't want to hear the answer to.

"So we killed twenty-five, against our thirteen. Did killing those twenty-five make any difference at all?"

Klein arched his eyebrows and pursed his lips, his hands parted in front of him in a gesture of supplication. "Lieutenant, I wish it had. But no, it didn't. The Talibs you guys killed are already being replaced by volunteers from Pakistan, and a few locals. And as far as we know, no members of Rahman's IED cell were killed or wounded."

"Shit," Klein muttered. Nunez had known that would be Durrand's answer. He kept his mouth shut and fumed in silence.

"And you know what else," Durrand said. "Rahman is telling everyone how disappointed he is that the Americans didn't get far enough into the valley to reach the IEDs he had planted. He says he would have destroyed another ten 'tanks' if the Americans had gone any farther."

"You think he really did have IEDs set?" Klein asked.

"Yeah, I think he did. Not ten, but probably one or two. Maybe it's best you guys didn't get that far. I mean, sour grapes and all, but I guess we can be happy that no vehicles were hit by IEDs."

Klein asked, "So is there any plan to get back in there and kill Rahman, like we should have when we had the chance?"

Durrand shook his head and said, "Right now, I don't think anyone has any plan or desire to go back into that place."

Nunez turned and walked out of Durrand's office without a word.

****

The Texas soldiers packed their belongings and staged them for the last ride back to Bagram. Nunez was quiet and distant most days. He spent a lot of time at the platoon's office, pretending to tend to the endless administrative tasks that needed to be done before they left. Most of the time he claimed to be working in the office he sat there alone, listening to an MP3 player, staying away from everyone. Wilson came in once and asked Nunez what his plans for homecoming were.

"No plans, Alex. I'll go home, just be a husband and daddy again, and I'll put my badge and uniform on and go back on the street when my terminal leave is up. That's all."

"When are you going to promote to First Sergeant? It's way past time."

"I'm not," Nunez said. "I'm done. My enlistment is up a month after we get home, and that's that. I'm through with this shit."

"Jerry, you've got, what, sixteen years in?" Wilson asked. "You need to become First Sergeant for a few years, then retire."

"I've got seventeen years. And I don't give a fuck about retiring. I'm done. If I want to get killed for nothing, I can do it in Houston, I don't have to come all the way over here. Fuck this. No more deploying for me."

"Damn, Jerry," Wilson said. "That's not the Nunez I know. I hope you get over that feeling, brother. We still need you in the unit."

"I won't get over it. And my wife damn sure won't. The unit will go on without me. Hopefully you guys won't deploy again anyway. It's not worth it anymore, Alex. Not if people higher up are too fucking scared to get out there and win."

Wilson frowned, then stood up and put his hand on Nunez's shoulder. "Don't give up yet, Jerry. We'll talk about it after we get home. Maybe you'll feel different then."

"I won't, Alex. We can talk, but I won't change my mind."

Wilson squeezed Nunez's shoulder, turned and walked out of the office. Nunez put his headphones back in his ears, losing himself in one of his favorite 70's songs, one that his soldiers called "old man music". He rested his arms on the makeshift plywood desk and laid his head on them. He had slept ten hours the night before, and it was the middle of the day. He closed his eyes and tried to force himself to stop thinking. Within minutes he was asleep.

****

Two days before their last convoy to Bagram, Nunez went to the command post at Firebase Pierce to make the platoon's preparations for departure. Several French officers approached him, shook his hands warmly and wished him a safe return. Nunez did his best to return their care, made a genuine effort to wish them a safe and joyous homecoming. He liked and respected them, and wanted them to return home to their families just as he was about to. But all he felt inside was that none of them, French or American, had earned the right to go home. Not until they accomplished their mission, and defeated their enemy.

The senior American officer on the base, a support battalion staff officer who had been assigned as a liaison to the French, asked Nunez to step into his office. He closed the door behind them and sat on the edge of his desk, then motioned for Nunez to sit down. The Major looked and acted like he had been in the military for decades, but he was younger than Nunez.

"I hear you're pretty pissed off about that fight in the Shkin, Sergeant," the Major said. "I just wanted to let you know that you guys did a good job out there.

You don't need to be upset about it."

Nunez glared hard at the Major, not angry at him, but furious at anything that reminded him of the pointless loss they had suffered. "Sir, I'm going to be pissed about it until the day I fucking die. If we weren't willing to get in there and win, we shouldn't have gone in at all. Now when I get home I have to explain to the family of one of my best friends, one of the best guys I've ever known, that he died for no god damn reason, in a fight that we lost."

The Major gave Nunez a curious look. "A fight you lost? You guys won. You didn't lose that fight."

Nunez looked back, eyes wide, incredulous. "Sir, what the fuck do you mean? We got stopped when we tried to advance into that valley. I mean, the lead guys got stopped within the first 500 meters. We had all these God damn plans to go in three kilometers, then hold ground overnight and kill a bunch of Taliban. We got ordered to run away instead. We didn't kill Rahman, he's still in the Shkin valley planning more attacks on our guys. We didn't accomplish anything, except maybe we killed some Taliban fighters they've already replaced with another bunch of inbred, brain dead fucks from Pakistan. We lost."

"Sergeant, I'm a little disappointed in you," the Major said. "You're infantry, and you're a leader. You shouldn't fall apart and give up on your mission just because you had casualties. And it's not like your casualties were that bad, you only had one man killed. That doesn't mean you lost."

Nunez's face tensed and he said "Fuh--" before he stopped himself. He had nearly said *Fuck you* to the Major. That probably wouldn't have gone over well.

He covered the near-insult by saying, "*First* of all, sir, taking *just one* casualty isn't the God damn issue. Yes we're infantry, we're prepared to take casualties. I'm not pissed because we lost one guy. I'm pissed because we lost one guy for no fucking reason. If we had lost him and won, that's one thing. The French lost a guy in Alasai, but he died in victory, not defeat. That makes things different, sir. We're all willing to take casualties if that means we win. If I had been killed out there, and we won, I wouldn't be too upset about it. But I am fucking pissed, and I'll always be fucking pissed, that we lost a good soldier in a fight that someone didn't have the will to win."

"Sergeant Nunez, you're looking at this all wrong," the Major said. "You need to remember that the Taliban told everyone that we couldn't set one foot in the valley. Those guys swore that we were too scared to even try it. Well, we showed them, didn't we? We did get in there, and we did kill some Taliban."

Nunez shot the Major a hateful look. His eyes asked, *What's this "we" shit?*

"Hold on, Sergeant Nunez," the Major said, holding his palm up. "I know what you're thinking, and we both know I wasn't there. When I say 'we', I mean all of us, the whole team. I wasn't out there, but I did everything I could to support you guys from here. We're all a team, aren't we?"

"Yesssir, I guess so," Nunez said, in a tone that reeked of insubordination. "We're a team. Sometimes I forget."

"Good," the major said, brushing off the snide comment. "So, what was the second thing?"

Nunez looked back, confused. "What second thing, sir?"

"You said 'first of all, the casualty wasn't the issue.' So what was second of all?"

"Oh. Uh¬...nothing sir, that was it."

"Hmm. Well, remember this, Sergeant Nunez. Sergeant Durrand says the Taliban are very upset that we entered the valley at all. So we did win. And this is an information war, Sergeant. If we call this fight a defeat, then it becomes a defeat. We can't take our victory and turn it around on ourselves. You know as well as I do that we can't kill our way to victory in this war. We have to convince the locals that we're serious about what we say, and what we did in the Shkin valley convinced them. We said we'd enter that valley, and we did."

Nunez let his head roll back and looked at the ceiling. Then he lowered his head again and said, "So, what really matters here is that we say we won? It doesn't matter that we lost two Americans and eleven ANA, then gave up and left?"

"I know this is hard to hear," the Major said. "And I doubt you've been to the counterinsurgency schools I've been to, so you don't understand what I'm saying. But yes, that's true. Holding ground doesn't always matter. Body counts don't matter either, not for us. As a matter of fact, in a counterinsurgency war, sometimes you don't want to kill a lot of enemy, because then you turn the families of the dead against us. So how many died on each side isn't the real issue.

What matters is that they said we couldn't enter the valley, and we did."

"Sir, we entered the valley, and the whole plan fell apart. The mission failed. It wouldn't bother me so much that it failed, if we were taking what we learned and saying, 'Okay, now we go back in there and do it right'. But we're not saying that. We're talking ourselves out of going back and winning the fight against them."

"Sergeant Nunez," the Major said, "you don't get it. You're still not hearing me. What you think decides victory in this war isn't what decides victory. This isn't World War Two, the measure of success is different. What we prove to the local population determines how much they believe us, and from that how much they support us. And that's why I say we won, because we showed them we mean what we say."

Nunez said, with acid in his voice, "So, Major, if we 'won', then I guess there's no reason to go back into that valley, is there? We defeated the enemy. The enemy still owns that valley, but we defeated them."

"That's right, Sergeant. Maybe someday another unit will find a reason to go into the valley, but you guys went in there and beat the Taliban. It was a victory, and don't call it anything else."

Nunez looked off to the side in disgust. *Oh my fucking god,* he thought, *what a load of bullshit.* He wondered what Gore would have said if he knew he was going into that valley to die, for a "victory" that only a dreamer with a gold medal in mental gymnastics could comprehend. He tried to figure out how it could have happened, how leaders could have forgotten that if you wanted to win a war, sometimes you actually had to defeat the enemy. He looked back at the Major, controlling his breathing, making sure he didn't explode when he spoke.

"Well, *sir,* since all that matters is what we say happens and not what really happens, why don't we just tell everyone we won the fucking war, and all go home?"

EPILOGUE

Nunez rolled to a stop in front of 1824 Tippit, an old wooden house off William Cannon road in south Austin. The house was in decent shape, way better than some of the other houses around it. A small flagpole stuck out from a tree in the front yard, with no flag on it. Nunez remembered a picture on Gore's computer, of him and his family in front of their house. An American flag was on the flagpole then. Gore's work truck, a truck Nunez had always seen at weekend drills, was parked at the end of the driveway. It was dusty and covered with leaves, no longer in use.

A few kids' toys were in the front yard but there were no kids outside. The front door was closed. Nunez had called to make sure she would be there before he left Houston three hours earlier, but the house looked empty. He wondered if she had told him she would be there and then left so that she wouldn't have to talk to him.

He knew he had avoided this meeting, pushing it all the way back to now, one day before he had to go back to work. Every time he had talked to her on the phone about it she had something else going on, some reason not to be there. The calls had been very formal, they had never even used first names with each other. Neither one of them had been comfortable talking on the phone. He felt like he had almost forced her to agree to meet him. But it had to be done, or at least he thought it had to be done. Maybe she would feel differently about it. He was at least going to make the effort.

He got out of his car and walked to the front door. One of the next door neighbors looked out his window at Nunez and Nunez looked back. A fat older man, arms and bare chest covered with tattoos, glared at him like a convict glares at a prison guard. Nunez looked away, not caring. He would see that kind of a look from ex-convicts every night, starting the next day when he went back to work.

He stopped at the door and reached for the doorbell, but didn't push it. He took a second to pulse-check himself. He was nervous, his heart beat way faster than normal and his breaths were ragged. He was more nervous standing at this door than he had been standing at the MRAP door, two months earlier in the Shkin valley.

This was going to be hard. He knew it and accepted it. It wouldn't be like the reunion with Quincy had been. He had expected that to be hard, but when the company saw Quincy at their welcome home ceremony there had been nothing but hugs and laughter, joy without anger. Quincy's father had even given Nunez a huge bear hug when Quincy introduced them and told his father, "This is the platoon sergeant I told you about."

Every soldier in the company had been angry at being ordered to go to the welcome home ceremony. It was the last obstacle the military had put between the soldiers and their families, and they just wanted it to be over with so they could go home. The soldiers had done nothing but bitch about having to go to the stupid ceremony at all. Some general had insisted that they have it, though, so they all had to be there.

Nunez's negative feelings had started to change when he saw Quincy. Then the General asked for all Vietnam veterans in the crowd of anxious family members to move up front. He announced to the returning soldiers, "Men, I know you didn't want this ceremony. But I ordered you to be here anyway, and this is why." He pointed to the four Vietnam veterans in the audience, one of whom was Quincy's father, and said, "I wanted you to have a welcome home ceremony, because those men never got one. They deserved one, and you deserve one. I'm doing what I can to make sure you never feel like when you came home, nobody cared." And at least for Nunez, anger over the ceremony went away.

Nunez tapped his pocket, felt the edge of Gore's dog tag.

Quit stalling and ring the doorbell, you chickenshit.

He pressed the doorbell. He couldn't hear any noise inside, didn't know if the doorbell worked. He waited a while, not sure if he should ring again, then knocked on the door. Nunez heard the sounds of small feet shuffling on carpet, then the curtain in the window next to the door pushed open. A little boy's face was in the window, round and blue-eyed, with his father's sandy brown hair. Nunez felt his eyes start to water, and willed them to stop. He waved at the little boy, and the boy smiled and waved back.

The door opened, and Nunez looked at the woman standing inside it. She didn't say anything at first, she just stood there looking at him. She was in her mid-thirties, heavyset, pretty but nothing special. Nunez thought she and her husband must have been perfect for each other.

"Hi," Nunez said. "I guess you're Deborah?"

"Debbie. You must be Sergeant Nunez."

"It's just Jerry. I'm out of the military any day now."

"Wow. Must be nice," she said, and Nunez realized that hadn't been the best thing to say.

"So, I guess there was something you wanted to tell me?"

"Uh...Debbie, I just wanted to see how you're doing. To make sure you're okay."

"You could have asked me that over the phone," she said. "I'm fine. The army people have been in contact with me, the life insurance money is coming through. Everything's taken care of."

She still hadn't invited him inside, and she didn't seem to have any desire to talk to him. He wondered if he should just leave.

"That's good. I also wanted to let you know, uh...if you need anything, you can call me. I can help out."

"I don't need any help. It's not like you would be here anyway. You live in Houston, nobody from the unit lives around here. We don't expect anyone to be here if we need help."

"I can come here if you need me to, Debbie," he said. "Seriously."

"If I need help I'll call my parents. I won't need your help." She turned and looked into the house at her kids and said, "Look, I'm a little busy. If you don't have anything else to say, I need to go."

Nunez sighed, not sure what to do. "Look, Debbie," he said, "I'm sorry if I'm bothering you. But I needed to tell you your husband was a great guy. I know someone from the unit has told you this already, but whoever that was didn't know him like I did. I didn't want you to feel like someone was just reading words on paper, I wanted you to hear it from someone who really means it."

"I know what kind of a guy he was," she said. "We were married a long time. He was a great guy, then he left and didn't come back."

He sighed again at that statement. What was the right response? "Debbie, it's not his fault he didn't come back," he said, trying to find the right words. "He always talked about you and the kids, he dreamed of coming back to you. If you're going to be mad about him not coming back, be mad at someone else, not him."

The woman's face furrowed in anger. "Who the hell are you to tell me who I can be mad at? You're not dealing with what I'm dealing with. You have no right to tell me anything like that."

Nunez held his palms up, wanting to calm her down and fix the mistakes he was making. He obviously hadn't chosen the right words. "I'm sorry, Debbie. That's not what I meant. I'm just trying to tell you that he would have come back to you if he could have."

"Well...I didn't mean to snap at you. It's just been hard lately. I'm easy to set off."

"That's...it's okay, Debbie, that was a stupid thing for me to say. My wife's been mad at me since I left, so I understand a little what you mean."

"I doubt you or your wife understand," she said. "My husband is dead, Jerry. He didn't just go away and leave me here to take care of four kids, he went away and died. And he didn't have to go. We were making enough money, there was no real reason for him to join the Guard. And even if he had to go back in, he didn't have to be a foot soldier. He was older, and he had already done his time. He should have just been a mechanic again, or something safe."

She looked down and thought for a moment. Nunez stayed quiet, waiting for her next sentence, knowing it would hurt. "You want to know who else I'm mad at, Jerry?" she asked. "I'm mad at whatever idiot let a thirty-five year old man with five kids go out and fight a war, like he was some eighteen year old with nothing to lose."

Nunez raised his eyebrows, inhaled and said, "Well, I guess that's me, among others. I let him fight. Me and everyone else in his chain of command."

She hesitated again. Her eyes squinted, but in confusion rather than anger. "Why would you do that, Jerry? Did you not know he had a family?"

"We all knew he had a family, Debbie. I have a wife and kids too, and so did our lieutenant and some of the other guys in the platoon. Having a family doesn't make anyone more or less valuable than anyone else out there. I'm sorry, Debbie, but that's how it is. Eli volunteered to be an infantryman, and he was treated like one. He wouldn't have wanted it any other way."

She rolled her eyes and opened the door. He backed away to give her room, and she went past him into the yard. Then she turned and said, "Jerry, why would he have wanted it that way? Why would he have given up what he had? Was it so that he could wear some stupid combat badge? That's not important, to anyone. He had everything he needed, right here with me and the kids. We aren't rich, but we were happy. Now he's gone, and what are we left with? Our kids get to grow up without him, they might not even remember him when they're older. My two kids from my first husband felt like he was their real father, and now it's like they lost a father twice. His daughter from his first marriage was part of this family, I love her like she was my own daughter. I don't even know if we'll ever see her again."

She started to tear up, not sobbing but almost there. "Do you know what Eli's god damn ex-wife did as soon as she found out he was dead? She got a lawyer to try to get some more of his life insurance money. He had set aside fifty thousand dollars to give her, just to cover child support and put extra money aside for his daughter to go to college, and his ex says that was just a gift and she should get more money for child support. Is that the way Eli wanted it? Did he want his family torn apart and his kids to grow up without him? Did he want me to be divorced once and widowed once, with four kids to take care of on my own? Did he want me to have to fight his stupid ex-wife for his money?"

"Debbie, you know he didn't want anything like that," Nunez said. "Nobody would. He went to Afghanistan because he wanted to protect you and the kids. It might sound stupid, but that's how he felt about it."

She laughed bitterly, and tears fell onto her cheeks. "You have to be joking. He was protecting us, by being over there? We're in more danger from the drunk next door than we could ever be from anyone in Afghanistan."

Nunez knew better than to even try to explain it. "Debbie...it sounds stupid, and I can't make you get it. But that's the truth. Just give him some credit. He didn't go running off to war because he thought it was fun, he went because he thought he had to."

"Well, he didn't!" she shouted. "And I'll be damned if I'm going to just forgive him, not when he left us like this." She turned and pointed. "You see this flagpole? He insisted on putting it in the yard, and he always had an American flag flying from it. While he was gone I made sure and kept it flying, because he always asked me about it and I knew it was important to him. The day they showed up and told me he was dead, I came out here and took it down. Because I don't buy that bullshit that you just told me, I don't buy that bullshit that he left us all here because he wanted to protect us. He left because he had some stupid patriotic idea about serving his country in a war, and because he watched too many war movies and thought it would be fun. I knew him better than you, Jerry. I don't believe for a second that he really thought he could die over there. He thought he would just go off to war, have fun and come home with some medals to show off. He couldn't have thought that war and those people were worth dying for. He couldn't have thought any of that crap was worth it. And it wasn't worth it. Nothing over there was worth his life."

Nunez's blood pressure had felt like it was rising for the last minute, while Debbie went off on her tirade. When he spoke, he had to make an effort to keep his anger in. "First of all, he wasn't fighting for Afghanistan or any of the people there. He was fighting for you, and your kids, and me and every other soldier he was with. He was doing something that was God damn important. I don't know why you feel like you have to tear him down, and tear down what he did."

A shocked look came over her face. She started to protest and he cut her off, saying, "You want to know if he thought it was worth his life to fight over there? Ask him."

Her eyes squinted again, in anger this time. "What the hell is that supposed to mean? Are you trying to make some stupid joke?"

"It's not a joke," Nunez replied, in a tone that sounded too harsh even to him. "Look at what he did, and take his answer from there. Did you know that on the day he died, when we went into that valley, he knew an American and several Afghan soldiers had been killed already? Did you know he knew that, and went in anyway?"

Debbie gave him a blank look and wiped her eyes. When she didn't respond, Nunez said, "I'm asking you for an answer. Did you know that or not?"

"No, I didn't know that," she said softly.

"Well, think about it. That fight wasn't about having fun. He knew we had already lost people. He knew there was a chance he would die. And he went in anyway, because it was his damn job. He could have gotten out of it. Only part of the platoon went on that mission, if he had taken me aside and told me he didn't want to go we wouldn't have taken him." He felt his anger rising, and was getting tired of holding it in. "If he had faked a sprained ankle or something before we left the outpost we wouldn't have taken him. If he had claimed he was seasick from the ride into the valley we wouldn't have taken him, we would have left him in the fucking vehicle!"

Check yourself, Sergeant Nunez. Check yourself. Nunez stopped talking, took a half step backward and got a grip on himself. He had almost let his anger get the upper hand. He was catching himself doing that a lot since he came home, getting angry at the slightest provocation.

"I'm sorry, I didn't mean to use that language. But Eli was one of my best friends, and he was a good soldier. He didn't think the things you say he did. He knew what the war was about, and he knew what the risks were. He thought you were worth risking his life, because he wanted to protect you from the people who want to come here and kill us. If you don't want to believe that, fine, don't believe it. But don't talk about Eli like he was some stupid ass kid who didn't understand what the hell he was doing."

Debbie's tears had stopped. She said, "I know he wasn't stupid. And I know he went there, even though he knew it was dangerous. I get that."

Nunez cut her off again. "No, you don't get it. He didn't go there even though it was dangerous, he went there *because* it was dangerous. He went there because of the risk, not despite it. He wasn't some damn victim, he made a choice to go there and fight because he knew someone had to, if we want our families to be safe. You can call that stupid if you want, but Eli didn't think it was stupid. He believed in it."

"How do you know this, Jerry? Did he tell you all this?"

"No, he never told me," Nunez said. "He showed me. He showed all of us."

She was quiet for what seemed like a long time. Nunez took a couple of deep breaths during her silence, forcing himself to back way down from the anger he had felt at Debbie's words. She finally looked up at him and said, "Maybe I can think about it that way, Jerry," she said. "If you can promise me that what I've been feeling is wrong. If you can promise me he died for something."

Did he die for something? Nunez asked himself. *Haven't you been pissed the last two months, telling people that he died for nothing?* Now that Nunez heard someone else speak the words he had been thinking, he wanted to punch himself in the face.

"He died for a lot of things. He died for you and your kids, and for me and my kids. He died because what he believed about himself was stronger than anything the Taliban could do to him. Tell yourself that, and tell your kids that."

"Don't tell me how to raise my kids," Debbie said, trying and failing to flush with anger again. "You can't tell me what to tell my kids about their father."

"Yes, I can," Nunez said. "About this, I can tell you what to say. I was there when he died, I know what he did and why he did it. And if you don't tell the kids, I'll tell them myself someday."

She went quiet again. Her eyes were red, but there were still no tears. She turned for a couple of seconds, looking toward the tree with the flagpole. When she turned back she asked, "Your colonel came here and told me Eli died a hero. He's getting a medal sometime in the next few months, and they want me to be there for the ceremony. Is that true, did Eli really die as a hero, or was he just telling me what he thought I wanted to hear?"

"Debbie," Nunez said, struggling to find the right words again. "Yeah, you can say he was a hero. I mean...it's not that simple. The truth is, he didn't do anything amazing, he didn't do anything other than his job. None of us did anything really heroic, we just went out there and fought the war. He held his position and kept up fire on the enemy, even though he was getting shot at. I guess...I guess compared to what some other soldiers have done in Iraq and Afghanistan, it wasn't particularly heroic. Compared to what you can expect from your average civilian back here...yeah, it was heroic."

Debbie pondered that answer for a moment. Nunez expected her to press him on it, but instead she asked, "Did he die instantly? They told me he died instantly, but I want to know the truth."

Nunez blinked away the tear that formed the moment she asked the question. He had known she was going to ask that. He had rehearsed how he would answer that question. He had spoken with his wife Laura, debating whether or not he should tell Gore's wife the truth. Laura had told him the best thing to do was to be honest, and despite his own feelings about it he had decided that if she asked, he would tell her what had actually happened.

Gore had only lived for a few moments after he was shot. He didn't have time to feel much pain. But Nunez knew that to Gore's wife, the knowledge that he had suffered any pain at all might be too much to bear.

Nunez braced himself. He closed his eyes and again imagined what Gore's death must have been. Gore braced against the machine gun, firing strings of lead into the enemy, yelling back and forth to Lyons. The sudden, unexpected enemy round that snapped his head back and blew his throat open, the pause as he let go of the trigger and maybe realized he was about to die. And his last act, his last pull on the trigger, a pull that he held as he dropped from the open window into a blood-drenched pile on the floor.

Nunez opened his eyes and stared into Debbie's. "No, he didn't die instantly. He lived for a few seconds after he was shot. After he was hit, he kept firing his weapon until he died."

The reaction was instant. Tears gushed onto Debbie's cheeks. Nunez stood in front of her, not sure if he should touch her hand, hug her, or just stand there. She put her hands over her face and her sobs broke through. He wondered if he had just done something unforgivably selfish, telling her a truth that she didn't need to hear. He reached toward her shoulder and said, "Debbie, I'm sorry."

She stifled a sob that was almost a scream. He jerked his hand back in alarm. She ran past him into the house, slamming the door behind her. He heard some commotion inside the house and saw the little boy's face for another instant in the window. The boy looked so much like Eli, and Nunez knew his twin brother must have as well. The sight of the boy made him start to tear up again. He stood in the yard, waiting for Debbie to walk back out the door. Minutes passed. She didn't come back outside.

Nunez held back tears as he walked to his car. He couldn't hear anything else at the house, didn't see anyone at the window. He got back into the driver's seat, started the engine, and took a last look at the house. There was still nobody at the door. He put the car in drive and started to roll, hoping someone would run out of the house and stop him. Nobody did.

He crept down the street, trying to stop the tears welling in his eyes. The road blurred in front of him and he wiped the tears away. It didn't work. He could barely see. He pulled over in front of another house. A Hispanic woman and two kids were in the front yard. The woman peered into the car window before she grabbed the two kids and rushed inside.

"Hey Eli," Nunez said, his voice wavering. "Check it out, she thinks I'm a Taliban. She thinks there's going to be a firefight out here." He half laughed, half sobbed at his own stupid joke. Then he remembered that he hadn't given Debbie Gore's dog tag like he had planned to, and he couldn't stop it any more. He put his hands at the top of the steering wheel, rested his forehead against them and burst into tears.

For the first time, he cried for his lost friend Eli Gore, over what had happened to Rodger Quincy, over what had almost happened to them all. He cried for the Civil Affairs soldiers who had been blown apart in front of him. He cried for the French soldiers and Marines who had died, and for the Afghan soldiers, both those who were lost and those who were condemned to lives of endless war and misery. He cried over how close his own children had come to losing their father, his wife to becoming a widow. He cried over the loss of faith, over his dead belief that the military he had devoted so much of his life to would never sacrifice men for no good reason. And he kept crying until the tears ran out, he made no attempt to stop them.

Several minutes passed before he lifted his head from the steering wheel and wiped his eyes. The woman who had gone inside the house and a Hispanic man were looking at him through a window, and the man was on the phone. Nunez took a few seconds to compose himself. He needed to quit feeling sorry for himself and get moving. If he wanted to be back in Houston before traffic got bad, he had to leave soon.

He pulled out his cell phone and called his wife. When she answered he told her he was already done, and would be coming back to Houston in a few minutes.

"The meeting is over already? That was quick. Did she not want to talk to you?"

"We said everything we had to," Nunez said. "I don't know if it made anything better, but it's done. I kind of feel like shit, like maybe I only did this for me, not for her."

"Did she ask about how he died?" Laura Nunez asked.

"Yeah, she did."

"And what did you say?"

"I told her the truth. She didn't take it well. I don't know if it was the right thing to do."

"It was the right thing to do, Jerry," Laura said. "If it had been Gore here telling me how you died, I would have wanted to know the truth. Even if it was hard to hear."

"Okay, Laura," Nunez said. "Okay, I know you're right. But it being the right thing to do didn't make it any easier. When I get home, lay with me for a while, just hold me. I need it."

"I will, baby, I'll be waiting for you. Hurry back. And be careful."

"I will, Laura."

He took one last look in the side view mirror. Gore's front yard was still empty, the flagpole still bare. Nunez thought, *I'll come back when she's had time to heal. I'll talk to her children. And when I come back, if she hasn't put that flag back up I'll put one up myself.*

Nunez pictured Gore at the Alasai combat outpost, dancing under the tiny American flag on the morning he died. *You earned the right to have a flag in your yard, brother. You earned it. What you did wasn't a waste. I know that now. I'm sorry I ever doubted it.*

"Jerry? Are you there?"

"I'm here, Laura." Nunez put the car in gear and got ready to pull out into the street. "I'm coming home now, okay?" He wiped away the last of his tears and drove away from the curb.

"I'm coming home."

CREDITS AND CONTRIBUTORS

Publishing: Tactical 16, LLC
CEO, Tactical 16: Erik Shaw
President, Tactical 16: Jeremy Farnes
Peer Editors: Brian Slaughter, Marilyn Pfaff, Karla Marshall
Cover Design: Kristen Shaw
Cover Photo: Thomas Goisque, www.thomasgoisque-photo.com

Special Thanks: to all those who so generously supported this project on Indiegogo, and an extra special "Thank You" to **Fred Tejan III** and **Paula Tucci** for going above and beyond to bring this project to life. Thank you, thank you, thank you for your kindness and generosity.

ABOUT THE AUTHOR
Chris Hernandez

Chris Hernandez is a former Marine and veteran Police Officer, currently serving in the Texas Army National Guard. He is a combat veteran of Iraq and Afghanistan, and served 18 months as a UN police officer in Kosovo. Chris lives with his wife and children in southeast Texas. Proof of Our Resolve is his first novel and is part one in a series of several books.

ABOUT THE PUBLISHER
Tactical 16, LLC

Tactical 16 is a Veteran owned and operated publishing company based in the beautiful mountain city of Colorado Springs, Colorado. What started as an idea among like-minded people has grown into reality.

Tactical 16 believes strongly in the healing power of writing, and provides opportunities for Veterans, Police, Firefighters, and EMTs to share their stories; striving to provide accessible and affordable publishing solutions that get the works of true American Heroes out to the world. We strive to make the writing and publication process as enjoyable and stress-free as possible.

As part of the process of healing and helping true American Heroes, we are honored to hear stories from all Veterans, Police Officers, Firefighters, EMTs and their spouses. Regardless of whether it's carrying a badge, fighting in a war zone or family at home keeping everything going, we know many have a story to tell.

At Tactical 16, we truly stand behind our mission to be "The Premier Publishing Resource for Guardians of Freedom."

We are a proud supporter of Our Country and its People, without which we would not be able to make Tactical 16 a reality.

How did Tactical 16 get its name? There are two parts to the name, "Tactical" and "16". Each has a different meaning. Tactical refers to the Armed Forces, Police, Fire, and Rescue communities or any group who loves, believes in, and supports Our Country. The "16" is the number of acres of the World Trade Center complex that was destroyed on that harrowing day of September 11, 2001. That day will be forever ingrained in the memories of many generations of Americans. But that day is also a reminder of the resolve of this Country's People and the courage, dedication, honor, and integrity of our Armed Forces, Police, Fire, and Rescue communities. Without Americans willing to risk their lives to defend and protect Our Country, we would not have the opportunities we have before us today.

More works from Tactical 16 available at www.tactical16.com or www.amazon.com.

Love Me When I'm Gone
The True Story of Life, Love, and Loss for a Green Beret in Post-9/11 War
By: Robert Patrick Lewis

And Then I Cried:
Stories of a Mortuary NCO
By: Justin Jordan

CPSIA information can be obtained at www.ICGtesting.com
Printed in the USA
LVOW07s1944190813

348672LV00006B/33/P